REBEL FIGHT

REBEL FIGHT

THE ROYALE VAMPIRE HEIRS, BOOK FIVE

by

GINNA MORAN

SUNNY PALMS PRESS

For Inquiries Contact:
Sunny Palms Press
9663 Santa Monica Blvd Suite 1158
Beverly Hills, CA 90210, USA
www.sunnypalmspress.com
www.GinnaMoran.com

To the biggest Orlando fan in the world, Brittany Graham, I'm sorry this isn't a sweet baby Orlando book, but you are officially another book closer to a good time with your second favorite O. XOXO!

1

BEAST—MODE

"SHE'S GOING TO POP OUT of me at any second," I say, groaning. "I just know it."

A hard thud taps against my belly from inside, and I automatically cup my stomach with my hand. The sensation of the baby moving is both incredible and alarming sometimes. I don't know what I expected from pregnancy, but this wasn't exactly it.

My belly jiggles with more movement, and I swear I see a hand or a foot, stretching against my skin. "Fuck, Jamie. I don't know how much more of this I can take. She's going to burst out from the wrong place."

Jameson chuckles. "Take a breath, Gigi. I think that's highly unlikely. You know how much force it takes to break through skin and muscle. Not to mention, she's the size of a cabbage or some shit."

"No way," I say, rubbing my hands over my giant belly. "She feels like a toddler already."

Jameson materializes next to me, giving me a once-over. Dropping to his knees, he rests his hand beside mine. He stares intently like he has X-ray vision to check on the baby without the ultrasound machine. We wait in silence, my belly going still like she wants to prove my ass wrong—that, or she knows Jameson is close and settles down, loving his presence as much as I do.

He smirks and kisses my stomach.

A wave moves across my stomach with the baby pressing against my skin. It's weird as hell that my super hearing can pick up on the noises of her shifting and thumping against my insides. I tense and brace for her to explode out of me, but it doesn't happen. She settles down right where Jameson's hand lingers like she wants to be as close as possible. Jameson grins and cracks up, the pure joy in his almost giggle sending warm love flooding through me.

"Come on, mini-beast. Let's practice those punches next. Your mommy loves feeling that you're as feisty as she is. Don't let her try to fool you." Leaning forward, Jameson brushes his lips to my round belly again, kissing my bare skin.

While I might freak out a bit over the sensation of another being growing inside me, Jameson is downright giddy—his enthusiasm and excitement make it a million times better. I enjoy how happy Jameson gets when he feels the mini-beast turning my belly into a punching bag.

"And jab right," he teases, grazing his knuckles to my skin. "Jab left."

The mini-beast thumps against my stomach again, turning Jameson hysterical with laughter. His fangs flash with his beaming smile, and he kisses my belly a dozen times, murmuring words of encouragement and love against my skin.

"Careful, Jamie," I warn, clutching his cheeks with my hands. His eyes sparkle with mischievousness, and I want to savor this moment. "You're getting her riled up. I think she knows it's you, because I'm starting to get hungry. Keep teasing her, and she might—"

Jameson reaches up and presses his index finger to my lips, cutting me off. Fake-glaring, he purses his lips and flares his nostrils. "Don't you even finish that sentence. How many times do I have to call Everett and have him explain that our mini-beast might turn you wild, but she's not going to smash through your gut to devour us all? We would see if she has fangs or claws, or whatever the hell else you keep imagining."

"That you know of," I tease, unable to help myself. It's just one of the many things I think about on a regular basis. I'm carrying a half-vampire baby, and no one can really prepare for such a thing that shouldn't be possible.

Reaching over, he snatches a stack of pictures from the nightstand. "I mean, look at her. She's perfect. She won't arrive snapping fangs and hollering for blood. Just boobie milk," he insists, resting a hand on each of my knees to open my legs. "Unless..."

It's my turn to cover his mouth. "Don't you dare even think the words. I'm not going to start squirting blood from my nipples or whatever twisted fantasy you keep thinking about."

"That you know of," he says, repeating my words back to me. He nestles his body between them and pulls me close for a kiss, making me stretch a bit because of the space my belly insists on keeping between us. "Though I do question how I'll survive the next two months if my brothers can't get here sooner. You're insatiable."

"And bitey." I snap my teeth.

His eyes flash silver. "Wild."

"Which is totally on you, Jamie."

He wags his eyebrows. "I'm only giving you what you need."

I blame Jameson and his dire need to ensure I never

have even a second to grow hungry for my desire to suck his neck day and night. He takes my nutrition seriously and will even have something prepared for me to eat during the day after I wake up craving his blood and allows me to satiate my dhampir nature with a couple love bites.

I laugh and comb my fingers through his soft hair, messing it up. "Well, what I need is control and some guidance on how to chill out the mini-beast. Because no matter what you say, I know I'm pregnant with a baby that wants to escape me only to devour the vampire population. You included."

His hand slides across my belly, and he nuzzles his nose to mine. "Your mommy doesn't mean that, mini-beast. She is just nervous. She knows you're not going to blast from her gut like the cutest cannonball you've turned her beautiful belly into. All you'll want to do is snuggle and sleep and suck the boobies."

"If you say so," I murmur against his mouth, groaning at the desire rushing through me at his closeness. My body is so out of whack these days. I sometimes worry I might ask too much of Jameson when his brothers can't make it here for days from the city. "But I'm nearly certain you're talking about yourself."

"Now that you mention it..." He nips his lip, sending a splash of blood into my mouth.

"You're trying to distract me," I say, mumbling as I

glide my tongue over his lip and suck it into my mouth.

"You need it. I can sense you're getting antsy and stressed, and I want you to know and believe me when I say Ev will ensure none of the freaky things crossing your mind happen. We'll all help, Gigi. I swear." He bites his lip harder. "Now let me give you what you want."

I flare my nostrils at the scent, his mouthwatering flavor nearly stealing my breath. The mini-beast feels as if she does a flip, jostling my belly enough to widen Jameson's eyes in panic. Jerking back, he presses both of his hands to my rolling belly like he's trying to keep one of my nightmares from coming true.

I laugh and rest my hands on top of his. It's funnier seeing him caught off guard than having it be me. "See? She wants out and demands that you better do more than tease us with a bit of blood. Hurry before she tries again. If you don't want her to give me enough strength to pin you down so she can have me take all of the blood she wants, you better comply." I grin with my words, finding more amusement that my stomach growls to prove my point.

"Shit. Did she just roar at me?" Jameson grabs the collar of his shirt and stretches it over his shoulder. "I think she did. That was not normal hunger sounds. That was—crazy as hell. Don't make her wait any longer."

I crinkle my nose and laugh harder at his teasing. "Uh-oh. Brace yourself. She's begging me to attack."

Throwing myself into him, I knock Jameson on his back and straddle his waist. I try to bend down to kiss him, but my pregnant belly gets in the way, and I frown. Jameson lifts an eyebrow, pressing his lips together to stop from laughing at my failed attempt to follow through with my joke.

I close my eyes and groan, scrubbing my hands over my face. "Damn it."

He breaks, unable to remain expressionless. His chuckle makes me laugh, and he rubs my belly again. Sitting up, he adjusts me on his lap so that I can reach him. "While I love seeing you try, I won't test my luck against your ferocity. Have at me, Gigi. Take what you—"

A knock taps on the door to Jameson's bedroom, drawing our attention away from each other. I tense at the sound of one of the Barons grumbling under his breath in the hallway. It's still too early for Cortland to wish Jameson a good day as I commanded him to do every single day to keep an eye on him. Closing my eyes, I try to decipher if it's Thaxton, who thinks I hide in Jameson's room to wait for him, but it's not him either. I don't think it's Freeport either, because I can hear him from a mile away, groaning over some dumb thing or another, keeping his space like I manipulated him to do...which means it must be Channing.

"Ignore his annoying ass," Jameson whispers under his breath, rubbing a circle over my lower back. "He'll go away.

He always does. He just thinks he is some kind of a boss over me since I'm not a part of the Baron bloodline. It's gotten worse the last couple days as the others have been demanding him to do more and more stuff while we sit around."

The knock turns into a bang on the wood. "Damn it, Jameson. I know you're in there. I heard you just shut off your TV. Open up or I'll break down the damn door. You were supposed to meet me ten minutes ago to take over my post." Channing's voice trickles through the door, his words grumbling with annoyance.

I frown at his comment. I don't have to see his face to know he wears his constant scowl. Channing is the Barons' poor attempt at growing their numbers again since they've lost more than half of their coven to either me or my guys. Freeport, Thaxton, and Cortland all fought over it, and then Freeport turned Channing anyway. The asshole brings nothing of value apart from a bad attitude and entitlement, thinking he's better than me because I don't have fangs. If the Royales and I didn't agree to use the Barons to our advantage and for extra protection, they'd all be dead and gone already.

"Don't make me go to Freeport," Channing adds, sounding more like a whiney asshole than the scary vampire he thinks he is.

I dramatically roll my eyes at Jameson and stretch my

neck to kiss him again. "Empty threats," I whisper. "Freeport won't open the door for anyone besides us."

"What does he yell at the guys tonight?" Jameson asks, stretching his neck to the side in offering.

I break my mouth from his and hover my lips an inch above my favorite spot on his shoulder. "Fucking-fuckers, I'm busy jacking off. Don't come in or I'll blow my load all over you."

Jameson shakes with laughter and reciprocates my soft kiss to his shoulder with one to mine. "Mik would appreciate that one."

"It was Bronx's idea."

Every evening, I sneak into Freeport's living quarters and wake him up only to mind manipulate him into thinking he controls the situation, though I've taken over. He always finds himself busy with scrutinizing the shadows of trees displayed on the security feeds that never show anything out of the ordinary on purpose. Mikkalo ensured it, using his skills to show only what we want them to show.

I have to admit, watching Freeport waste one day after another is one of the most satisfying things in the world. I thought having to keep up the mind manipulation would be utter torture, but Jameson and I have turned it into a game. Revenge isn't just sweet. It's fucking delectable. Having the power that I do feels like I'm on the verge of being totally diabolical.

"Jameson," Channing calls again, his voice rising in anger. He pounds his hand on the wood, refusing to give up. "I mean it. It's your turn. If I have to see Cortland make another lap around the property blindfolded, I'll lose my shit. These guys can be fucking insane. Freeport threatened to blow a load on me. Like what the fuck kind of threat was that?"

"It kept you away, didn't it?" Jameson comments.

I stifle a giggle.

"Why don't you just join Cortland instead of bitching? He's training, which is something you should do. I heard the others discussing your worth. You need to start proving you're capable of keeping up." Jameson shifts me as I suck his skin without biting.

I can't stop the laugh from bubbling from my throat. I had almost forgotten that I commanded Cortland to run laps until he felt the heat of the sun. That fucker annoys me more than even Freeport and Thaxton combined. He acts as if I somehow already belong to him, because like Thaxton, he thinks I'll end up killing Freeport to eventually make him next up on the chain of Barons who think they're entitled to me.

"What the fuck?" Channing snaps, hearing my voice. "You're with *Gwen*? Freeport's going to love this. You're one crazy bastard to think you can sneak behind—"

Jameson disappears from beneath me and rushes to the

door so quickly that my brain barely registers that I'm resting on my knees instead of in his lap. Flinging the door open, he releases a growl and snatches the scrawny vampire by the shirt. Channing throws a punch, missing Jameson's face by at least six inches. Swinging Channing forward, Jameson throws him to the floor and unsheathes a blade from beneath his jacket.

"If you think you can control me with threats of ratting me out like the fucker you are, you will be sorely disappointed." Jameson's muscles ripple in his arms as he prepares to fight. "I might not be of the Baron bloodline, but I've been alive a long fucking time and will show you what you face trying to test me. I'll kick your ass straight to the city."

I suck in my bottom lip and shift onto my ass for a better view of the show. Jameson looks so incredibly sexy all protective and broody, ready to cut this guy's heart out. Channing struggles for a second until he feels the prick of Jameson's blade penetrate through the back of his shirt. Grumbling, Channing clenches his jaw. A deep rumble from his throat reverberates through the air, sending a shiver up my spine. The noise steals my amusement, leaving me cold and on edge.

"You wouldn't fucking dare, Jameson," Channing mutters, turning his brown eyes toward me.

"Fuck yeah, I would," Jameson says, sinking his knife

deeper between Channing's shoulder blades. "You're just lucky Gigi is damn good at what she does or else you'd be offering her your final blood donation, and we'd hate that. That sexy mouth of hers is mine."

Snarling, Channing shoves his hands into the ground, thrusting himself up despite Jameson lodging his knife in his back. Blood splatters on the floor, sending the scent of something savory, like roasted garlic and balsamic vinegar through the air. And hell. What is wrong with me? I'm never much in the mood for something other than sweets, but my belly flips as the baby stirs, sending ravenous pain shooting through me.

"Ja-Jamie." I clutch my stomach, feeling an elbow or something press against my tight skin. The pain freaks me out a bit, and I can't stop a gasp from escaping my lips.

"Fuck. Gwen." Jameson swings and punches Channing, knocking him out of the way to race to me.

I bend forward and squeeze my eyes shut. "Get him out of here. Something is—"

Jameson yells out, the pain in his voice radiating through me as if it's my own. Glass shatters, and I force my lids to flutter open. Jameson drops to the floor with chunks of the now broken mirror. Channing caught him off guard and threw him across the room. The last thing I expected from tonight was for this new Baron asshole to choose confronting me instead of Jameson.

I don't get the chance to move before Channing snatches my wrists and hauls me from my spot. Spinning around, he uses me as a shield to protect himself against Jameson's wrath. Channing locks his fingers through my blond hair and yanks my head to the side, sniffing my throat like the creepy perv I knew he could be.

"I've always wondered what the big deal was about you," he says, whispering into my ear. "Everyone always fighting and threatening each other. And for what? You're nothing special, and in a few weeks, that pussy of yours—"

My belly rumbles with the sounds of my blood hunger, and I swear to the universe the baby thrusts itself forward in an escape attempt. It startles Channing, making him stumble, and I break my hand free of his and lock it around his throat. Something powerful comes over me, and I lock my gaze to his, my whole body trembling with the urge to bite. I knew I was toeing a line of self-control, but damn it, I think he went too far.

I can't even think before a command screams from my mouth, echoing through the room. "Don't fucking move! Don't speak! Your blood is mine!"

Jameson grabs my shoulder, trying to pull me away. "Gwen, wait—"

Jerking Channing around, I thrust him into Jameson, sending the two of them to the floor. I hop on top of Channing, now frozen in my mind manipulation, and drag him up by his shirt. Jameson stiffens in shock, his wide green eyes blinking as Channing's blood splashes across his face. I tear into the bastard's throat again and again, the mini-beast shifting and moving, seemingly dancing with delight inside me as I yank Channing's head by his hair so hard that I decapitate him to drink from the blood spilling from his neck.

"Shit. Shit. Shit." Jameson chants the words, his eyes locking to mine. I can't even manage to stop even knowing that he's on the verge of panicking. "Gwen, if you need more, let me bite my arm for you."

His words snap rationality back into my mind, and I pull away from Channing's throat and cover my mouth in shock and disgust.

"Oh, fuck," I whisper-hiss, scrambling off Channing and Jameson.

My ass hits the floor, and I struggle to push to my feet. My stomach growls and moves with blood hunger. I catch sight of my silver flashing eyes in a broken piece of the mirror on the floor. My mind screams at me to chill the hell out, but my body argues otherwise and insists I return to my kill to drink more.

"Gwen," Jameson says, risking his safety to move closer to me. "Gwen, hey. Look at me."

A rumbling growl escapes my lips, and I jerk my attention to Jameson. He holds his hands up in surrender and takes an automatic step back. My soul wails in agony, knowing that he might fear me, but once again, my body couldn't care. I'm starving. I feel as if a monster will burst from my belly and kill me if I don't give in to her demand.

Jameson darts to the other side of the room and snatches his com device from his nightstand. I stalk him, clenching and unclenching my fingers. Even the ring of the video call doesn't break my focus on Jameson. My emotions run hot and wild, more out of control than ever. It's like the pregnancy forces a disconnection between my instincts as a dhampir and my human rationale. All I want is for the world to stop, but I also really want to taste more of Jameson's blood. I want to sink my teeth into him and hear him moan in pleasure. My mouth waters just at the thought of a longer, hotter taste of him.

"Uh, brothers. I think you need to drop what you're doing and get the hell out here as soon as you can," Jameson says, darting toward the other side of the room when I get within a few feet of him. "Our girl is extra hungry, and I need backup."

"It's going to have to wait, Jameson." Bronx's voice echoes through the line, though I can't see the video stream of him. "Just do your best. Gwen can't be—"

My dhampir nature kicks in, and I fly so fast at Jameson that the world blurs around me. He gasps as I shove his back into the wall, lifting him off his feet. Locking his fingers through my hair, he yanks my head, keeping my teeth from his throat. I thrash and snap my teeth, in full-blown beast mode.

"Fuck!" Jameson yells, trying to spin me away instead of shoving me back like he should. "Ev! Mik! Someone needs to get here like fucking yesterday."

"Holy shit," Mikkalo says.

"Dandelion, don't!" Bronx yells at the same time.

"Gwen, you don't want to do this." Everett's soothing voice cuts over the com device next. "Just look at me. Follow my voice for a second and find the com device. I'll help you through this, okay? Just don't kill Jameson."

"If you do, you'll get only bananas for eternity," Bronx adds.

I ignore them, my stomach turning wild with need and desperation. I can't think of anything else besides drinking Jameson's delectable blood.

Jameson groans, his sharp fangs peeking from beneath his lips. "Take care of our girl, brothers. She's going to devour me now."

Covering his face with his arm, Jameson blocks his neck and releases me. I sink my teeth into his forearm, moaning so incredibly loud as his blood fills my mouth. My heart races, thudding in chaotic beats against my ribcage. The red tint of my vision clears, and I grab Jameson by his hip and pull him into me. Even thinking I'm about to rip him apart, his body arouses to mine, and his erection presses into my hip.

I gather the fabric of his shirt in my hands and rip it open, brushing my lips to his taut chest. "You taste so good," I murmur, nipping his skin hard enough that blood splashes my mouth.

His tense muscles loosen. "Oh, fuck. Thank fuck. You're not going to drain me."

"I feel like I might," I murmur, biting him again.

"Jameson, get out of there," Bronx commands, his voice trying to steal my attention. "You need to before she loses control again."

"I'm not going anywhere," Jameson responds. "She needs me."

Everett groans. "So do we."

"Hang up the com device, Jamie." My voice practically purrs with my words. Shit. Did I really just say that? "You're mine." Fuck. I did.

"Jameson," Bronx warns.

"I'm going to set off a security breach, Gwen," Mikkalo says, his voice smooth, reminding me how much I love hearing him say my name when he gives me his blood. "I'm sorry."

The mini-beast kicks like she agrees with my thought.

Bronx growls and something smashes on the other end of the line. "Do it now. I'll cancel everything. Ev, get Rio on the line. I think we need to start making plans."

I don't get a chance to hear whatever else he says, because a loud alarm screeches through the air. It steals my senses, turning my vision foggy. My legs drop out from under me, but Jameson catches me before I hit the ground.

A figure darts into the room from my peripheral vision. I blink through the haze as Thaxton hovers over us, his eyes wild as they roam from my body to where Channing lays dead on the floor. Mouthing something I can't hear over the alarms, Thaxton points at Jameson.

"I'm so sorry, Gigi," Jameson says in my ear, his voice breaking through the torturous noise. "Thaxton's right. I need to bite you with venom."

Ah hell.

Fiery pain explodes in my shoulder.

The last thing I see is Thaxton reaching down for me.

2

REUNITED

COLD SWEAT DRENCHES MY BODY. I can't move my limbs, but the sensation of pins and needles prickling across my skin promises it won't be long until I can. My dark vision shifts to maroon as someone shines a flashlight at my lids. A cool finger caresses my lashes, and blinding light follows.

"Gwen? Hey, Gwen. It's me." Everett flashes the light in my other eye for a second before turning it off. His fingers graze over my forehead with his gentle, familiar touch.

"You're going to be okay. We're all here. Everything is going to be fine. Just take a few breaths and open your eyes."

My body thrashes, my consciousness returning at full force. I attempt to jerk upright, but my pregnant belly gets in the way, and I fall back onto the soft mattress of my familiar bed. I feel like a turtle stuck on its back, annoyance about not getting up as quickly as I'd like rushing through me.

I groan and growl, trying to get up again, in desperate need of blood.

A dozen familiar scents dance through the air, and my stomach aches and roars with its never-ending hunger. Panic ignites inside me. I heave a few breaths, trying to settle my racing heart and mind. I hate feeling so disoriented and out of control. So starved.

"Get back and give her space," Everett says, touching his cool hand to my clammy forehead again.

"Damn, she's wild," Mikkalo murmurs.

Bronx crosses his arms over his chest. "So hot."

Jameson growls, drawing my attention to him, giving me the space Everett demanded. "You two aren't helping. She gets easily set off by hunger or lust. Maybe don't prod at the beast until she gets what she needs."

Everett's handsome face draws my attention to him as he hovers by my side. Giving me a once-over, he examines me from my head to my toes for a moment. Happiness lights his face, and he greets me with a sexy smile that would surely melt the panties off me if I were wearing any. He doesn't back off at my wildness and helps me sit up. Adjusting a couple of pillows behind me, he ensures I'm comfortable with the position.

He grabs a glass of ruby liquid from Mikkalo and offers it to me. "Here, drink this. Nice and slow."

I flare my nostrils at the scent of a mixture of my guys' blood. They usually make sure that I have extra on hand, but they had to push their visit a couple of days, which meant I rationed it in fear of having to ask Jameson to give me extra. I guess it really fucked with me, and that's why I lost control.

"I don't think that's possible. I'm starving. It's taking everything in me not to jump on you and bite your throat." At dhampir speed, I flick my hand and grab the front of Everett's shirt, pulling him closer. He manages to keep the glass of blood steady while freeing himself from my grip on him.

"You can do that later, I promise. But for now, drink." Everett ever so slowly offers me the large glass of blood.

I lick my lips, focusing on the four sets of hands all touching a part of me. Blood seeps between my barely parted lips, and I wring my hands together as not to steal the glass and chug it like the wild beast I've become wants to. Jameson squeezes my knee, drawing my eyes to him as he clutches a pitcher of blood bigger than my head. He winks at me and mouths that he's ready for more of my sexy mouth, which sets off my stomach again. Blush blooms in my cheeks, feeling everyone watch our quiet conversation.

"Someone should take that from him," Mikkalo whispers, like any sudden noise might set me into action to tackle Jameson. "I'm jealous as fuck. She's so fucking sexy all wild and bitey. I need her to look at me like that."

"Like she wants to murder you?" Bronx quips, subtly shifting toward Jameson. He freezes when I lock my gaze on him and glare. I challenge him to say something else, but he tightens his mouth and raises an eyebrow.

"Did you hear that?" Mikkalo mutters, lowering his voice. "I think she growled."

"Hot, right?" Jameson says, chuckling. He pats my leg. "I don't even think she realizes it, but she does it all the time. You should feel it vibrate on your skin when she's devouring you. I love it."

"What else is different?" Everett asks, snapping his fingers by my ear. His voice remains even, though his eyes flash silver with his desire, triggered by Jameson's remarks. And damn. Now I'm horny as fuck. "Gwen? Hey. Look at me. I'd prefer to hear it from you. Tell me anything you can think of that's different from the last time we talked."

I whip my head up to drag my stare from his growing hard-on and narrow my eyes on the empty glass in his hand.

Once again, I inhale a few deep breaths. "I feel murdery. Starving all the time. It's like no amount of blood is enough. I thought it was worse before, but...fuck. Come here. I want my mouth on you."

"Damn," Bronx murmurs under his breath.

"I can see why Jameson asked for help. I want to wrestle with her until she pins me down and bites the hell out of me." Mikkalo smiles at me. "Though I might have to use some chains to give me a fair advantage."

"Good luck, Mik. She can't be tamed. She's even wild in her sleep, if she can even manage to close her eyes. Her sleep has been shit too recently," Jameson adds, turning back to Everett.

"You try sleeping with the mini-beast treating your insides like a fight ring," I snap, glowering at him. "And you don't help, always teasing her and trying to get her to go wild for fun. You're asking me to bite."

He smiles. "Well, yeah."

Our gazes lock, and once again, my stomach roars like crazy. I have a feeling that Jameson's venom bite made things worse, because all I can think about is the pulsing vein in his neck and the ones traveling up his arms as he flexes his muscles in anticipation, expecting to have to catch me at any second. And fuck. I want so badly to launch myself at him. I need to chill out.

"Damn, anyone else getting jealous?" Mikkalo comments, but I don't look at him. I can't take my gaze off Jameson's delectable throat, silently calling for me to lick it. "I want our girl to get what she needs, but hell. Jameson is one lucky bastard. I want her to take from me and not him."

Mikkalo's words slap some sense into me. I knew that all my extra time with Jameson could possibly affect everyone else, but this is the first time anyone has mentioned their feelings out loud.

"I agree," Everett says, failing to remain expressionless. The corners of his blue eyes crinkle, and he shifts his jaw as he pauses. "We know that these circumstances are neither of your faults, but I think some space will do you a bit of good, Gwen. Jameson too. It might help ease your blood hunger for him and prevent your dhampir nature from wanting to push him to his limit since he doesn't want to set boundaries. His venom bite also draws you to him even more now."

"I don't want space or boundaries. We like how our relationship with each other is, and I'm sorry you feel we need a break, but can't we just figure something else out? I'll give you all the attention you need if it helps." My mouth spits the words before my mind realizes I've just responded to Everett with something I hadn't planned to say. I sound whiny as hell and a bit possessive. I take a breath. "I'm sorry. I just mean, I—"

"Dandelion, listen to your health keeper. We're not

suggesting anything but giving him a chance to recover from your ravenous appetite and fill yourself up on us instead." Bronx clears his throat and swipes the pitcher from Jameson's death grip, nearly sloshing the elixir from the container. He moves to my other side, giving Jameson a warning look so that he doesn't try to follow him. His eyes flash with pops of silver, and he reaches out and combs my messy hair from my damp forehead. "We all have your best interest in mind and the same desire to test our own limitations against your sexy ferocity."

"Be careful with that. You're going to be in huge trouble if you spill even a drop," I say, ignoring his comment.

He raises an eyebrow and purposely swirls the pitcher, sending the contents to the top in a whirlpool. "Am I, now? I'd like to see that. So, how about you give Jameson's body a small break from your teeth?" Bronx asks, sitting on the edge of the bed beside me. He dips his finger into the blood and coats it across my bottom lip, seriously testing me. "You know he can't resist that naughty mouth of yours, and the way you look at him—it's time to look at me like that."

I smirk as he graces me with a smile, slowly licking the blood from my lip before snatching his hand. I suck his index finger into my mouth, listening to the change in everyone's breathing. "Make me."

"I'm not sure my brothers want to know what I have planned to do so," he teases, his voice deepening with his lust.

"Fuck, brother. Look at her eyes." Everett holds the empty glass to Bronx for a refill like he needs to give me an offering next to steal my attention. "You might need some assistance, and I'll gladly help." Easing the glass away, he wipes the blood from my lips and kisses me. "We've missed you, Gwen. Especially your brand of teasing."

"Hell yeah. More than I ever knew possible." Mikkalo crawls onto the bed by my feet and moves my legs onto his lap, preparing to gather me in his arms the second he can. "How is my wild one, anyway? Apart from the hunger and pregnancy?" Bending closer, he touches my cheek with one hand and rests the palm of his other one on my belly. "You look in dire need of a bubble bath and a massage while I feed you."

I bob my head, licking my lips, loving his suggestion. "You have no idea. Your brother is amazing with distracting me by fulfilling my other needs, I forgot some of the things only you can provide. Will you remind me?"

"What are these supposed other needs? Food, blood, and orgasms." Jameson taps his finger to his hand. "I'm not missing anything."

I grin at him. "That's right. You're not from you. You're perfect."

Mikkalo chuckles and play-punches Jameson. "Don't worry, brother. Gwen and I just have some catching up to do."

"That goes for all of us," Bronx says, grazing his fingers over my belly.

Everett waits to see if I motion for another glass of blood, but I shake my head. He swings his attention between me and Jameson, remaining expressionless toward our teasing. "Not to question what you think our girl needs, but have you been ensuring her human needs? Like what about regular exercise? Fresh air? Are you making sure she is drinking a ton of water?"

Jameson and I glance to each other and nod at the same time, despite being well aware that he carries me around if we ever leave the room. Sex is my cardio, and the only fresh air I get is when we decide to switch things up and make love on a big picnic blanket near the garden and behind the hedges where no one can see. As for water? Licking it off Jameson in the shower counts, right?

"What about the movies?" Bronx adds, tilting his head, looking at me incredulously.

Damn. I was hoping he wouldn't bring those up. He goes from lustful to birthing coach in a split second, the reminder of our daughter coming kicking him into preparedness mode. Keeping busy and learning certain things he never expected he'd have to seems to help with his nerves a bit. Out of the four of them, Bronx is the most freaked out.

I remain silent, staring at Jameson.

Bronx knows my answer before I can even open my mouth with one of the million excuses I had weeks to come up with. "You didn't watch even one? I sat through every single one of them to pick out which of them I thought you would tolerate, dandelion. I hope you didn't make me do that for nothing. I'm not the one giving birth. You need to be more prepared so it's not as scary to you. I know you worry about the whole process."

Jameson groans and palms his forehead. "Seriously, Bronxy? Gigi is good. No need to add horror movies to the mix. We've read the stuff Rio sent."

I crack a smile and bat my eyelashes. "Plus, it wouldn't have been for nothing, Bronx. I can't punish you properly when you're in a bad mood, so this is second best."

Bronx play-growls and flops down on the pillows beside me, gathering me into his arms before anyone else can. The coolness of his form does nothing to diminish the heat rising in me at his closeness. Fuck. I've missed his embrace and cuddles more than I realized—all of my guys', really. Snuggling his face into my throat, he inhales a breath of my scent and makes me shiver as he presses a kiss to the nape of my throat. The mini-beast must really enjoy his presence and my reaction to it, because she presses heavily near the spot where he holds me, making my belly look lopsided.

And then she kicks.

Bronx gasps in surprise, and I'm nearly certain it's the

first time I've heard such a sound escape his mouth. He leans away from me and drops his gaze to where my belly jostles. "What the fuck is going on in there? Ev, call Rio. Now. She is trying to break out. Isn't it too early? We still have things to prepare and arrange."

Uh-oh. My tough guy looks like he's on the brink of panicking.

I clutch his face with my hands and lock him with my gaze. "Just breathe. This is a normal occurrence. Right, Jamie?"

Jameson tips his head back and barks a loud-ass laugh, bouncing on the edge of the bed in his amusement. "Hell yeah it is. Now get your ass together and shut the fuck up about the baby busting out, Bronxy. Gwen already thinks the mini-beast will explode through her gut at any second. She doesn't need you agreeing with her."

Bronx's eyebrows shoot lower on his forehead, and he flares his nostrils with another deep breath. "She's worried about her gut?"

Fuck. Me. He better not go there.

He leans back a bit to look past my bulging belly. "I'd be more scared of—"

Everett leans over me and slaps his hand over Bronx's mouth before he can say what I know is on his mind. "Everything is going to be fine."

"And it's time to make things even better for our girl.

No more birthing talk." Mikkalo takes his chance to pull me into his arms, using Bronx and Everett's distraction against them.

I smile. "Definitely not. Kisses and cuddles instead."

Brushing his lips to mine, Mikkalo meets me for a kiss, not even reacting to all the damn blood I feel dried to my face. He slides off the bed with me in his arms, and purposefully avoids every reflective surface, knowing how self-conscious I get.

"That sounds like a great plan. Why don't you draw her a bath? I can bring the equipment in and perform her exam while she relaxes," Everett says, rubbing his hand on the back of his neck. "I'd rather get this out of the way now instead of waiting much longer. It'll help with everyone's nerves."

The strange tone of his voice sends a blip of worry through me. I know all my guys are as nervous as I am, but it takes a lot to make Everett's voice quiver. Butterflies feel as if they flutter through my stomach, and I clutch onto Mikkalo, letting him kiss me again like it's all he needs in this world to survive.

Mikkalo barely makes it into the spacious bathroom when I realize I was so happy to see my guys that I had nearly forgotten the reason that brought them here. I snatch the doorframe, my sudden strength nearly throwing Mikkalo off balance, and he back steps to catch himself.

"Wait, before you guys start barking commands around here, what the hell happened after...my little incident, Jamie? How long have I been out? I can't believe you bit me with your venom." Redirecting my worry helps ease the anxiety blooming inside me over Everett's comment. If something is wrong...fuck, I can't think about it. Everything is fine with our baby. I know it. I feel it. But maybe it's me he's worried about.

Jameson materializes in front of me, pouting out his bottom lip. "I'm sorry, Gigi. You can bite me a dozen times for that. I was caught up and afraid that Thaxton might do it himself, and the last thing we need is to have to command the Barons to venom bite us so you'd get the blood you want. I did what I thought you'd prefer."

"You made a good decision." I nod my head, puckering my bottom lip out to mirror his. "And I'm the one who needs to be sorry. I wish you wouldn't have had to do it in the first place. But so you know, you're my hero. We love you. I can't wait to be able to show you exactly how much."

That gets a smile out of him, and he kisses my forehead. "And speaking of Asshole Thaxton. I'll be back in a bit. I need to toss Channing's body into the sun and clean up the mess."

"What? Really?" I ask, tilting my head. "You're hiding it?"

Shrugging, Jameson says, "Thaxton told me to. He said

he'd keep his brothers busy until our mess was taken care of. He thought Channing caught you waiting for him, so he's covering his tracks." He shudders like he can't even stomach the thought of me and Thaxton together, which neither can I. I hate having him think we're secretly together behind Freeport's back. I know Thaxton enjoys the thought way too much every time I see him. "Such a dumbass. I can't wait until we can get past all this bullshit and finally let him know the truth before you rip his heart out."

I hate how Thaxton looks at me like he's in love with me because I mind manipulated him to believe I mess around with him behind Freeport's back. It was our attempt to put a wedge between the Barons, and it works well enough, but I still don't like it.

I nod and puff a breath out, trying to shed the thoughts of our power play from my mind. I don't want to think about the Barons any longer. "You can hold him for me while I not only rip his heart out but also break it into a million pieces."

"Damn straight." Jameson kisses me again, the thought bringing a wicked smile to his face. "Now try to be good for Ev and Mik. They can't punish you how they like at the moment."

I tip my head back and laugh. "Never."

Bronx groans and stretches his arms over his head. "Why don't I help you, Jameson? We can get the job done faster that way," Bronx says, getting off the bed. He tightens his jaw to remain expressionless. I know him, and right now, I can sense he is as worried as Everett and doesn't want to show it, which is why he's asking to go with Jameson.

"That's probably a good idea. There is only so much space in my tub, and if you hang around, I will expect you all to pile in with me," I tease, offering him a reassuring smile, so he knows I'm okay with what he needs to do for himself in this moment.

"I'd also like to sweep the property," he adds, glancing at Mikkalo and Everett. "Just in case. Things are too quiet in Crimson Vista. It leaves me a bit on edge."

"What doesn't do that, Bronx?" I stick my tongue out at Bronx playfully.

He grumbles under his breath. "Yeah, yeah. Maybe you can work with me on some stress relief later."

Heat crawls up my body at his innuendo. And fuck yes. I could desperately use his distraction. "I think we could all use that."

The four of them devour me with lustful gazes as my comment sinks in. Tingles blossom between my legs, my residual blood hunger threatening to turn into intense lust at any second. I don't know how we could even accomplish much in my current giant-bellied state, but I do know they can get creative as hell.

Jameson smacks Bronx on the back. "Fuck. Let's hurry

and get back here. I want to give her everything she wants."

They each kiss one of my cheeks, and Mikkalo sets me on the counter between the double sinks. He turns the hot water on in the garden tub, sprinkling in a mixture of powders, salts, and way too much bubble bath, just the way I like it.

Everett disappears and reappears just as quickly, pushing in a cart of medical supplies he keeps in my wardrobe. The scent of mint and lavender fill the air, helping to ease my tight muscles. Despite where we are and our circumstances, this quiet moment seems so normal and perfect. I want more. I want this to happen every day and just be able to enjoy a simple life without the rest of the shit show that comes from being a dhampir.

Grabbing a washcloth, Mikkalo wets it in the sink and runs the soft material over my face, cleansing my skin as the bath fills and Everett sets things up to monitor the baby. Gracing me with another handsome smile, Mikkalo kisses me, his excitement and desire set off by my closeness prevalent as his erection bulges against the fabric of his dress pants. I flick open a button on his dress shirt first, eagerly making my way down to expose his chiseled abs and sexy as hell body to me. Fuck, it makes me yearn to lick and kiss and bite him how he likes.

"I want you to join me," I say, unhooking his belt and easing it open.

"Anything you want," he murmurs, letting his pants drop to show off the length of his erection through his briefs. His muscular thighs nearly make me drool as I imagine all the times I've sunk my teeth into them.

He's so sexy with his smooth, velvety dark tanned skin, rippling with his bulging muscles. I trace my finger across the hard bone-like texture of his abs and to his pec. I want to bite him there, too. Everywhere, really.

Mikkalo's pupils dilate under my scrutiny, the copper rings around his irises shrinking with his sizzling gaze. I caress my fingers over his clean-shaven face as smooth as the rest of him, and slip my finger between his lips, pricking myself on his fang, teasing him with my blood.

Humming with his heavy desire, Mikkalo kisses me softly, tugging my shirt over my head. His eyes rove over my body, and he drinks me in like I'm still the most beautiful woman he's ever seen in his life. I ease my hips up for him to tug my stretchy shorts off, showing I'm not wearing panties. He licks his bottom lip in longing, so ready to take me right here on the counter. It takes Everett holding out the jelly-feeling belt to wrap around my belly to stop the both of us from pouncing. Because damn it. I want to.

"This will only take a couple minutes. Rio is waiting for the feed to assess baby girl's measurements and whatnot." Everett helps Mikkalo situate everything before allowing him to carry me to the tub. "Do you have any questions you'd like for me to ask him? Any concerns?"

I shrug. "I don't think anything he says will assure me that my stomach isn't going to blow up and a beast will come out with a mouth full of fangs."

"That's not going to happen, Gwen," Everett says, hitting a button on the machine. We all stare in silence as the mini-beast comes into view, stealing my breath away as always. The baby sucks her thumb, her body curled in the fetal position. Like she can sense us watching, she smiles.

Mikkalo chuckles and cuddles me from behind. "He's right. I still don't see any fangs."

"She's so beautiful," I murmur, overcome with emotion. I blink my eyes to stop the tears from spilling. There is just something enchanting about getting to see her while I feel her subtle movements like she's calm because we are.

"Just like her mom," Everett says, tapping his finger to his com device. "And I'm so in love with the both of you."

A ring sounds through the air, and Everett frowns, accepting the call on his com device. Rio's gruff voice drifts through the air with his greeting, and I squeeze Mikkalo's hand. He wouldn't be video calling this second if something wasn't wrong.

I nearly lose my shit, waiting in dread and anticipation.

"Gwen, hey. The baby is fine. Perfect," Everett says, snapping me out of my whirling thoughts. "Take a breath."

I inhale, my body shuddering as the anxiety leaves.

"I didn't mean to scare you, Gwen, but as your obstetrician, I like to make sure I can relay information personally to you," Rio says, his picture lighting the bathroom wall, though I know he can't see me in return as Everett continues to hold the com device. "You are measuring much farther along than you should be, and I think it has to do with your dhampir nature and the circumstances of your pregnancy. I want you on around the clock care from this point forward, okay? Take things easy."

I nod my head, my thoughts fluttering. I mean, I thought I had at least two months. But now? Fuck. We're not ready. I'm not ready.

"Everything will be fine. I'll stand by ready and waiting if you or Everett needs anything," he adds. "I will do what I can from here in the meantime. Now, do you have any questions? Concerns? Have you thought about your birth plan?"

My mind whirls, and I can't seem to find my voice to respond.

Everett clears his throat. "I'll let you know if she thinks of anything and discuss all the possibilities to make everything perfect for labor and delivery."

"Good," Rio says to Everett. "Don't worry about things yourself, either. She is in your capable hands. You're absolutely prepared for anything."

"Thanks, Rio," Everett says, smiling at his assurance.

"Talk to you soon."

The line drops, Rio not being one to drag out small talk, especially knowing I'm in the Royale Region's greatest health keeper's hands. He once joked that if he didn't know any better, he'd think Everett was out to steal his title for the most renowned OB in the region.

Turning to me, Everett grins. "See. I told you everything was fine."

"Better than fine. We're going to be parents sooner than we thought. Bronx is going to freak," Mikkalo says, shifting me to look at him.

I bob my head, a small laugh escaping my lips with my words. "He's going to freak? I'm the one already freaking out."

Everett kneels next to the tub and takes my hand. "Don't worry, Gwen. I'm here, and I'm not leaving. Ever."

"What about you, Mikkalo? Bronx?" I rest my head to his chest. "I don't want any of you to go."

Mikkalo kisses my shoulder. "Then we won't. Screw the region. You and our baby girl are the most important things in our world."

3

OUTMATCHED

EVERETT COMBS MY DAMP TRESSES over and over again, absently keeping himself busy as I suck on Mikkalo's shoulder. Each of them has two bite marks. Mikkalo's on his pec and shoulder, and Everett's on each side of his neck. But it seems that no matter how much I drink, the ache in my stomach refuses to leave. I don't know if it's now because of my nerves or knowing that Rio thinks I could give birth at any time, but damn it. I can't get enough blood. I can already hear Jameson joking the reason might be that

I'm prepping to release the beast.

"Gwen, want me to bite my arm?" Mikkalo asks, keeping his voice low as he massages lavender oil into my calves, sitting between my legs. "I think you're just giving me a hickey."

It's been a while since I've had to stretch my body to fit his muscular form, but I have to admit, it feels amazing. Everett might've been right about exercising, especially since Jameson and I have been a bit creative navigating around my big belly.

"Oh, huh?" I murmur, pulling away from his shoulders and out of my wandering thoughts. "I'm sorry. I was just thinking and savoring the taste of your skin. Enjoying your hands on me. I don't need any more blood this second."

Twisting his body, Mikkalo turns to face me. Everett sets down the brush on my nightstand and scoots until he's beside me, and I can nestle into his arm. I snuggle my face to his chest and brush my lips to his collarbone. I can't help myself. The attention the two of them have showered me with makes me only crave more.

"What's on your mind?" Mikkalo asks, pulling my legs across his lap to get even closer to me, smothering me with his delectable scent. "Maybe we can help you sort things out."

I shrug and sigh, not even sure how to put my thoughts into words. "It's hard to explain. I'm excited and scared at the same time. Everything has been so calm and easy lately that I'm afraid of what's going to happen after...this." I wave at my stomach, still struggling to process the huge change our lives are about to go through. "We haven't even thought about her name, and we can't just keep calling her baby girl and mini-beast."

"I think Jameson will tell you otherwise," Mikkalo teases, grinning at me before rubbing his cool palm across my bare belly. The baby presses forward and kicks.

I groan with a shiver at the soft sensation of his hand and what it does to me. Shaking my head, I whisper, "Mikkalo, you better not encourage him."

Everett chuckles and kisses my temple. "I'm sure we'll get it figured out, Gwen. Something perfect will come, and we'll know."

"I hope so," I murmur, resting my hand on top of Mikkalo's. "I just wish things were...different? Better? I can't think of the word I'm looking for. All I want is not to have to constantly creep into Freeport's room every day or think of something creative to keep the others busy." Because really, it's getting exhausting. This wasn't supposed to go on this long. The Barons should be dead with their ashes blown to the wind.

"It won't be for much longer. Just until baby girl makes her arrival and we can assess what we need to do to ensure we're good," Mikkalo says, trailing his fingers over my belly again, watching for the crazy jostling. But the mini-beast is finally settled and content it seems, only shifting and moving a bit, used to me sleeping during the day. "And then we'll take care of the problem."

The Problem with a capital P, he should say. None of us has talked much about my rebel brothers, but they cross my mind every time I get to talk to Ashton and Declan. I know Silas and Grayson are causing trouble somewhere just outside the territory because rebel activity has been reported several times over the last month, and now we're just waiting for them to show their faces.

It's the main reason the Barons are alive. Their strength and knowledge of Blood Rebels give us an advantage. Their power will help us survive any sort of threat the rebels make, and it'll be their lives on the line and not ours.

As much as I want to pretend that Silas and Grayson have just moved past everything, I can't. If I've learned anything by now, it's that they don't give up on the rebel fight. They will continue to think vampires control me or I'm a traitor. With our baby coming, it's more important than ever that we use what we can to end this shit show.

I slowly nod my head, agreeing with his words, my response a bit late. Silence fills the room, but it isn't uncomfortable. It's comforting and warm and snaps my focus from what goes on in the world outside our little slice of safety and to the melody of our pounding hearts, beating in perfect sync with each other that it's hard to distinguish them apart.

"I don't want to think about them anymore," I say, my voice turning breathy. "I don't want to think at all."

I draw my finger up Everett's knee, tracing my way up to his bare thigh. The three of us remain naked from our quiet bath that stayed only that—a relaxing soak to calm our nerves—and now that I'm feeling more in control and less in shock from Rio's announcement, I can't help craving more of Everett and Mikkalo's attention.

Gliding my finger up Everett's pelvis, I watch his body awaken into full force. I lock my eyes to his, the blue depths of his ocean gaze flickering with flashes of silver desire. I lace my fingers over his prominent girth and trace my tongue between my lips.

"Is this okay?" I ask him, smirking, knowing it's a silly question to ask because his desire for me leaves him breathlessly nodding his head. "I've missed you both. I want to show you how much."

"I'd like that," they both say in unison.

Mikkalo's cool lips caress my calf as he stretches my leg up to duck beneath it to get between my knees. I squirm, tightening my fingers around Everett's cock while meeting Mikkalo's lusty, heavy-lidded eyes. Their dark depths, with the beautiful copper rings, rove over my face. The warm slickness of Everett's pre-cum drips on my hand with his excitement, turning as slippery as lube with my stroking of his shaft. He hums in pleasure, massaging his hands over my breasts. It turns me on so much that tingles burst between my legs before Mikkalo can even lower his body down to taste me like he wants.

Touching my chin, Everett guides my face toward his, kissing me sensually at first, tasting and teasing me. He slides his tongue into my mouth, exploring the taste of my kiss. I moan a breath and glide my tongue over his, deepening our kiss with my fervent fingers jerking him off with the tightness and quickness he enjoys.

The familiar click of Mikkalo's fangs sounding through the air makes me moan, craving his bite, and I shiver at the sensation of him gently scratching them up my thigh. He nips me on my hip, tasting my blood, and I kiss Everett even harder, more passionately. My hand turns desperate to give Everett the same pleasure Mikkalo gives me, and I cup Everett's balls and massage them with my fingers.

"Feels amazing, Gwen," Everett murmurs, flexing his cock.

"Mmmhmm," I murmur and moan, enjoying the sensation of Mikkalo's mouth on me.

Mikkalo hums in his throat, the rumbling noise vibrating across my skin. Warmth builds even more between my legs, my body begging and craving for him to continue his slow exploration to kiss every inch of me, like he maps my body with his mouth.

I move one of my hands from Everett and rub my fingers over Mikkalo's dark, cropped hair in desperation. I guide his head to move to the spot I want, and he teases me with a soft kiss between my legs until he shifts the folds of my body with two of his fingers to expose my clit to him.

I gasp and moan, leaning into Everett so that he can steal the sexy whimper from my mouth. Our tongues glide against each other's, and he hums as I stroke my hand up and down his shaft. Mikkalo kisses, sucks, and licks my clit, dipping two fingers inside me to discover the arousal he causes. The pressure sets me off, and I moan incredibly loud, throwing myself back on the pillows. An orgasm grabs hold of my muscles, tensing my entire body, and I arch and squirm through the pleasure that seemingly never wants to end.

Everett grunts and cums, splashing his warmth over my hand. I could watch exactly what I do to him over and over again, loving that I turn him on and satisfy him.

I reach out for Mikkalo as he slows and kisses each of my hips. "I want to see you cum next."

He groans and pushes up on his arms, his muscles flexing and moving and he crawls on top of me, meeting me for a kiss. He holds himself up, ensuring he doesn't put any weight on me. I savor his mouth on mine, the feeling of his abs lightly brushing my belly, and the thump of his erection flexing between my legs.

"I want her on top," Mikkalo murmurs, rolling off me, only to have Everett materialize behind me to lift me up.

I gasp as he sets me on top of Mikkalo as he holds his cock in place ready to slide it between my legs. The pressure sends my body shuddering in ecstasy, and Everett digs his fingers into my ass cheeks without letting me go, guiding me up and down in a rhythm that makes me pant and moan.

"You're so sexy," Everett murmurs, shifting my hair with his nose.

He nips me with his fangs, and I moan and reach up to clutch the back of his neck. I stretch and meet his mouth, feeling so hot and beautiful, more wanted than I've ever felt in my life. Mikkalo arches up enough to play with my clit, and I squirm, my body wanting to explode all over again. The sensitivity of every molecule on my body turns every touch intense.

"Tell me how I feel to you." Mikkalo's eyes flash silver, his desire and hunger for me intertwining in a wave I can feel when our minds open for each other. I don't know if he does it or if it's me, but I love it. I live for these moments, feeling my soul merge into one with the men I love.

"Good," I say, the word coming breathlessly.

"Give him more than that." Everett kisses below my ear.

My mind spins with a dozen sensations, and I scrunch my nose in bliss, leaning my head back against Everett as he eases my legs open even wider, giving Mikkalo better access to my clit.

Mikkalo rubs me harder with his fingers, the sensation mind-blowing. "You feel so wet and warm. Fucking incredible. I'm addicted to your scent, your taste, your voice."

I smile through another wave of intensity, loving how he describes me. Touching my chin with his free hand, he locks his eyes to mine again. "Now tell me more. How do I feel to you?"

My mind opens once again, and I say, "Like love and desire and pure ecstasy. It feels like you're igniting sparks right between my legs and like I'm going to explode at any second. Everett controlling my movements is driving me crazy in a good way. I want more. I want to feel like you're fucking my brain out. I want the two of you to make me scream."

Everett releases the sexiest noise I've ever heard, and he tugs me back to rest my back to his chest while Mikkalo braces my legs and thrusts into me. His balls slap my ass, and Everett's fangs click in my ear as he bites his arm. The scent of his blood sets me off, and I moan and snatch Everett's arm, drinking his blood while Mikkalo rocks hard and fast until I reach my peak again.

My body clenches his with my release, and Mikkalo

sinks his fangs into my calf, giving me a pleasure bite in the only place he can reach. Everett bites my shoulder at the same time, and they suck just a bit to satiate their craving for me.

Tensing his muscles, Mikkalo pulls out and strokes his cock a few times, cumming on my pelvis, knowing I wanted to see exactly what I do to him. My body relaxes as Everett cradles me against him and Mikkalo sets my legs down.

"I love you, Gwen," Mikkalo says, cleaning me off with a discarded towel. "I can't wait for this to be the rest of our lives."

"Just living to make each other happy," Everett says. He snuggles in close. "Raising our daughter to be the fiercest being the universe has ever met."

"The sound of that...it's perfect." I pull the two of them close to me, savoring the slowing of our heartbeats and breathing. If only Bronx and Jameson were here, I'd ask the universe to stop spinning so this moment would never end.

The alarm on my com device chirps, snapping me from my blissful haze. I rip myself from Everett and Mikkalo, and nearly eat shit as I try to scramble off the bed. Everett catches me by my arms, swinging me up for Mikkalo to catch. I screech in surprise. Patting Mikkalo's chest, I release a breath and wiggle until he sets me on my feet.

"I'm late," I say, spinning on my feet for the nearest thing to throw on. "I have to get to Freeport before he wakes up. If I don't—fuck, where are my clothes?"

Everett materializes in front of me with a clean dress that hikes up in the front because of my huge belly. He helps me step into panties, and Mikkalo offers me a small blade in expectation. I automatically take it and tuck it into the hidden pocket on my hip. I won't need it, as I never carry weapons these days, but I know it'll make Mikkalo feel better.

"You guys have to stay here," I say, turning and placing my hands to their chests before they stalk me into the hallway. "Thaxton and Cortland might be around, and I can't risk missing Freeport."

"But Gwen," Mikkalo argues.

I shake my head. "I do this every day, okay? His room is only a few doors down."

Mikkalo looks ready to toss me back to the bed to tie me up, but Everett grabs him by the elbow, keeping him back. I peek over my shoulder at them once more and close the door, tiptoeing down the hallway as quietly as I can. I hear Cortland watching what sounds like porn through his door, and I shudder at his soft moan. Ugh.

Thaxton's room greets me with silence as I pass, but I don't stop to press my ear to it. I don't have a lot of time. Minutes at most.

Striding the remaining ten feet to Freeport's living quarters, I ease one of the heavy double doors open and peer into his pitch-black room. The only light illuminating the plush gray and blue, silver-threaded rug comes from the hallway light behind me. My eyes adjust to the darkness, and I shuffle my way across the room and to the king bed with a huge, ornate frame with metal twisted into roses across the headboard.

I reach what's supposed to be my side of the bed and ease myself onto it. Freeport's form remains still, and I stare at the ceiling and hold my breath.

Oh, fuck.

Oh, no.

My pregnant belly prevents me from getting up fast enough, and Freeport releases a growl from across the room. His com device glows a second before the lights in the suite flick on. His sharp fangs protrude from his lips, and he bares them, growling.

My fear instincts buzz like crazy, and I reach for the blade in my dress. Freeport snatches my hand and rips it free, rushing at me from his spot so quickly that I can't stop the scream escaping my mouth. Freeport rams his hand into my chest, winding me, and my eyes widen at the strange milky haze of his gaze.

"Where have you been, Gwen?" he asks, his sharp voice tensing every muscle on my body.

"I was—I was just getting something to eat." I lock my hand around his wrist, terrified he might do something more to hurt me.

He roars in my face, blowing my blond hair from my forehead. "Don't lie to me! I've been up for hours. I suspected Thaxton lied about the possible rebel threat and saw what you, Thaxton, and Jameson had done to Channing. You made a treacherous mistake, my dhampir. I know what's going on."

"Please, it's not what you think," I say, flicking my gaze around the room, looking for something, anything I can use to protect myself with. I thought Freeport was more of just an annoying asshole before, but right now, I'm scared out of my mind.

"Not what I think? You can't lie to me!" he hollers.

I wince. "Channing tried to bite me, so I killed him. That's all it was. Please, you have to calm down. You're freaking me out."

"Liar! I saw the Royales arrive!" he yells, shaking the bed with his anger. "I know my brother has been jealous of me all along, and now he's trying to rise against me and take my heir. The baby is ours. It belongs to me."

"You're crazy!" I break my arm free and swing my fist at his head, knocking him away. Panic kicks my ass in gear, and I roll over, scrambling to get to my feet.

But I'm too slow to get off the bed. I couldn't run far even if I tried.

"Freeport!" Mikkalo shouts from the door. He bangs

his fists on it, shuddering the heavy wood from the force of his strength. "Open up! If you hurt Gwen—"

"You'll do what exactly?" he calls, keeping his focus on me. "You're powerless against me. I don't know what happened with my mind manipulation on Gwen, but I'll fix this. I'll drain Gwen into compliance."

Loud thuds bang against the door as Mikkalo tries to break it down.

Another muffled voice hums through the air, and my fear pours through me in waves. It's Cortland. I hear the sounds of fighting.

The door shudders again, the snarling and growling of Mikkalo and Cortland growing louder. It's hard to think or react, my fear instincts clutching me. Everett shouts, joining in.

Freeport grabs my chin, forcing me to look at him. "Don't move."

"Gwen, fight!" Mikkalo yells and heaves, his back sounding as if it smashes into the door.

"Fight, and I'll make it hurt," Freeport mutters, his voice lowering. Leaning in, he meets my gaze, his eyes freaking me out. What is wrong with them? Why do they look like that?

"You don't want to do this," I say, searching his eyes, waiting for the familiar darkness of his hatred to course over me with a mind link.

It doesn't come.

"I do. So badly," he murmurs, extending his fangs. "It's all I ever think about. I can already imagine your taste."

I reach up and push my hand to his collarbone, using all my strength to keep him back. "You don't," I command. "You will release me and return to sleep. You won't wake up until—"

Freeport snarls and gnashes his teeth. "I knew it! I knew you were doing something, and now I know what it is. You fucking bitch. I'm going to cage you for this until my heir comes and then I will feast on your blood and drain you dry."

Fuck. He did something to his eyes. I can't manipulate his mind.

Inhaling a deep breath, I scream as loud as I can, startling him enough to loosen his grip.

Jabbing my fist at his chest, I attempt to crush his sternum and take his heart. Pain swells in my knuckles, and blood pours from my hand.

What the actual fuck? Some sort of spiky chest plate hides beneath his baggy shirt. He really was paranoid and prepared. The worst kind of enemy.

Throwing me back, he pins my arms with one hand and jerks my head to the side with the other.

I grind my teeth and thrash, but I can't break his hold.

Someone yells my name.

All I can think about is my daughter and what will happen to her if I fail. If Freeport gets his way.

"No!" I scream, doing everything I can to fight him off.

Nothing works.

I'm outmatched.

4

CRAVING REVENGE

"FREEPORT, STOP!" BRONX'S DEEP, THREATEN-ING voice knocks the dread out of me, filling me with re-lief. It gives me the second I need to block his bite by shov-ing my arm into his neck.

Unfazed by my gesture, Freeport snaps his attention toward Bronx filling the doorway to the massive wardrobe. I wiggle beneath Freeport's weight. He's not quick to move, assessing the situation. Realization sinks in, and Freeport growls deeply, his body vibrating on top of me.

"Face me like the powerful shithead you think you are," Bronx says, taking a step closer without jumping in to fight Freeport. He's waiting for him to get off, his need to protect me stopping him from testing Freeport. If Freeport wanted to make us suffer, he'd try to get in a bite before Bronx even closes the space.

Loosening his grip on my arm, Freeport snatches the blade he stole from me from the bed beside us and prepares to fight. He obviously underestimates Bronx and his ability to strategize like a diabolical genius, because Freeport doesn't even see the other figure blur toward us. Laredo rushes Freeport from his spot against the wall. I have no idea how long he's been standing there, maybe just before Bronx yelled, but I'm so thankful to see him. It's a rare emotion that reminds me of the moments of my life with my brothers and before the Royales.

Breaking my arm free, I sucker punch Freeport in the nose, sending his blood squirting at me. I wince at the warm liquid and press my lips together. I refuse to taste even a drop of his blood. The scent sends goosebumps prickling over my body. Laredo takes advantage of Freeport's distraction and drags him off, keeping out of his view.

Locking him in a chokehold, Laredo swivels to face Freeport at Bronx. His jaw twitches as Freeport tests Laredo's strength. All I want to do is get off the damn bed, grab the discarded knife from the floor, and sink it into Freeport's heart. Maybe kick him in the balls, too.

Bronx races toward the two vampires and rams his fist into Freeport's gut. He does it again and again, winding the asshole. Unsheathing a dagger from a hidden place in his jacket, Bronx aims the sharp point at Freeport's throat. The psycho smiles, leering with his fangs, taunting Bronx to rile him up even more. His strangely milky eyes dart away from Bronx to land their gaze on me. I can't get over it. What has he done?

"Did you really think we'd willingly just give up our girl and daughter to you?" Bronx asks, his fangs protruding from his lips. He nicks Freeport with the knife on his jaw near his ear, and a trickle of blood winds down Freeport's neck. "Or that Gwen would just comply after being raised all of her life to rebel against anyone telling her what to do? You've made a huge fucking mistake."

Freeport doesn't respond, keeping his gaze locked on me. I scoot off the bed, relief filling me as my feet touch the rug. Anger pulses through me along with the thudding of my heart. If I didn't know any better, I'd think it would launch from my chest in an attempt to collide into Freeport and send his own heart exploding out his back. I haven't felt this helpless in a while, and I hate it. I never knew I could empathize with an animal stuck on their back and unable to get back to their feet. Fuck, next time I see a roach or something, I'll make sure to flip it over.

I glower and ball my hands into fists. "Of course he did, Bronx. This fucker is not only full of himself, but he's also stupid as hell. How he even survived in the human world before the Vampire Uprising is beyond me."

Freeport breaks at my comment and snarls, trying to fight against Laredo's quiet restraint. "You will regret this, dhampir! You have no idea what I'm capable of!"

Bronx loses control of his rage and sinks his teeth into Freeport's shoulder, injecting him with his venom. A holler escapes from Freeport at the intense pain that comes with such a bite. Who knew I'd enjoy the sound of Freeport's torment so much. It sends my belly rumbling with my dhampir nature.

Freeport snarls and thrashes in Laredo's arms, and Bronx does it again. Heaving a few breaths, Freeport scowls, his sharp features scrunching in agony. A painful tear drips from Freeport's lashes, and I notice the milky white substance coating one of his irises shifts and exposes the deep color of his eyes.

"I'm going to kill you!" Freeport yells, fighting more vehemently in Laredo's arms. Laredo's silence unnerves me a bit as I can't decipher the steeliness of his expression. I know he doesn't want Freeport to know he's here, and it takes everything in me not to say his name. To beg him to end Freeport.

"You think you can kill me?" Bronx scoffs, the shuddering, strained noise mocking Freeport. "I should rip your head off and be done with you. Your coven has been nothing but a pain in my balls, and it kills me that Gwen ever had to deal with you in the first place," Bronx says, swinging his big fist at Freeport's gut.

"Then do it. Give my brother the satisfaction of knowing he won," Freeport says, flicking his attention to me, his voice quaking as he tries to catch his breath. "But know this. Even if I die, Gwen will never be a Royale. She will always belong to the Baron bloodline as will the power she'll birth."

Bronx hollers in agitation and swipes his blade over Freeport's throat, sending his blood pouring down the front of his shirt. Yanking Freeport back, Laredo growls at Bronx, stopping him from taking Freeport's head. The two of them standoff, looking ready to fight with Freeport between them. I can't believe what I'm seeing. Laredo swore he was on our side, but here he is, protecting the Baron asshole.

"Laredo!" I screech, fisting my fingers. Annoyance pushes me into doing exactly what I didn't want to do by alerting Freeport to who restrains him. I waddle forward, my belly making it damn near impossible to look or act intimidating. So I try to lower my voice while baring my teeth with my glower. "Whose side are you on? I trusted you even though you've done nothing but fuck with my life. What the hell? Why are you protecting him?"

The scent of Freeport's blood smacks me in the senses.

I cover my nose and mouth, trying to keep my wild body in check at the sight of Freeport's blood. Jameson's venom must've worn off enough, because my stomach growls in deep-seated, feral need to consume the blood of every single one of my enemies. The urge to launch forward and sink my teeth into Freeport's throat is only kept at bay because Bronx steps back and blocks my way. His buff, hulking body acts as a chiseled wall, and I can't get around him, his movements identical to mine like he knows exactly what I'll do and when.

I give up and steady myself, bracing on his shoulders to stretch on my tiptoes. Bronx's closeness floods me with relief and kicks all my fear away. With him, I'm not afraid of Freeport. Now that we touch, I know I'm utterly and completely safe. He won't let anyone hurt me.

"Gwen," Laredo argues, narrowing his eyes at me. "You have to understand."

"Just answer my girl," Bronx snaps, his muscles flexing, sending a vein in his neck bulging. "Don't try to excuse this bullshit. He needs to die. Look what he tried to do. Enough is enough."

"Please, you both need to listen and hear me out." Laredo digs his fingers harder into Freeport, sending blood pooling around his nails. "I am and always will be on your side, Gwen. I know you both want to kill him, and he should die for his crimes, but we can still use him. He has information that is of value," Laredo finally says, speaking up. He clenches his jaw like the words physically bring him pain. "I swear. You have to trust me. I want him dead as much as you. I know you don't think he will become of use, but I promise you that I will get what we need from him. And then you can take his head."

"I want his heart, too," I say, my chest heaving with my anger.

Freeport tries to thrash free, but Laredo's strength keeps him in place. He presses his lips to Freeport's ear. "I'll help you to ensure it hurts him as badly as he hurt you."

"No." Bronx straightens his back. "It's not worth the risk. There are other Barons left we can control."

Freeport visibly stiffens, but the wound on his throat leaves him incapable of responding. Bronx punches him in the jaw, guaranteeing it. I move with Bronx, remaining close with each of his movements. The satisfaction of seeing Bronx so protective and in need of revenge courses through me. He's sexy and hot, and I never knew how much I liked watching him defend me.

"Dandelion, go to the door and let my brothers in," Bronx says, keeping his eyes trained on Freeport. "This must be done."

Laredo flashes his fangs. "Bronx, listen to me. I mean it. We shouldn't kill him. The rebels are preparing to try to seize part of the territory. I've seen them facing the dangers of exploring territories outside of Donor Life Corp to do so. Freeport knows things that we can use against them. He helped start the rebel uprising. Please, you have to trust me." Laredo flicks his attention to me, locking his gaze to mine as I remain firmly in my place, using Bronx as a shield. "Please, Gwen. You know I wouldn't ask for this otherwise. You have been my sole purpose since the moment we met."

Fuck. Fuck. Fuck.

But I want Freeport dead, and currently, the mini-beast grows wild, moving and shifting my stomach, trying to coax me into dashing forward to draw my tongue across Freeport's bloody throat. Who knew one of my pregnancy cravings would be death? Beating hearts. Severed heads. Waterfalls and rivers of my enemies' blood to swim in because baths of it just isn't good enough. Why couldn't the baby want pickles or something? A banana. Blood drizzled ice cream.

"Gwen," Laredo repeats, the desperation in his voice staunching the urge of my crazy-ass blood hunger. Because now I want ice cream with syrupy blood over it. "Please. I just need a bit more time. You will—we will—get our revenge."

I inhale and exhale a long breath. It takes me ten long gasps to settle the beast inside me, thinking about Laredo's reasoning. It had been our plan all along. Bronx and I both know it. These horrible circumstances today trigger us to think and act with our anger.

"Maybe he's right, Bronx," I finally say, pressing my face into his back to breathe in more of his scent.

"And if he's not?" Bronx argues. He reaches behind him to grab my hand like he needs more than my closeness. He needs to know he has me. "What if we hadn't arrived today? You could've been killed. Jameson too. I just don't know if the risk is worth it anymore. You're too far along. It has to be taking a toll on you. I know how mentally exhausting mind control can be."

I lick my lips, squeezing his fingers. "I'm good, really. It's not so bad. And now that you're here, it'll be better. We can seize control over the Barons in a more permanent manner. I just need to know what went wrong and why my mind manipulation faltered. Something snapped it out of him, which is why he managed to pull this shit. I'm afraid I can't protect you all, so we need to control them other ways."

"It's not your job to protect our coven, dandelion. It's mine, and I'll figure it out. But for now, I need you to manipulate him into doing everything I say, okay?" Bronx says, pulling me into his arms. "It's important to get this right."

I bob my head, my chest tightening. What if I screw it up again? I shove the thought away and motion at Freeport's strange eyes. "I just need you to remove whatever the hell he put on his eyes to keep me out. It's why I couldn't fight him off."

"All right." Bronx clenches his jaw and turns to Laredo. "Hold the fucker still. I'm going to make sure this hurts."

"What the hell is this?" I ask, staring in surprise as Bronx carries in a king-sized mattress to add to the bedframe he put together next to my bed. He plops it down and swivels his torso, gracing me with his gorgeous smile. I love his broody face, but damn, the happiness practically glowing in his expression leaves me weak in the knees.

"What does it look like?" he asks, continuing his mission to stretch a mega-sized sheet across the two mattresses. His biceps bulge with his effort, and I admire every inch of him as he does something completely out of his normal behavior. "I'm getting things prepared how we need. After everything we've been through, I've decided it was time to give up the idea of a staff and start doing things for myself." He straightens his back and puffs out his chest, proud as hell over his work. "Now what do you think? I think it'll work."

I laugh and stroll forward. "It's huge and totally unnecessary. The bed was fine before. I'm not that much bigger." I stick out my tongue and turn sideways to give him a view of my bulging belly. "This cannonball will only keep like a foot between us. But thanks for thinking of my comfort...or yours."

He chuckles and shakes his head. "The king is crowded when we all try to squeeze in it, and we've decided until our daughter arrives, we're all sharing a room."

Our daughter. I'm so in love with the sound of it. I love how my guys accept her as their own whether or not she'll share a blood bond. It's exactly how I imagined and hoped, knowing that we will raise her as a coven, together like we do everything else we possibly can.

I raise my eyebrows and tilt my head, deciding to poke his beast side just a bit more. I've missed teasing the grumpy brute and can't wait to see how he responds. He can't just toss me around or throw me on the bed how he likes. This pregnancy brings out the softer, sweeter, more adorable side in all of them.

"Hmm. No one asked me," I tease, already loving the idea of being sandwiched between the four of them. "Maybe I like being crowded. Caged in. It's easier to snack on you as I please when someone's arm, chest, or back is always near."

Bronx's eyes flash silver and he play-growls, raising his hands in front of him. "You know what, dandelion? Your bratty ass is asking to be punished."

I laugh and screech, trying to get out of the way as Bronx strides across the room to me. Reaching the loveseat of my sitting area, I swipe a pillow and throw it at his head. He dodges out of the way but doesn't expect that I'll be so fast to grab another, and I spin on my feet and clock him square in the face with it.

He huffs and scoops me up, my waddling ass not getting far with his use of vampire speed. Carrying me like a bride, he slowly, torturously closes the space to the bed. I tip my head back and laugh as he gently sets me down like he might break me at any second. He licks his lips and kneels on the edge of the bed, his eyes roving over my body. Arousal hardens his body in excitement, his playfulness turning into lust. Lying back, I stretch my arms over my head, totally failing at being sexy with my pregnant belly, but that's not my mission.

Bronx crawls closer, thinking I'm silently inviting him to join me. "Dandelion, I—"

I hook my fingers to one of my fluffy pillows and whack him again.

I shriek and giggle as Bronx tears the pillow open with his teeth, sending downy feathers all over me. I grab a handful and throw them into the air, watching as the white feathers blow across the room in the wind from the ceiling fan. Bronx smiles, showing off his perfect teeth, and I automatically grab for his shirt, wanting to see him out of it. His muscles flex under my desperate exploration of his taut pecs and abs as I make my way down to the enormous bulge threatening to burst through his pants.

"I'm so happy you plan to stay," I whisper, pulling him to me by the back of his neck until he lies down beside me.

"I was worried."

"I will—our coven will—never leave you again." His full lips brush to mine, and he absently rubs his hand across my belly, waiting to see if the baby kicks.

He laughs and smiles the second she does, and I snuggle against his neck and lick his throat. He hums at the sensation of my teeth lightly scraping his skin. I nip him hard enough to leave a mark but not draw blood. I'm a bit nervous about it, knowing how much his taste sets me off. Bronx's blood always tests my wild side and affects me in a way unlike his brothers, and now that I'm constantly on the verge of losing myself to my nature...I don't want to risk it.

"Dandelion, you're torturing me," he murmurs, his fangs clicking in my ear. "I want you to bite me. Let me take care of you."

"Maybe you should let me take care of you instead." I glide my hand over his belt until I stroke the hard length of his shaft.

He moans and kisses me harder, biting my lip to taste my blood. I shift on top of him, my savage desire controlling my actions. My sex drive is utterly crazy, my lust and need wanting to control me every minute of the day.

Someone clears their throat, and Bronx sits up and glowers, enveloping me in his arms protectively.

I sigh and wave my hand. "You need to learn how to knock, Laredo. We're obviously in the middle of something."

"I did knock." Laredo smirks, the side of his lips curling up, revealing a dimple on his cheek. "You two must've been too busy squealing and moaning to hear me."

I struggle to slide out of Bronx's embrace and off the bed. Bronx must feel my frustration about not being as nimble or fast as I'm used to, because he quietly lifts me up and sets me on my feet. I straighten my dress, pulling it down as best I can to ensure I don't give Laredo a view of my panties. Bronx looms behind me, following my waddling gait as I close the distance to Laredo. I expect Bronx to growl and yell, maybe even pick Laredo up by his shirt and toss him out, but he remains his silent, threatening self behind me.

I straighten my back, accidentally bumping my belly into Laredo with my attempt to get into his face. I'm too proud and annoyed to step back, so I push closer and try to herd him back. But fucking shit. He doesn't even budge, not even when the mini-beast kicks him.

"I know you didn't knock, Laredo. I have better hearing now, so don't lie to me." I poke him in the chest, surprised by how hard his pec is. He must've been working out a lot lately.

"I'm not lying—"

I grab the front of his shirt and lock my gaze to his, my eyes trapping him in place while opening his mind. He freezes, unable to break away. "I said don't lie." A growl escapes my lips, and Laredo's eyes turn solid silver as he tries to resist my unintentional mind manipulation. "Now tell me if you knocked on the door or not."

Laredo's fangs peek from beneath his lips. "I didn't."

I fucking knew it, and it pisses me off that he entered my room like a fucking creep. "Why not? Don't you know that makes you a damn perv?"

"You wouldn't have answered," he argues, his voice monotone. I could force him to stop trying to excuse his behavior, but I don't want to cross a line. I just want the truth.

"You couldn't have known that, and you know it." I dig my fingers into his scruffy cheeks, heaving a breath into his face.

"Fine. If you must know, I wanted to interrupt you. I wanted to piss off your mate and stop him from always getting what he wants. I'm fucking jealous. You were always supposed to be mine." Laredo's nostrils flare with his words.

I don't respond, letting his words sink in. He's always been clear about what he wanted from me, and at one time, I would've given in. I mourned him when I thought he died. But then, if he hadn't abandoned me and faked his death, I'd have never ended up with the Royales. Who knows what my life would've been like.

I inhale a deep breath and then exhale, letting the annoyance flow out of me. "I'm sorry, Laredo. This is hard on all of us, but sneaking around, continuing to lie to me—"

Bronx clears his throat. "Fucking trying to cock-block—"

I bonk my back into Bronx. "Interrupting my time with my mates and one of the dads of my baby, and being resentful and jealous instead of trying to understand me like I'm trying to understand you...it has to stop. I'm about to have a baby. I don't need the stress that you're putting on me. You don't have to be here. I don't even know why you are at this point."

I break my stare, not sure if I really want to hear the truthful answer in his soul. I have too much to deal with and don't need to add Laredo to the mix.

Laredo shakes his head, squeezing his eyes shut for a second. "You're afraid of the truth."

I shrug. "I don't know if I even care. Now, just tell us why you're here. You didn't really come to be a creep."

He grazes his tongue across his bottom lip, drawing my attention to his mouth. "I have a surprise for you."

"A surprise?" I ask, twisting my lips to the side. Swiveling, I glance at Bronx behind me.

Bronx lifts and drops his shoulders without saying a word.

"Well, it's actually for you and your brothers," Laredo says, remaining expressionless.

My eyes widen. "Wait. Ashton and Declan are here?" I spin and face Bronx. "Why didn't you tell me they were coming?"

"They weren't supposed to come for a few more days." Bronx darts his gaze to Laredo.

Laredo smiles, his cocky-bastard grin savoring the fact that he obviously took my guys' surprise and twisted it into his own. "It couldn't wait."

I smack Laredo on the shoulder. "Whatever. I don't care who brought them. Just take me to them. I'm so happy they're here."

5

FAMILY REUNION

"GWENY! HOLY FUCK, YOU'RE GOING to pop!" Ashton materializes in front of me at vampire speed and presses his palms to each side of my belly. Leaning forward, he kisses my cheek.

"Shit, you're right, Ash." Declan stands up from his seat, moving at his human pace.

Snaking his hand between Ashton and me, he pokes my protruding belly button. He smacks his lips together, creating a popping sound. My brothers laugh and squish me into a hug between them. I rake my fingers through their hair, tousling their tresses. Even now, they remind me of our childhood together with their teasing.

"But you're stunning," they say at the same time and grin at each other. "Dad would've been so excited."

I laugh and pat their heads. "That was creepy as hell. Did you guys practice that?"

"The whole damn way here," Laredo mutters from the hallway, staying out of the way.

Bronx offers his hand to each of my brothers and surprises them by tugging them in for a hug. Joy swells inside me. I never dreamed of a moment like this, and it couldn't be more perfect—except if things had been different with the rest of my brothers.

I push thoughts of Grayson, Silas, Kyler, and Porter away. I hate that I sometimes miss them—at least, who they were to me before we were separated. I know I shouldn't carry any guilt, because they were the ones responsible for their own decisions, but it doesn't hurt me any less. It's best just to forget.

Ashton and Declan's matching, wide-ass grins help.

"Where's Jameson?" Ashton asks, pulling away from Bronx's bear hug. "He seems to be taking good care of you, Gwen."

My grin widens. "The best. And he's around here somewhere. Probably taking a much needed break from my teeth."

Declan grimaces. "If I didn't suspect he liked it, I'd feel bad for him having to deal with—"

"A beautiful, ravenous, ravishing, extra-bitey beast." Jameson steps through the front door with Mikkalo, the two of them carrying giant crates on their shoulders like they weigh nothing. "Also, no Gigi. I don't ever need a break from you. I'm just catching up with Mik. If you hadn't realized, this fuckhead only ever talks to me for minutes before asking to talk to you."

I crinkle my nose at Mikkalo. "I wouldn't take it personally, Jamie. Mikkalo can't help himself when I show him my..." I bare my bottom teeth as blush crawls up my neck to blossom in my cheeks.

Both of my brothers groan from behind me, and Bronx roars a laugh and smacks them on the back. Everett enters the house with his brows peaked on his forehead. He shakes his head with a smirk. At least I only brought up my video chats with Mikkalo, because if my brothers—or any of my guys, for that matter—knew the fun things Everett came up with to help ease missing each other, I don't think my face would ever recover. I already know the second he gets a moment alone with me, Everett's going to ask to recreate some of the things I teased him with.

Like he can read my mind, Everett winks at me and whacks Mikkalo and Jameson with the duffle bags hanging from his arms as he slides between them. My heart picks up pace and heat swells between my legs. I clench my thighs together and try not to glance at Everett anymore, my thoughts wandering to places I never want them to leave.

Jameson groans and drops the crate at his feet before rubbing the back of his neck. "What the fuck is that about?"

Damn.

Everyone's gazes fall on me, and I keep my eyes glued to the floor.

I suck my bottom lip between my teeth and murmur, "Boundaries, Jamie."

He scoffs and strides across the room to me, scooping me up to bury his face in the crook of my neck. "I don't know what those are anymore, Gigi. I'll accept your answer for now because your brothers look ready to cover their ears and run, but I will find out later. Even if I have to tickle it out of you. Because, fuck. That reaction? I need to be the reason. Your body got hot enough that I could smell your blood warming from across the room. You even whimpered."

I laugh in exasperation and wiggle until he sets me down. "Go finish unpacking and make sure your brothers get settled, and maybe—if you're good—I'll reward you."

He pumps his fist in silent victory. "You heard our girl. Get your asses moving. There's no time to waste."

Jameson pushes Bronx toward the hallway leading to

my room, and Mikkalo strolls past me and kisses my shoulder and touches my belly like he can't resist. Laredo glides from his creeper spot and plops onto the couch, folding his arms over his chest. Holding my hands out to my brothers, I hook my arms through each of theirs, and drag them to the sitting area with a huge entertainment center, a black leather couch that I don't like to sit on now because I feel like I melt to it, and a wide ottoman with a top that turns over to create a table. Shelves of ancient books rest in built-ins on the walls, and a heavy, back-world velvet curtain covers a dark tinted window, ensuring it looks like night all day long.

I choose to sit on the ottoman, crossing my legs at my ankles. "You have no idea how happy I am to see you two." I slightly turn to Laredo. "Thanks for arranging this."

Laredo nods slowly, his features softening. "Anything for you."

I blink my weepy eyes and turn back to my brothers. "How is Crimson Vista, Ash? Bronx says you've adapted so well." I look to Declan. "And what about you? Where's Macon? I didn't think he'd let you out of his sight." It still feels unreal that Declan chose to remain with the Bowman Coven, but he swears he enjoys it.

Declan smiles sheepishly, a warm tint peeking through the scruff of his beard. "This guy arranged for two sisters to transfer into the Bowman household in exchange for time away under Ashton's protection...also, Mac knows I won't leave Jessa for long."

"Jessa?" The name squeaks from my mouth.

"I wish you could meet her," Declan adds.

I bounce in my spot, excitement coursing through me. I knew finding a woman and starting a family was something all of my brothers wanted.

And then my face falls.

Declan is a carrier of the dhampir mutation. While it's rare, it's still possible. What that would mean for my brother and his future family...

Leaning forward, Declan rests his hand over mine and shakes Ashton's knee. "I already know what you're thinking, and I don't want you worrying about me, okay? You have enough of your own things to worry about. Trust that I can take care of mine."

"He's right, Gweny. This visit is supposed to be fun. Nothing heavy. It's been far too long that we all got to be together that I don't want to waste it. I want to see your badass self in action, putting the Baron fucks in their place. I want to see your silly as hell pregnant waddle. I want to see the Royales taking care of you, so I know they'll take care of our niece." Ashton flicks his attention to the commotion in the hallway as my guys stroll from the hallway and back to the door, acting as if they're not eavesdropping on our conversation.

Declan wiggles his fingers at them. "I just want to see the look of sheer panic on their faces when you go into labor. I bet a thousand stipends that Bronx passes out."

Ashton tips his head back and laughs, his voice ringing through the room. "I accept. I'll double it and bet that it's Mikkalo."

I reach out and press my index fingers to each of their mouths, knowing damn well that Bronx and Mikkalo hear. Jameson's soft laugh and quiet bet to Everett that he agrees with Declan proves it.

I don't remove my hands from silencing my brothers until my guys pass by again, carrying more stuff from the vehicles. If I didn't know any better, I'd think they were planning for all of us to move into the Barons' estate permanently.

Declan and Ashton laugh and joke for a moment more, filling me up with happiness that starts to deflate the longer I try to hold onto it. I have to keep reminding myself that this is just a visit. Once I give birth, things will change. How much exactly? I don't want to even think about it.

"Gweny?" Declan says, drawing my attention to him. Reaching out, he runs his finger under my eye, smearing a tear I hadn't realized leaked from my lashes. "What's wrong? You know you can talk to us about anything."

I sigh and scrub my cheeks, flicking my gaze to Laredo and back to my brothers. "I'm sorry. I don't mean to. It's just—" I rub my hand over my stomach. "I'm a bit emotional these days. I can't control it. I am happy. I swear." Emotional is an understatement. I could handle some crying. But the outrageous hunger and wildness? I hope my brothers never see that side of me.

"But you're worried?" Ashton pries, joining his hand with mine.

I shake my head. "No, well, yeah. But I was just thinking about what it would be like if this was permanent, and you guys never had to go. I've been thinking about all the changes that have hit us so suddenly, and...I can't stop wondering what it would be like if Silas and Grayson...fuck. If Kyler were alive. If Porter—"

"I found Porter, Gwen." Laredo's smooth voice cuts through my moment of spilling my heart out. He's been so quiet. It's easy to forget he sits at the opposite end of the sectional.

I bring my hand to my chest, feeling the thrums of my racing heart. "What?"

Declan and Ashton swivel on the couch to face Laredo, staring at him in silence.

He nods at me in confirmation, never breaking eye contact. "There are many things I regret in life, and separating you from your brothers is one of my biggest ones. I feel as if the path it led Grayson, Silas, and Kyler would have been much different if I had figured out how to keep you together." Laredo stands from the couch and shuffles to drop on his knees in front of me. Clasping my hands, he draws them up to his chest. "I know bringing Porter won't make up for my actions, but I hope it will help."

I sit in shock, trying to process his words. I don't know whether I should be cautious or excited. He only said he found Porter. He doesn't have him yet. If he did, Porter would be here. And then? Fuck. Porter and I weren't on the best terms. Laredo killed Porter's best friend after catching me sleeping with him. If he blamed me for that, there won't be any reason for him not to blame me for Kyler. For Silas and Grayson. Fuck. He could even blame me for Ashton, despite Silas biting him with venom.

But the smiles my brothers give Laredo are enough to shove my concerns to the dark recesses of my mind, and my body floods with happiness and relief. If Laredo located Porter, we can figure out how to get him back. It'll stop me from thinking the worst of the worst.

"As soon as I talk things over with the Royales, I swear to you that we will bring him home," Laredo adds.

More tears swell in my eyes, and I throw my arms around Laredo's neck, giving him a real hug. He sinks into me, breathing in my hair, his stomach pressing into my belly. He gently smooths his hand up and down my spine, trying to push away my trembles.

I ease away and smile, staring into Laredo's sparkling

eyes, the flash of silver lighting streaks of steel across their fathomless depths. Laredo caresses his thumb over my jaw, and the second his eyes lower to my mouth, I know exactly what he plans to do. I don't get a chance to react or move, to even make sense of what is happening, before Laredo molds his lips to mine, kissing me like the hundreds of times we've kissed in what now feels like another life altogether.

My stomach jostles, the mini-beast shaking my sense back into me, and I jerk away and touch my mouth like his kiss burns me. My emotions surge in a wave of confusion, spinning around my mind like a cyclone hell-bent on destroying my life. Swinging my hand, I slap Laredo in the face, my palm stinging at the force hard enough to jerk his head sideways. I shove him back and manage to push to my feet with only a little effort, and I squeeze my eyes shut and bolt toward the front door.

I need air.

Lots of it.

I also need to get away from the man who thinks because we once had a past life together that he assumes my affectionate gratitude meant he could kiss me.

"Gwen, wait. I'm sorry," Laredo calls out.

Ashton growls and something crashes. "Don't chase her, Laredo! You've done enough."

Cool air engulfs me, and I bow forward, clutching my

knees. My emotions crash through me, sending me reeling. Two warm hands steady me from behind, and Declan's familiar scent engulfs me. He spins me around and gathers me into a bear hug, rubbing soothing circles between my shoulder blades.

"What was he thinking?" I ask, my voice rising into the night.

Declan huffs. "I don't know—"

A figure materializes behind him, and Thaxton flashes his fangs and he rips my brother away from me. "What are you thinking, Gwen? Who the fuck is this? You're mine!"

Bending Declan's neck, Thaxton exposes his throat. Panic freezes me in place. I try to speak, to move, to do something, but my body fails to react.

My fear instincts buzz wildly, and all I can do is hold my hand up and say, "No."

Declan yells for help, Thaxton drags him away.

Declan hollers, and then silence falls through the dark night.

6

COMPLETE CONTROL

MY BODY KICKS INTO ACTION at the heavy silence, and I rush toward the shadow of the house Thaxton dragged Declan into. I don't get within ten feet of it when Bronx materializes in front of me. He picks me up, wrapping my legs around his waist. I clutch onto him as a sob escapes my lips, my inability to get my words out tearing me apart. It takes Bronx spinning around at a gurgled noise to get my shit together.

I open my mouth to scream for Declan, but my brother

crawls from the shadows on his hands and knees until finding his footing. He braces against a tree, his face pale from fear. I gasp a breath of relief, spotting Jameson and Everett surrounding Declan, ensuring he's okay. I don't see any blood or bite marks, and Everett gives Bronx a nod and disappears with Declan. Jameson follows suit, clutching a dagger, protecting them from another surprise attack.

"He's going to be fine," Bronx says, stroking his big hand along my back. "Are you okay? He didn't hurt you any?"

I swallow and bob my head. "I'm so-sorry," I manage to say, but nothing else comes to me. My foggy mind refuses to process anything that just happened.

Bronx kisses my cheek with a soft smile but doesn't comment. He turns to Mikkalo, now visible in the dim outside lighting. "Mik, stay on guard. Gwen needs to get into this asshole's head." Bronx adjusts me in his arms to cradle me instead of setting me on my feet. And I'm glad for it. My nerves are shot. First Laredo surprise kisses me and then Thaxton tries to kill my brother. This night keeps getting worse and worse. We should be celebrating and settling in. Enjoying our newfound time together, and not dealing with the Barons.

I'm so done with them and these games.

Mikkalo wields a sword, his muscles rippling with his fighting stance. I search the weapon for Thaxton's blood, but the shiny metal is clean. Two pairs of silver eyes blink from the shadows, and I realize Laredo restrains Thaxton in place, holding a short blade against his throat. Thaxton flares his nostrils, narrowing his eyes on me. He looks as if I'm the one in the wrong. Like I've betrayed him. Fucker.

"Gwen, I don't understand," Thaxton says, his voice bellowing through the night. "I thought you liked me. We've been together for weeks."

Bronx carries me the two dozen feet across the yard, and it takes everything in me not to whimper and beg for him to just take me back to our room. I don't want to deal with this now. I just want it to be over with.

"It's been all in your head, Thaxton," Laredo says with a growl. "You were wrong about Gwen only birthing power. She is power incarnate and more magnificent than anyone could ever imagine."

Thaxton bares his fangs as recognition settles in. "Brother. I should've known you were too smart to get killed."

"I'm not your brother," Laredo snaps, his voice reverberating through the air with another guttural noise from his throat. "The Barons were merely a power source for me. I'm with Gwen. Always have been."

"Yet she's with the Royales." Thaxton glowers at Mikkalo and tries to break free of Laredo's hold. He snaps his teeth, not even caring that Laredo's knife cuts his throat.

Mikkalo aims his sword, catching it to the front of Thaxton's shirt. "Enough! You will not argue over our mate."

"She won't be yours for much longer," Thaxton mutters. He once again tries to break free, but he can't figure out how to escape the points of the weapons surrounding him.

Fury crashes through me, and I launch from Bronx's arms, summoning my dhampir speed with my anger. I haven't moved this fast in a while, and the blurring world seems to fill me with electric energy, zinging power to my core. The baby moves like crazy, shocking me a bit, but I suppress my surprise. I stop a foot short of Thaxton, next to Mikkalo, wrapping my hand around Mikkalo's wrist. Before Thaxton can even react, I shove the sword into his chest. Thaxton's mouth falls open in surprise, and I tug Mikkalo back to watch Thaxton's blood soak his shirt.

"You think you're in control but you're not. Nothing between us was ever real. I was using you." My silver eyes reflect back to me in Thaxton's saucer gaze.

His jaw twitches, and a gurgling sound escapes his mouth as he tries to push air through. "Gwen." Thaxton's eyes flick back and forth as he searches my face for the truth he doesn't want to believe. It's in this moment that I know how powerful my mind manipulation is, because I can see Thaxton's heart breaking before my eyes.

I hum in appreciation, a dark part of me satisfied for turning into the monster the Barons turned me into. In another lifetime, I might feel a teensy bit bad for the mind games. For playing with Thaxton's heartstrings until they snapped. But now? Fuck no. He deserves every ounce of pain I inflict on him. He deserves more than I can even think to bestow.

If it wasn't for Thaxton, for his former coven head Rochester, and for the rest of the Baron assholes, both of my parents would be alive. My brothers would all be safe and happy. Together. Laredo wouldn't have felt the need to constantly manipulate my life. I'd have—it doesn't matter, I guess.

Because as much as I wish things would've been different for my family, I wouldn't change things for me. Every terrible thing in my life brought me to this moment. It gave me a protective coven of powerful men—ones who not only take care of me but also accept that they need me to take care of them too. It brought me a life I never imagined possible and so much more to look forward to. It also gave me so much more to fight for.

The control the Barons think they have on me ends now. I'm no longer going to manipulate them to think things are normal and in their favor. I will manipulate them to know that I'm the biggest threat they'll ever face and the only way they will ever survive is to bow to me and the Royales.

Stepping closer, I punch my hand into Thaxton's chest. He hollers and clenches, his body turning rigid. His warm, squishy insides engulf my hand. The power of my blow breaks his sternum, and I feel the rapid beats of his wild, frightened heart.

"I want you to know how fragile your life truly is," I say, locking him in my stare. His mind opens to me, and a shockwave of his emotions drags a soft gasp from my lips. I suppress the collision of his emotions with mine. I will not be distracted at the strangeness of my power. "You will know and accept that regardless of your eternity, your power stops short of what I can do. To me, you're merely like a mortal, and I can and will do with you as I please. You will obey me and stand by my side as my puppet."

"Careful, dandelion," Bronx murmurs, his voice low in my ear as he fills the empty space next to me. "You don't want to ask too much. The mind is fragile."

"If he were human," I respond, squeezing Thaxton's heart tighter.

Laredo shifts behind Thaxton. "Gwen—"

"No, Laredo. I know what I'm doing, and I will handle this." Stepping closer to Thaxton, I get into his face, leaving only an inch between us. His eyes turn solid silver as I bury my very essence into his mind, hypnotizing him with my power. Another wave of hot emotions crashes over me, and

I smile at the exhilaration that follows. "Isn't that right, Thaxton? You will let me handle everything from now on."

"Yes." Thaxton's robotic voice agrees.

"You will know that Laredo has always been alive, and he was doing the right thing by keeping you away from me. You will accept that I'm Gwen Royale, and the Royales are my mates. You will not question our authority, and if Freeport or Cortland tries to betray us, you will end their lives. Do you understand?"

"Yes," Thaxton says.

"Now, gather your brothers. You will ensure they remain in line. I expect dinner and a celebration for the Royales arrival. Laredo will assist you." I slide my hand from Thaxton's chest cavity and smile. "You will all bow and swear loyalty."

Thaxton wobbles on his feet and shakes his head, snapping out of the hold I had on his mind. Bronx pulls me to his chest as Mikkalo steps in front of me, protectively sandwiching me in between them. Laredo tests Thaxton, slowly releasing him, I wait in silence, pressing my lips together, afraid that if I even breathe, he might snap out of it.

Thaxton straightens his shirt, studying the blood for a second. "My apologies for my rash behavior, Ms. Royale. I hadn't realized you invited guests." Swiveling on his feet, he looks at Laredo. "I'm happy to have you and the Royales home. I think we should celebrate such an occasion. Will you help me, Laredo?"

Laredo remains stiff, the sinewy muscles on his arms rippling. He curls his fingers into fists and glances at me. I nod and wait for him to obey, and without another word, Thaxton and Laredo disappear.

I exhale a long breath upon their departure and sink against Bronx until he lifts me back up into his arms. Exhaustion courses through me, and I can't stop my head from resting on his shoulder. Manipulating Thaxton like I had took a lot out of me, but if this is the only consequence to get such a command to stick, it was totally worth it.

If only it also didn't leave me worried about Freeport and Cortland. I didn't feel like this after putting them in their places.

"You're going to have to manipulate Freeport and Cortland one more time to include the information about Laredo, dandelion. I wish you had just left him out and allowed for him to deal with his own mess with the Barons." Bronx's smooth voice remains even, but I don't have to ask him to know he's more worried about me than he lets on.

"I just—I'm tired," I say, closing my eyes. "The fewer secrets we have to keep hidden, the better."

Bronx nods. "Maybe next time give us a bit of a head's up. Finding you outside—"

"I'm sorry for that. It was careless. I didn't think things through, because Laredo—" I snap my mouth shut, my mind whirling all over again as I remember his stolen kiss. "Laredo kissed me. He kissed me and—"

Mikkalo growls and disappears, abandoning me and Bronx outside. Bronx grumbles under his breath and shouts for Mikkalo, but a crash sounds from inside the house. Several guttural growls vibrate through my bones, and the world spins as Bronx carries me at vampire speed. Mikkalo pins Laredo to the dining room wall and punches him in the gut.

"Mikkalo, stand down!" Bronx shouts, closing the distance.

Jameson snatches me from Bronx and moves me to the corner to cage me behind his muscular body. I bump my belly into his back and link my fingers to his shoulders, using him to stand on my tiptoes to get a clear view of the drama unfolding.

"He kissed our girl!" Mikkalo yells, ignoring Bronx while ramming his fist into Laredo's gut again. "He nearly got Declan killed!"

"And we will discuss it. In private with Gwen. Now is not the time to fight. If Gwen thinks this is necessary punishment, she will say so. Until then, back the hell up. She needs you to concern yourself with her, not that asshole." Bronx grabs Mikkalo by the shoulders and hauls him back. "That goes for everyone. Gwen is our number one priority."

"So you're okay that he kissed her?" Mikkalo asks, his

face lining with anger.

"Did you even think to let Gwen finish talking when she was trying to confide in us? What if—" Bronx shuts his mouth and shakes his head. "We will talk about this later, understand? Right now, Gwen needs to eat and get the celebration she requested. She needs us to listen to her and do things her way."

Mikkalo swipes his hands down his face, smoothing out his features. He abandons Laredo and comes to me and Jameson. Jameson shifts enough to allow Mikkalo into his protective cage. I grab onto him and lace my arms around Mikkalo's neck, hugging him close, wishing none of us were ever in this position in the first place.

"I'm sorry," Mikkalo murmurs, caressing his lips to my ear.

"Don't be. You've done nothing wrong. I appreciate you looking out for me as my mate." I lean back and kiss Mikkalo softly. "And don't tell Bronx, but he might be right. I just want to celebrate that you guys are here and not think about all the other bullshit right now. Can I feed you a little? I want to more than anything right now."

Mikkalo loosens his clenched jaw and nods his head, finally settling down enough to keep the silver blinking in his eyes in check. "Whatever you want, Gwen."

I smile. "Maybe a little taste of you as well."

Mikkalo cracks a smile and exhales, the tenseness in his

muscles fading. I kiss him once more and nip his lip. Familiar stomping footsteps clomp down the hallway in the direction of the dining room, and I tense, steeling myself for Freeport's arrival. Cortland appears in the doorway first, gliding far more silently that I didn't hear him approach.

My heart sinks into my stomach, and I race as fast as I can to him and cup his face between my palms. "You always knew Laredo was alive," I say, opening his mind so easily it feels as normal and effortless as inhaling a breath.

Freeport growls, the guttural noise shuddering through me. Panic explodes inside me, and I fear that maybe my mind manipulation in his bedroom didn't stick. Maybe I've done it too often that he's grown used to it. Maybe—

Freeport steps in front of me, and I snatch him by the shirt and swing him toward the wall. Locking my gaze to his, I say, "Look who has come home, Freeport. Aren't you happy to see Laredo? You were right. He wasn't dead."

Freeport's eyes flicker silver and a strange pressure erupts in my mind. He's resisting. I can feel it in my soul. I should've known that I couldn't keep this up forever. Freeport is powerful. He's older than the Vampire Uprising.

Another growl escapes his lips, and I pinch his cheeks.

"You always knew Laredo was alive. You knew he was out handling the Blood Rebels," I say, imagining ripping his mind open to climb inside. The pressure in my head lessens, and I heave a breath, watching Freeport's features soften.

"Welcome home, Laredo," he says, splitting his hard mouth with a smile.

I release Freeport from my hold, and it's like he takes a part of me with him. Dizziness steals my senses, and Everett calls my name.

The world vanishes.

7

PSYCHO

"WHERE IS SHE?" FREEPORT YELLS, his voice stinging my ears.

"You speak as if you will claim Gwyneth as if she doesn't belong to Galveston." Thaxton's low voice soothes the pain in my head Freeport leaves behind. "Careful, brother. You don't want him to think you plan to ensure he doesn't get her."

Something thuds against the closet door, and Laredo tightens his fingers over my mouth. With his other hand, he rubs his fingers up and down my side, trying to get my human rationale to settle down.

Tugging my head to look at him, Laredo whispers, "Don't make a sound. I will make sure they never claim you." His eyes flicker as our minds connect, and my muscles relax, the fear inside me fading with the sound of footsteps and the slamming of a door.

Laredo removes his hand from my mouth and eases the closet door open. Crossing the room, he locks the door and motions for me to step from our hiding place. I follow him to the expansive bookcase where he plucks an old leather-bound tome from the shelf.

"I'm sorry they scared you, but I couldn't leave you alone. You get in too much trouble these days, my beautiful dhampir."

Standing beside him, I watch Laredo crack open the book and pull out a weathered paper—a map. I always wondered where he'd gotten the ones he previously used to move us around while ensuring we get to stay among rebels.

"Where is that?" I ask, tracing my finger across the brittle paper.

He smiles. "Our next home."

I shake my head. "I don't want to move again."

"But Gwen—"

"Gwen, fuck. Gwen, let me sit up." Bronx's voice drags me from the confusing dream—memory of Laredo—one of many that like to sneak back to me in my sleep.

I push the thought away and bonk my head...into Bronx's taut, but definitely bloody, back. "Fuck," I say, trying to figure out where I am and what I'm doing.

"Ease up, dandelion. You're pinning me down," Bronx says, trying to move his arms.

Whoa.

I jerk upright and stare at the three bloody bite marks across his upper back. I straddle him, wearing only a sheer nightie that stretches over my belly. My nails dig into his wrists, my restraint so tight that his hands turn slightly red from my strength.

Damn it, does he smell delicious.

A strange purr escapes my lips, and I release Bronx's wrists to slide myself low enough to stretch down and drag my tongue across his back. I moan, his sweet, mind-blowingly delicious blood coating my mouth. Lust ignites inside me, my blood hunger quickly transforming into blood lust, and I climb off of Bronx only to grab his sides to roll him over.

"This is the kind of wakeup call I've missed," Bronx says, gracing me with a smile.

He arches up only to snatch me from the bed beside him to set me down right on his huge hard-on throbbing from his boxer-briefs. I moan at the sensation of his thick girth flexing between my legs with only the cotton of his underwear keeping us apart. He obviously was the one to dress me in the bare minimum, and I can't help smiling and grinding against him.

His eyes darken with lust, and he fingers the hem of the nightie and lifts it up to get a better view of my body. Licking his lips, he hums his appreciation. "I love it when you soak me."

I crinkle my nose and giggle, my voice breathless. "Even being near you turns me on."

He hooks his fingers to my hips and slides me forward until my knees hit his pillow. "Good, because I've been dying for a taste. I've missed every inch of you."

"Which there's a lot more of now," I say, stretching my neck to meet his gaze from over my belly.

He chuckles and slides me back just enough to stretch up to kiss the bottom side. "Then you know exactly how excruciating it has been to be away. Now hold still. I plan to enjoy you for the next few hours. It won't be often that I get you all to myself."

I comb my fingers through his dark hair. "If I keep sleep-biting, you might."

He adjusts my body again and hums. "I guess I'll have to turn you wild."

The vibration of his satisfaction buzzes across my skin from his deep voice. I squish his head between my thighs in excitement, a low moan of pleasure escaping my mouth as he kisses the sensitive spot between my legs, slowly, sensually teasing me for a moment before gliding his tongue along the seam of my body to suck my clit. Electricity ignites through every cell on my body. The anticipation of him going from teasing to passionate makes me squirm. He purposely tortures me by taking his time, proving he wasn't kidding about savoring every inch of me.

I clutch the wooden headboard with one hand and use my fingers to spread myself wider, showing Bronx that I want him to kiss me harder. I want him to flick every nerve-ending on my body with his tongue until I scream. It's what he wants and enjoys. Prodding at my dhampir nature until I turn heavy with desire and wild with need is one of his favorite things to do.

He moans as I roll my hips, riding his face in a way that makes me pant. With his hands, he guides me back and forth on his tongue, knowing that with my strength in the moment, it might be impossible to hold me still. My long hair cascades down my back, sweeping across my waist. I can't stop imagining exactly what I look like in this moment, pregnant and needy, desperate for relief only my mate can bring.

A whimper escapes my lips and I lean forward, attempting to get a better view. Bronx's eyes turn to mine, alight with flashes of silver, and then he surprises the hell out of me by rolling his tongue at vampire speed.

I gasp a moan, my eyes widening, my face scrunching with pleasure. He's never done this before, and the second he wags his eyebrows at me, I know the cocky bastard has been holding back so he purposefully doesn't make me cum as fast as he can. Pleasure grows more intense with the wave of cool tingles crashing over my body at my impending orgasm.

But then he slows back down, prolonging the sensation of my near peak.

"Bronx," I gasp, smacking my hand against the wall, needing something to hold onto. "I was so close."

He hums his agreement, the vibration zinging through me. I squeeze my legs around his head, my body begging and pleading for relief. Bronx slides one of his hands across my ass cheek until he tightens his hold on me to sink his fingers between my legs, making me gasp. He caresses my g-spot, and I moan so embarrassingly loud that vampires across the world might hear me.

My body prickles with bliss, every inch of me reveling in the sensations Bronx creates with his mouth, tongue, and fingers. He guides my body against his face with one hand, adding pressure and pleasure.

And then he sends me over the edge by nipping me with his fangs, craving to taste even more of me. The teasing pleasure bite tenses my entire body with an orgasm, and I slap my hands to the wall to brace myself, letting it consume me. My fingers and toes curl, and I scream out, the shock of my orgasm's intensity seeming to shut my mind down to ride the pleasure wave crashing through me. Bronx moans at my reaction, nipping me again to lengthen the time of my tightening muscles, and I feel as if the ecstasy might never stop to let me catch my breath.

Bronx groans and eases me onto the bed next to him. Grinning, he wipes his face with his hand and pops his fingers into his mouth like he can't get enough of me. I grab his cock and stroke the length of it through his underwear, feeling his hard excitement flex under my fingers. He doesn't let me climb back on top of him, and instead kisses my jaw and works his way over my shoulder, silently guiding me to lie on my side.

He curls his body to spoon mine from behind, sliding his arms around me to glide his fingers over the sheer fabric over my nipples and map his hands down my belly and to my hips. He rubs a smooth circle from my hip to my ass, shifting my nightie up. He kisses my shoulder and tugs his cock free from his boxer-briefs, wasting no time to take them off. I gasp at the pressure of his body aligning with mine, his tip slipping and sliding against my arousal.

"You are so beautiful, Gwen," he murmurs, shifting my hair from my throat to kiss my sensitive skin there too. My skin warms him, our passion filling me with everything I could ever want from him. "I love you. I love you more than anything in the world. You are everything to me. I had no idea how much I needed this moment with you until now."

I lick my lips and reach behind me, lacing my fingers through his to pull him even closer. "I've missed you. Your kisses. The way your body feels against mine. How you know exactly what I need. I'm so happy you're here."

"And I'm not leaving you ever again," he responds. "Never."

"That's all I want. Us together."

He moans his agreement as he slides into me completely, hugging and cuddling me from behind.

The even thrusts hit me just right, and I gasp and moan, savoring the pleasure of our lovemaking. Bronx doesn't get wild or rough like I expect him to and this side of him stirs warmth in me like he wants me to know that he's capable of being anything and everything I need. That he can fill me with love and passion while still igniting unforgettable pleasure. Sliding his arm between my neck and the pillow, he offers his body to me to give me everything I need to satisfy me on every level.

I lick his smooth, taut skin and suck his arm for a moment until my wild nature grabs hold of me, and I sink my teeth into his forearm, filling my mouth with blood. His fangs click in my ear, his muscles rippling and moving with his ecstasy, and I savor the sweetness of his blood. Bronx scratches his fangs along the back of my shoulder, his hands tightening around me as he thrusts harder and deeper, releasing a sexy moan. The sensation of his cock sliding in and out of me steals my breath, fogging my mind with love, lust, and an ache that only giving him what I know he desires can cure.

I clutch the sheet between my fingers, bracing my body, gasping at the pressure of his powerful thrusts. He spanks my ass cheek, sending a burst of tingles over my skin. He sucks my shoulder hard, leaving his mark, and his hand desperately slides across my pelvis and in between my legs as he rubs my clit.

"Bite me," I say, my words coming out long and breathy, demanding.

He releases the sexiest noise, like a growling moan. The pinch of his fangs ignites another orgasm inside me, my body remembering the dozens of delicious bites he's given me before.

Molding his lips to his fang marks, he sucks my skin only long enough to savor me how he craves. My gasping moans turn into a burst of quick screams of pleasure until Bronx bites me again as he cums, clutching onto me with his final thrusts.

My mind whirls with pleasure and desire, with love and passion, and I can't stand facing away from him another moment longer.

Like Bronx can hear my thoughts, he slides out of me

to help me roll over. His hands grab mine and he twines our fingers together, resting them against our chests. His beautiful eyes capture mine, and without a word, we open to each other.

Neither of us says anything, just staring into each other's gazes, feeling the whirlpool of our emotions blending and tangling as if our souls morph into one entity.

I lean forward and kiss him again, my whole body still buzzing and warm.

My muscles relax, and I snuggle close, listening to the sound of his heart. The rhythmic melody of the steady beats lulls me into a state of calm and bliss.

If a familiar female voice didn't creep in from beneath the door, I might've fallen asleep. I definitely wouldn't have sat up. Bronx tries to pull me back to him, but the woman laughs outside the door.

I frown. "What is she doing here? It's the middle of the day...right?"

Bronx arches upright and kisses my shoulder. "I might've told Brooklyn what was going on, and she invited herself. I wasn't expecting her so soon, but...you'll have to talk to Ashton."

I grimace, my eyebrows lowering on my forehead. "I know she's your sister and all but—" I snap my mouth shut.

I know I don't have to remind him that his blood sister was part of the coven that killed Kyler. Nor do I have to remind him that she caused a shit-ton of problems. I can't exactly blame Brooklyn, but I also don't have to like her. She's unpredictable.

"I'll tell her she has to leave," Bronx says, nuzzling his nose to mine. "She'll understand. She knew she was supposed to wait until I talked to you."

Damn. How can I agree? He's not arguing or anything.

I sigh. "No, it's fine as long as you think we can trust her. I know she's covenless now, and I'd honestly prefer to know she's not hiding in the shadows, thinking of a dozen ways to plot revenge."

"She wouldn't, dandelion. She knows you're mine for eternity, and she accepts that you're no longer a threat to my power or standing. Fuck, Brooklyn knows you enhance my strength and will protect me better than I can myself." Bronx smirks and brushes my hair behind my ear. "She might've also already proclaimed herself as the Royale aunt."

"Oh, jeez," I mutter.

He chuckles. "You can thank Ash for—"

The door to my bedroom flies open and bangs against the wall.

Bronx growls and disappears from beside me, blocking Freeport's way before he can enter the room. I snatch the sheet and wrap it around myself, unable to get to my feet before Bronx swings his arm and punches Freeport in the face, knocking him back.

"Gwen, I need to speak with you!" Freeport shouts, dodging Bronx's second swing. Flying into the room, Freeport glares at me from the edge of my bed. "I don't know what exactly is going on here, but I know you're behind this."

Bronx grabs Freeport from behind, pulling him away from me.

I blink a few times and try to make sense of what is going on. I know my mind manipulation didn't falter, but maybe it also didn't work completely. If I failed, he'd have come in here throwing daggers or something. Instead, he's annoyingly confrontational.

"Get out of here and wait until the evening if you have qualms you need to settle," Bronx snaps, getting between me and Freeport.

Mikkalo and Jameson materialize in the room, both armed and ready to fight if need be.

Thaxton and Cortland come in next, and I groan and pull the blankets up higher. I'm about to scream at the two fuckers to get out, but then Laredo leads both my brothers into the room. At least Brooklyn seems to keep her good sense, because she remains in the hallway with her hands on her hips.

"Seriously, what the fuck?" I ask, meeting everyone's gaze one at a time.

"I tried to warn them how dangerous it is to interrupt a

starving, pregnant dhampir," Jameson says, remaining expressionless. If only he were joking. "No one would blame you if you ate someone's heart."

I groan and scrub my hands up my cheeks. Turning my attention to Freeport, I wave my hand at him. If I'm supposed to be in charge around here, I guess I need to act the part. "What is so important that you risk your life interrupting my time with my mate?"

He growls. "You might have these fuckers bowing before you, but I will not stand by and act as if they're more powerful than me. I demand to be treated as first in line. You will not force Thaxton and Cortland into my space as if they're—"

"What the fuck? You did not come in here for this." I frown as his wild eyes dart around the room. Fear prickles on the back of my neck.

Freeport's muscles ripple with his tense body. "I want to challenge everyone here and prove my place."

Bronx growls and shoves him. "Get the fuck out."

"No," Freeport snaps.

Before I can open my mouth, Freeport unsheathes a blade from beneath his jacket. My eyes widen as he vanishes and reappears across the room. A scream blasts from my mouth at the same time he swipes his dagger where everyone clusters together.

Blood drops fling like bullets, pelting me across my

face.

"Stop him!" Laredo shouts, shoving my brothers back.

I can't form any words.

I can't think.

All I can do is watch as blood spurts from Cortland's headless body as he falls.

8

FOOLISH

"GWEN, I DON'T THINK YOUR mind manipulation worked completely," Laredo says, calling out over the glass shattering.

A vase of flowers spills across the floor. My vanity table falls over next, and the mirror cracks. Ducking, Laredo avoids getting a chair to the face as he dodges out of the Barons wrath aimed at each other. I tense, the growls and snarls setting off my fear instincts. Clenching my fingers into fists, I suppress my nerves, letting my rage swell inside me at the destruction these assholes cause. They're lucky I'm not attached to any of these belongings or else they'd already be dead.

The mini-beast kicks and moves, reacting to my emotions, and the edges of my vision shadow with red. Hunger swells inside me, and I flare my nostrils as I inhale a few deep breaths, catching everyone's delectable scents.

"You assholes need to stop," I say, my voice low and even, a weird grumbling noise lacing my words.

Thaxton shoves Freeport into the wall as the two remaining Barons fight harder than I've ever seen two vampires fight. Blood sprays from hard punches and venom bites, permeating the air. My stomach growls in protest, screaming that I shouldn't allow all of their blood to go to waste despite them not being my guys. So greedy. I rub my belly and remind the mini-beast that we have standards, and there is no fucking way I'm going to start licking Baron blood off the floor.

Bronx, Jameson, Mikkalo, and Everett create a muscular shield between me and them, and I scoot to the edge of the bed and stand up to peer over their heads for a better view. And damn. It's worse than I thought. These fuckers are going to tear my room completely apart.

Reaching up at lightning speed, Mikkalo catches a broken chair leg and throws it at Freeport, impaling him in the back. Freeport stumbles, and Laredo attempts to get in the middle of the fight, but Freeport manages to snatch the broken wood from his back and swings it at Laredo.

I suck in a sharp breath. "Laredo, fuck."

"I will have what belongs to me!" Freeport hollers and dodges out of Thaxton's way, avoiding the point of his blade.

Laredo listens to me and backs into the sitting area and rubs his hand across his chin. His eyes dart around the room as he tries to strategize what to do next. I, on the other hand, only want to watch Freeport and Thaxton kill each other.

That is, until my loveseat barrels across the room and collides into Bronx and Jameson. It knocks them back and sets me the hell off. Anger rushes through me. I can't even grasp what is truly happening. All I know is that Freeport is a psychopath, and if I can't stop him, he might go after my guys next. He is obviously stuck in some weird kill mission.

"Freeport, stop! That's enough!" I yell, cupping my mouth with my hands like if I can project my voice loud enough, it might send him dropping to his knees. "You need to calm the fuck down. I don't know what's going on, but I'm pretty damn sure killing Thaxton like you had done to Cortland won't solve your problem. And if even a piece of dust touches my guys again, I'll take your head. So fucking stop, you psycho!"

Freeport materializes a foot in front of my guys, and I

nearly catapult over their heads, thinking Freeport might attack them next. Jameson spins and catches me, setting me on the floor behind him, blocking my view of the psycho vampire. I grab his shoulders and try to peek over him, struggling to keep my balance on my tiptoes as I bump my belly into his back. He remains firmly in place, his solid frame harder than concrete. Every muscle ripples, and I grip him tightly, afraid he might charge.

"If you take a breath, drop your weapon, and back the hell up, I will talk to you," I say, waving my hand, motioning Freeport to step back. He's far more intense than usual, and I wonder what the fuck my mind manipulation might've done to his brain. No one really knows what I'm capable of, but at least it's this fucker who I get to experiment on.

Freeport bares his fangs, shifting on his feet. He inches forward and growls, ignoring my command to back off. "Talking won't accomplish anything. I need to—"

Thaxton appears behind Freeport and latches his fingers to his shirt. Spinning so fast that the two of them blur, I startle and jump in place as Freeport suddenly collides into my bedroom wall. He sinks into a huge crater from the impact of his body, and Thaxton bends forward and slams Freeport down over and over again, hitting his head to the debris littering the floor.

I gape, saucer-eyed and open mouthed, wondering how

much trauma a vampire skull can withstand. Thaxton roars with his movements, the sound scary as fuck. I expect Freeport's head to explode at any second, but he manages to jab his thumbs into Thaxton's eyes. Ramming his hands against Thaxton's chest, Freeport shoves him off and flies back to his feet. Blood pours from Freeport's eyes, nose, ears, mouth, and I gag at the sight of how flat his head looks in the back, his face now wider from the blows.

Heaving a few deep breaths, Freeport sweeps his gaze across the room and narrows his eyes on me. "Gwen! You fucking bitch! I don't care if you are on the verge of birthing power. I'm going to murder you for this."

Oh, fuck.

"Brother, don't you touch her!" Thaxton yells, covering his bleeding eyes with his hands, unable to see the world as he wobbles on his feet.

"It must be done. We have failed by not getting to her early enough. She has far greater power than we realized. She can control our minds!" Freeport roars, extending his fangs longer than I've ever seen them. "I demand we be done with her. You can take her heir for us. This ends here."

A wave of panic explodes inside me at his words, and I clutch my stomach. What the actual fuck! Bronx and Mikkalo launch forward at Freeport while Jameson rushes Thaxton. Everett scoops me into his arms and spins on his feet, trying to strategize getting the hell out of this room.

Freeport's anger erupts his back-world strength, and he overpowers Mikkalo, throwing him into the wall. Sinking his fangs into Bronx, Freeport tears into his neck and sweeps his legs out from under him. Laredo materializes behind Freeport with his blade, but Freeport spins and sends Laredo slamming into the wardrobe. Everett growls deep in his throat, shifting me to his back as he prepares to fight. My heart collides against my ribcage over and over again, making it hard to breathe. I don't know if Freeport moves faster, but it feels like an eternity passes before my guys recover and regroup to counter attack.

"Thaxton, I command you fight beside me!" Freeport yells, cracking his neck. His solid-silver eyes focus on me, trying to get into my head from ten feet away.

Thaxton holds his hand up. "Brother, please—"

Jerking his attention to Thaxton, Freeport flies at him and pushes him against the wall. He grabs Thaxton's hair and bangs his head so hard that I can hear the crack of Thaxton's bones. Realization settles through me. He's not fighting his brother. He's trying to ram my mind manipulation out of him. If he does...fuck.

"You must obey me as your leader!" Freeport shouts, keeping his attention on the rest of my guys as they form a semi-circle around him.

Laredo flashes his fangs. "It's over, Freeport. I've done nothing but try to keep you alive, thinking you could benefit us, but I was wrong."

Freeport growls and swings his arm, getting everyone to step back again. "This is your one and only chance to join me, Laredo. You are dead otherwise. You will not stand in my way of power."

"Freeport," Thaxton mumbles, his head lolling from his injuries.

Freeport cups his brother's cheek. "I'm sorry I had to do that. Give it a second. The truth will break free."

Groaning, Thaxton blinks his bloody eyes. His vision must return, because he looks past Freeport and locks his gaze on me. I freeze under his intense stare. If Everett wasn't blocking my belly, Thaxton would probably hone his attention on it next.

"How could you?" Thaxton murmurs, his voice deepening in anger.

Fuck. Fuck. Fuck.

"I was foolish to think the kin of Gwyneth would be anything other than a risk to our coven. Look at what she's done. She's torn us apart. She's nearly wiped us out." Freeport fists his hands, extending his fangs again. "You must get our heir, and I'll take care of the—"

Thaxton crashes into Freeport, cutting off his words. The move surprises the hell out of everyone, and my guys rush back to my side. Laredo joins them, and I stare in complete shock, trying to figure out what's going on with

Thaxton. I thought he was accusing me of betrayal, but he seems hell-bent on taking out his brother.

"Thaxton, stop!" Freeport shouts, trying and failing to block a strike to his face. "She manipulated you!"

Thaxton grabs Freeport and restrains him, turning his brother to face me. "How could you ask me to destroy someone so beautiful and incomparable on your behalf, Freeport?" Darting his gaze to me, Thaxton narrows his focus. "If Gwen has found you unworthy, then you are no longer entitled to live. How dare you think I will put you over the power of our future."

Whoa.

I wiggle in Everett's arms, not giving him a choice but to set me on my feet so that he doesn't drop me.

"Brother—" Freeport snaps his mouth shut, his silver eyes widening. Blood drips from five holes in the front of his shirt.

"I've heard enough! I've sat idly by while the rest of you ruined everything. I have one job, which is to protect and preserve the Baron dhampir line and you want to destroy it. I will not allow it. You've failed her while the Royales have risen to a place you never could have." Thaxton tightens his grip on Freeport and turns his eyes to Bronx. "Misters Royale, please accept my offering as proof of my alliance. I will give you the honors of taking his head."

Is this a trick?

The question flits through my mind over and over again. Bronx shifts and looks at me, thinking the same thing.

"You can't do this to me, brother! She's in your head!" Freeport shouts.

Thrashing with all his strength, Freeport manages to break free. He zooms at us, snapping his fangs. I tense in fear, his rage turning him deadly. Laredo launches at Freeport, getting in the way. Punching his hand into Laredo's chest, Freeport tries to take his heart.

"No!" I scream, pushing through Bronx and Mikkalo, moving too fast for anyone to stop me.

Laredo's face scrunches in agony, and I cry out as if his pain were my own. The world slows, and my speed dissipates, my body stalling on me. Freeport twists his hand inside Laredo's chest, his sharp features lighting with victory as Laredo's bones crack.

A wail rips through the air and blood spatters across me. I grab Laredo as he falls forward, but Bronx intercepts and stops him from crumbling to the floor. An uncontrollable, wild urge tightens around me, and I snarl, the vicious sound sinking deeply into my bones. It takes a moment to register Thaxton gripping Freeport in his arms. Blood sprays from Freeport's severed arm, and he howls and thrashes.

I launch forward, my blood starvation consuming me completely. Jabbing my fist, I punch Freeport in his chest.

Bones crush under the force of my hit, and I fall onto Freeport, sandwiching him to Thaxton. I sink my teeth into Freeport's neck, ripping and tearing at his flesh until blood pours into my mouth, satiating the burning rage and starvation inside me. I can no longer hear or see, my dhampir nature determined to drain Freeport dry.

Cool hands lock around me, dragging me up from my kill. My body reflexively fights, and I land hard on my knees. Crawling forward, I attack Freeport again, ramming and shoving my hands inside him, ripping him apart piece by piece. I'm afraid that if even a limb remains intact, he'll heal and come after me again. And I'm done. I'm done with all this bullshit. No one will ever threaten my baby or my mates again. I will embrace the deadly beast inside me to ensure it.

"Dandelion, please. They're dead. They won't hurt you ever again," Bronx says, his soft voice prodding at me, trying to break through to my soul.

"Hold her as tight as you can, Bronx." Everett's words try to rip me from my blood hunger, but I can't break away from my mission of total Baron annihilation.

Two buff arms wrap around me from behind, dragging me off the floor. Bronx murmurs my name into my ear, tightening his grip over my chest and hips, trying his best to pin me in place without hurting me.

"Careful, Ev," Jameson warns. "I had to inject her with

my venom last time to stop her."

"I don't want to risk that. Just back me up, Jameson," Everett says, his blurry form stepping into my line of vision. "Mikkalo, help Bronx. I need you to prepare if I can't get through to her."

Gentle fingers touch my cheek, and I snap my teeth, my wild aggression making it hard for my mind to realize that Everett touches me. He risks getting closer until his blurry form sharpens, and I can distinguish his blue eyes flashing silver with his concern.

"Gwen, look at me and don't look away," Everett commands, capturing me in his stare. "You are safe. You don't have to fight anymore. Freeport and Thaxton are dead. No Baron will ever hurt you again. Do you understand?"

"No." The word automatically escapes my mouth as his mind manipulation opens me on another level for him.

"I don't think she realizes that she took Thaxton's heart with Freeport's." Laredo's words tug at my attention.

I snap from Everett's gaze and jerk my attention to him. "Laredo, get over here." Did I really just say that?

"Stay back, Laredo. She's tensing. I think she might try to attack you," Bronx says, shuffling back with me.

Laredo steps forward, locking his eyes on mine. "I don't think—"

"You've been hiding shit, Laredo! I want you to come

clean!" I thrash and try to break free, bucking my body with my dhampir strength.

Everett jumps in front of me again and grips my face in his hands. "Gwen, stop. Close your eyes. Sleep."

My mind snaps to his command, and I lose myself to darkness.

9

WILD

BLOOD FILLS MY MOUTH, COATING my tongue. It awakens me from the strange, all-consuming darkness I've been trapped in for who knows how long. I can't move or see or speak, but I can swallow, and my stomach roars, begging me to drink faster.

"Gigi, it's okay. I have a lot more to offer you. If you open your eyes and tell me your favorite thing about me, I'll let you have at my neck." Jameson's soft words trickle through the darkness holding me captive. "Nice and easy. I need to know you're in control."

More blood coats my tongue, and I moan a breath of satisfaction as it helps subdue the agonizing hunger swelling inside me. Fingers glide over my bottom lip, wiping my mouth. Jameson's familiar scent coaxes my body to relax, and I finally manage to flutter my eyes open and peer up at the ceiling.

Jameson leans over me and smiles, his green eyes sparkling like I'm the best thing he's ever seen. "Tell me your favorite thing about me," he says, combing my hair from my forehead with his hand. "I only need one thing, and then I'll allow you to drink properly. Just don't tell my brothers. They haven't had the honor of taming your beastly side like I have, and you've kind of scared the shit out of them."

I try to sit upright, but a leather restraint around my wrist doesn't allow me. "What the hell?"

He chuckles. "Sorry about the ankle bar. Apparently Mikkalo had some kinky shit planned for you and decided that was better than what the Barons have on hand that is a whole lot less fun."

I frown and try to move again. "You think this is really going to restrain me?"

Jameson shifts on the bed next to me and gives the arm chain a hard as hell tug. "Damn straight. Mik calls you wild one for a reason and won't go half-assed when it comes to something he thinks you'll enjoy."

My mind whirls with a dozen hot as hell thoughts. Mikkalo loves teasing my feral nature, but he especially loves controlling it. Pleasure bites and working me up until I practically pounce on him is his specialty...

I shake the thoughts of Mikkalo's hotness from my mind, and say, "Uh, but why do I have to tell you my favorite thing about you? Am I...in trouble?" I can't stop the smile from crossing my lips at my words.

Jameson purrs deep in his throat and bows into me, caressing his lips to mine. "So much trouble. You bit Everett in the shoulder so hard that he's still healing."

I frown. "Oh, no. Fuck."

Jameson nuzzles his nose to mine. "He'll survive."

"Just release me so I can make sure myself." I yank at the wrist cuffs again. "Please."

"Like I said, tell me your favorite thing about me, and I will. Bronx's orders. I can't release you until I know for certain that you're not in beast-mode. As soon as I know, I'll let you out and you can bite me how you like. I'm sure you're starving. It's been like five seconds since you've consumed blood." Jameson straightens up and grins, loving this way too much. He obviously isn't going to relent, so I sigh and lean back.

"I like your butt," I say, tugging against the restraints more. "I like it so much, that I'm going to bite it the second

I'm free."

Tipping his head back, Jameson laughs loudly. "I fucking love you, Gigi. Come here." Jameson hits something I can't see and the restraints release me from my spot on...not my bed. This isn't my room. I think it might be Cortland's room, but I can't be sure because I never stepped foot into it.

I shudder and sit up. "I seriously fucking hope you changed these sheets. You know how often Cortland jerked—"

"Worse than Bronx," Jameson interrupts. "And yeah. I moved the bed from my room, because there was no way I ever wanted to see you on that fucker's, even if he's out roasting in the sun with his brothers."

My mind whirls, gathering and sorting through the memory of what the fuck happened. Freeport killed Cortland, and I killed Freeport and Thaxton. I know I did. I remember someone—Mikkalo? No, it was Laredo—saying that I took their hearts together.

I scrub my hands over my face, shocked by the lack of blood staining my body. My fresh nightie screams of Jameson's choice, the baby doll silhouette something I know he loves on me, especially now.

"Here, let me feed you, Gigi," he murmurs, pulling me onto his lap. "You can bite my ass later. Right now, just let me cuddle you for a bit and assure myself you and the mini-beast are okay. I know everything was so fucked up."

I lean in without comment and graze my lips to his, sweet and sensually, trying my best not to go wild. I think he's had enough of my savagery to last a few days. I've had enough of it. That's for sure. I just want to give him what he wants by fulfilling my needs. If cuddling close and feeding each other will ease his nerves, then I'll personally build him a blanket fort to shield out the world.

Snatching a blanket, Jameson does it for me like he reads my mind, but instead of going all out, he simply wraps the two of us in the big blanket and adjusts my legs around his waist. I hook my fingers to his shirt and tug it off, pulling him closer by his neck to lick his throat. He cups my breast through the nightie and eases the material down with his cool fingers. My skin buzzes under the sensation of the flick of his thumb against my tight, sensitive nipples.

I moan and tease him with my teeth, wanting him to feel my anticipation. "I want you so badly it hurts. I ache everywhere."

He bends his neck and adjusts my body until I feel the bulge of his erection press against the fabric of my panties. "Bite me first. Let me satiate your hunger."

A whimper escapes my lips, and he grinds me against him, teasing me like crazy. It's enough to prod at my nature that I sink my teeth into his neck, filling my mouth with blood. I hum at the warmth and sweetness flooding my mouth. The baby kicks like crazy, turning me into a punching bag. Jameson chuckles and rests his hand on my stomach, tapping his finger on every spot he feels the mini-beast press against. I smile and continue to suck and swallow, hugging him close and savoring his tender words of love whispering in my ear.

"You hang in there a bit longer, mini-beast. Bronx will have a coronary if you arrive before he's ready, though I already told him he better get used to it. You're going to be just as uncontrollably wild as your mommy." Jameson laughs at the next round of kicks to his comment. "Little rebel."

I ease my mouth away from my bite and plant a kiss to his mouth, unable to resist. He's so adorably sweet in this moment that I crave giving him every ounce of my affection. Jameson grins against my lips, cupping my face to kiss me deeper. His excitement flexes between my legs, tempting me to push things farther, hotter, exactly how he desires. It's been days instead of hours since we've had sex together, and I'm sure he misses it as much as I do. It's me and him a lot, and I have to prove that even with his brothers around, nothing will change. He's always been my biggest confidant, and I'll do everything to ensure all my guys get what they need from me.

"I love you," he whispers, reaching between us to test me for a reaction.

I moan as his fingers tug the fabric of my panties aside. "I love you too—"

A growl escapes Jameson's mouth, the vibration of his threat ricocheting through me in a startling burst. He grabs me and hoists me against his chest, catapulting to his feet. Thrusting the blanket off, Jameson zooms to the shelf and snatches a blade from Cortland's massive weapon collection.

"Put the dhampir down," a woman says, her husky voice stays low with her words. "I don't want to shoot a pregnant woman, but I will if I have to. I know she'll heal."

Jameson tightens his hold on me and spins away. The woman fires her gun, missing us by a foot. Swiping his com device from next to the bed, Jameson smacks the screen and sets off a screeching alarm. It'll hurt the woman's ears, but it's not intended for her. He wants to drop any rebel vampires that might've come with her. It wouldn't be the first time, though all the Barons are dead now.

"Gwen, go to the wardrobe. You'll find an access door to a secret passage," Jameson says, pressing his lips to my ear. "Stay on guard. Don't hesitate to hurt anyone who comes after you. I'll take care of the rebel."

Setting me on my feet, Jameson rushes toward the rebel woman, not even flinching as she fires her weapon. As hard as it is for me to run, I listen to Jameson and put my safety first, hugging my belly protectively. The woman shouts, but I don't stop to look at her or what Jameson does. Another round of gunfire goes off, and a bullet plunks into the wall two feet from my head.

I screech and scramble into the wardrobe, spotting a man flinging open the bedroom door. He narrows his gaze on me and aims his gun, not even caring about what his actions could mean. Jameson swipes the blood from his mouth and charges him, yelling at me to go.

I grab a rolling rack of suits and block the doorway the best I can. I can't lock the rebels out, but I can at least make it more difficult to target me. Flinging my hands through the hanging clothes, I look for the access door to whatever secret passageway Jameson mentioned. After Bronx and Laredo had saved me from Freeport by entering the room through his closet, I should've known there would be more. I guess having rooms without windows means there must be another way to escape—I just wish I knew what I was looking for.

"Little sis, boy you've gotten huge." Silas's voice stops me in my place, and I spin around and spot him standing next to the open panel of a hidden door. Fuck. Of course he would know of the Barons' secret passageways. He was a Baron before they renounced him as their brother and had him banished from Donor Life Corp.

Darting my gaze around the wardrobe, I look for something to use as a weapon. I'm not going to act as if this is some sort of reunion with my brother. He severed our familial bond the second he tried to barter my existence for his eternity. The selfish prick.

"How about you don't make things hard on yourself and just come with me. I've arranged a nice home to raise my heir, and you will get the things you need without all of the bullshit that comes with—"

I snatch a dress shoe off the rack and chuck it at Silas as hard as I can. He doesn't expect my sudden speed and accuracy, given to me by my dhampir nature through my desperation. It clocks him in the face so hard that his nose pops and blood pours down his chin. Hollering, Silas rushes toward me, his crooked nose clearly broken, and I grab another shoe and throw it.

The second he ducks, I snatch a metal rod from the wall and yank it free. Clothes teeter and fall, but I still manage to whack Silas in the gut with the end. He locks his fingers to the rod and yanks it away, nearly making me fall forward. I catch myself on a shelf. Silas swings the rod, trying to knock me down, but it gets stuck on the wall, giving me the chance I need. I charge into him, hunkering as low as my belly allows, and smash my shoulder into his gut. He flies off his feet, his strength no match for mine. I climb on top of him and hiss, my anger and hurt turning my vision red.

"Freeze!" I shout, locking my hand to his neck. "Don't move or speak or even fucking breathe, Silas."

His eyes widen, the silver in his irises flickering so fast it looks as if his eyes turn metallic. Baring his teeth, he shows off his fangs. His cheek muscles twitch, and he remains placated beneath me, trapped in my mind manipulation.

"Why are you here?" I ask, heaving a breath.

"The elders want the dhampir-hybrid," he responds, his deep voice even and monotone, sounding weird as fuck.

Tears burn my eyes. "What do they think they're going to accomplish?"

"What the Barons failed to do." He doesn't elaborate, nor does he react when one of my tears splashes his cheek.

"Where is the rebel nest?" My whole body shakes as I run a dozen questions through my mind, wondering what the fuck I should ask that can help us.

"It's—"

"Gwen!" Jameson's yell cuts through the air, snapping my attention away from my brother.

I don't have a chance to move or react. Silas hooks his hands around me and hops to his feet, acting as if I weigh nothing at all. I slap my hands to his face. Silas growls and snaps his teeth. So I smack him hard enough to jerk his head sideways. A gunshot pops through the air, stealing my senses. I blink, clearing the stars peppering my vision. Everything happens so fast that all I can do is brace myself as Silas tries to make a run for it.

"Gwen!" Jameson hollers again. "Rip his fucking head

off!"

Jameson's command kicks my instincts on, and I lock my fingers around my brother's neck. Snarling, Jameson throws something—no, someone—at the wall, and the rebel woman lands hard on her back.

"Silas, we gotta go. They're coming!" The woman rolls and gets to her feet, stretching her hand out to my brother.

Reaching out, Silas grabs her by the hand and drags her closer. I take advantage of his distraction and try to do exactly what Jameson commanded, and I sink my teeth into my brother's neck, biting him as hard as I can.

He yells and thrashes, swinging around, trying to get me away from him. I pull back and prepare to bite him again, but the rebel woman yanks my hair, trying to rip me back. She grabs a gun from Silas's belt and aims it into the bedroom, firing it at Jameson again and again. Fisting my hand, I swing my arm, needing to take Silas's heart. This is it. This is what needs to be done. I'll never live peacefully as long as he's living and breathing. With Silas has come nothing but destruction to my life. I will not allow him to ruin my daughter's life as well.

"Silas, watch out!" Grayson appears in the doorway to the hidden tunnel and raises his gun at me.

Fearing for the baby, I throw myself away from him and scramble toward the bedroom. The woman shoots for Grayson, and a bullet whizzes past me. Jameson grunts as it lodges into him. He staggers forward, falling to his knees next to me. A dagger glitters from his hand, and with perfect accuracy, he throws it, sinking it into Silas's chest. Silas disappears with the rebel woman and Grayson, slamming the door closed to the secret passageway. A boom rings through the air, shaking the world around us. I expect the roof to cave in. I expect a dozen rebels to attack in an attempt to steal me away.

But nothing happens. Silence fills the air.

"Fuck," Jameson says, his voice shaking. "Are you okay?"

I nod, my body trembling. "I—I think so. But something's wrong."

Sliding his arm around me, Jameson shifts to his knees. "Shit. Let me help you get up. Someone else is—"

A growl sounds from the hallway, and I snap my attention to a filthy vampire with crazy silver eyes.

He doesn't even make it a foot into the room before I launch at him, flying across the room at vampire speed. I crash into him, knocking him on his back. Ramming my hand into his chest, I shatter his sternum.

I take the fucker's heart.

10

REBEL THREAT

"JAMESON, GRAB HER. GET HER back to the bed," Everett commands, his voice pulling me from my blood hunger. "Everyone else, give her space."

I release a deep growl, my emotions running wild. "Stay back!"

"Rebels," Jameson says, his labored breath trickling from behind me. "They—"

"They're gone." Mikkalo's voice stirs my humanity, pulling me from the crazy fear freezing me in place, keeping me locked onto the dead vampire. His shadow looms across the floor, and he braves touching my back. "Gwen, they're gone. You can relax. No one is going to hurt you or our baby girl."

I gasp a breath and wipe my hands across my face smearing blood on my cheeks. I feel on the edge of losing control again. Scrambling away from Mikkalo, I hold my palms up, silently asking everyone to stay back. It's now that I realize who surrounds me. Mikkalo, Everett, and Jameson stand the closest, looking a bit bloody, but it mostly doesn't belong to them. Their clothing has been ravaged with bullet holes, but the wounds already coagulate, and I spot Jameson trying to hide a glass of blood behind him. He knows I'd never expect him to refrain from drinking what he needs. I guess my current state freaks him out enough to not want to risk it.

Standing near the door, Declan and Ashton hover together next to Brooklyn. I rub my messy face again, feeling self-conscious and gross. It's funny, and slightly ridiculous, but I'd prefer she never saw me like this. She doesn't wear blinders toward my grossness like my guys do. As for my brothers? I've seen them in worse positions, so I don't give a fuck.

"Please, stay back. I don't feel so good," I say, trying to clear the stinging tears from my eyes.

Everett ignores my pleas and materializes at my side.

"Come on. Let's sit down."

My lip quivers. "It's taking everything in me not to attack and bite you. I'm scared. I don't want to hurt you."

Taking a step away from me to give me space, Everett slowly trails his eyes down my body. "Everyone who isn't the father of Gwen's baby, please get out." He shifts and turns to Ashton. "Go find Bronx and take over, Ash. Brooklyn will watch your brother."

No one argues, following Everett's commands. Jameson shuts the bedroom door and leans on it, inhaling a breath. Motioning to me, Everett gets me to shuffle to the bed. I squeak at the sight of a dead body and spin around, crashing into Mikkalo. I don't even have a chance to react before he relocates me to the bathroom and abandons me outside the shower he flicks on so quickly I miss him doing it.

Everett fills the empty space Mikkalo leaves behind to take care of the mess in the room. Biting his arm, he fills a glass with his blood and hands it to me. I accept his offering and chug the sweet, warm blood in a few gulps, wanting to fill my belly as quickly as possible. It does nothing to ease my nerves, and the baby feels as if it somersaults inside me, and I groan and hug my arms across my torso. A cramp steals my breath, and I cry out, the sudden tightening of my muscles making me wobble on my feet.

"Fuck," I say, shuffling backward to lean on the counter. "Shit."

"Can you describe your pain?" Everett drops to his knees and presses his ear to my stomach while touching it with his hand.

I groan again, curling forward to brace my hands on his shoulders. "It's—I don't know. Fuck, make it stop. It hurts. Everett..." I squeeze my eyes shut and dig my nails harder into him.

"Try to breathe. In through your nose and out through your mouth." Reaching up, he links his free hand through mine, letting me nearly crush his fingers. "Don't panic."

He falls silent, just continuing to listen and touch my stomach until the cramping subsides, and I can breathe again. It doesn't last long, but hell. It felt like eternity. Everett's brows knit together, and he stays on the floor a little longer, eyeing my face in his peripheral vision while using his vampire senses to examine me.

"Is she okay?" I finally ask, worried because he's not quick to tell me what's on his mind as usual. "You don't think something is wrong, do you?"

He bobs his head and gets to his feet. Taking my hands between his, Everett holds them against his chest. Sparks of silver dance across the blue depths of his eyes, and he offers me a soft, reassuring smile. "She has a nice, strong heartbeat. It's you I'm focusing on. I've been training day and night to prepare for after her birth, but I've been relying on Rio for you for more than the basics."

I blink a few times and purse my lips. "Should we call him in case? Do you think she's coming? Damn it. I'm not ready."

I now feel like I fucked myself over by ignoring all the information and videos Bronx and Everett sent my way. I don't know why, but a part of me still can't believe I'm going to be a mother, despite this giant stomach and mini-beast practicing her combat skills and using my insides as a punching bag. Another part of me is scared as hell. From what I know, this experience will be far from pleasant. One of the movies I tried to watch started off with a woman screaming. So, yeah. I shut that shit off.

"I don't think so, but I want to get you cleaned up and resting, Gwen," he says, offering me another glass of blood. He kisses my forehead while I chug. "I think you were experiencing Braxton Hicks, which are basically like warm-up contractions. I'd like to examine you to be sure, if that's okay. I need to know if I should panic Bronx or not."

I lick my lips clean and ease the straps of my nightie down. "Will the exam hurt? Be awkward as hell for us? I love you, Everett, but I worry this might ruin me for you."

His brows furrow, his face scrunching in confusion. "Helping you through this in the way I know how will not ruin you for me. Even if I wasn't your health keeper, it still wouldn't ruin anything or change how sexy and incredible you are to me. You're my magical, beautiful mate, Gwen.

While I'm nervous about being a dad and scared if I'll be a good one, I am ecstatic. I never thought I'd be so lucky."

My heart swells at his words, and I kiss him, feeling loads better about our circumstances. "Our daughter is the luckiest baby girl in the universe having you as one of her dads. She already loves you all so much."

"And I love her so much and you," he murmurs, helping me undress out of the bloody gown. His eyes roam down my body, and he nudges me toward the shower. Stripping down, he joins me under the hot water and washes my hair, cleansing my body and checking for injuries as he does so, not getting carried away by the fact that we're both naked, slippery-wet, and in need of a serious distraction.

A knock thuds against the door, and Bronx peeks his head in. "Can I come in?"

"Yeah," Everett and I say in unison.

I smirk and hug my arms around him, burying my face into his taut chest to listen to the thrum of his heart beating. Everett plays with my damp hair, his body so close that even with Bronx coming in, it doesn't turn my attention away from my rising desire.

"We're almost done." I stretch my hand out to draw a heart on the foggy glass.

"So are Jameson and Mikkalo. I'm sorry about everything. We failed you by not expecting the rebels to take advantage of the situation," Bronx says, closing the space to the shower. He peeks over the foggy glass like he needs to see for himself that I'm okay.

I stretch on my tiptoes and touch his cheek. "You couldn't have known. We haven't heard from them in a while."

He clenches his jaw. "Still. I'm sorry. We won't let anything like this happen again. Laredo is sweeping the property and setting traps. We're no longer going to assume alarms will work to keep the rebels away. If they cross onto the property, they won't make it out alive."

Jeez. It sounds like Laredo is setting up death traps, and I'm not sure how to feel about it. I mean, fuck, I don't want rebels getting anywhere near me, but the thought of someone walking into some twisted trap...I shudder to even think about it.

"The rebels now think we're an easy target because the Barons are gone," Bronx adds.

I stiffen at his comment, trying to remember the information I extracted from Silas. He's right. My brother mentioned something like that. "Wait. How did they even know? It hasn't been long at all, and none of us has left the—shit. Do you think Brooklyn—"

"Easy, dandelion. It wasn't my sister. She's been with Ashton this entire time. She wouldn't betray us like that." Rubbing the back of his neck, he flicks his gaze to Everett and back to mine. "I think it's been in the works for a while. They knew exactly what to avoid to slip past security. They also knew where to travel to access the escape tunnels. Mik suspects they've been strategizing since you moved in here and were waiting for the perfect opportunity to take advantage of the situation."

I reach for the shower knob and turn it off, desperate to get out of the hot spray. I need cool air, some more blood, water, possibly something to eat, and to just lie down for a bit. My mind whirls. I have so many questions and worries and not many answers. I want to process what happened.

Exhaustion sneaks up on me, and I worry if I don't rest and relax, I'll experience more pain. The Braxton Hicks or whatever need to chill. I don't need those kind of preparations. Now is not the time for me to be going into labor—not until we figure out how to take care of the rebels first.

"So what now?" I ask, stepping out of the shower, glistening with water.

Bronx's dark eyes travel the length of my body, drinking in the sight of me standing naked before him. With the desire that crosses his face and bulges against the zipper of his pants, I would think I wasn't about to give birth if I didn't know any better.

Bronx blinks, clearing his silvery, lusty gaze. He grabs a towel off the rack and holds it up, but isn't quick to give it to me. He instead motions for me to spin around and comes up close behind me, stroking the absorbent material across my bare shoulders and down my back. Everett wraps a towel around his waist and stands in front of me, studying my reaction as Bronx fulfills his sudden mission to dry every inch of me instead of answering my question.

Everett doesn't say anything either, but he caresses his hand to my breast and smiles. His body hardens in arousal, his towel-covered cock insisting to dry my pelvis with his flexing.

I shake my head, snapping myself from my desire. I realize Bronx didn't answer my question.

"Bronx?" I prod again as he shifts my legs open to glide the towel between my thighs, slowing down just a bit. I shiver at the sensation and clutch Everett to keep my knees steady. "What now? What's the plan?"

Everett clears his throat. "I already told you, Gwen, remember? I want you off your feet and resting. That is the only plan happening now."

I glare and pat his bare shoulder. "You guys better not start acting like every little thing might send me into labor. It's not an excuse you can use to keep me on a damn need to know basis. I want to know what your plan is involving the rebels."

Bronx grumbles behind me and smacks my bare ass. "You bet your sexy ass that's exactly what we're going to do."

The sting of his palm makes me jump, and I clutch Everett tighter. I exhale a breath and try to turn around to retaliate, but Everett doesn't let me. And then Bronx spanks me again before running his cool fingers over the surprisingly exhilarating heat he leaves behind.

"Damn. You should spank her more often," Everett teases.

"I plan on it. I can't think of a better way to get her to stop arguing." Standing flush against me, Bronx shifts my damp hair and leans down, kissing the skin below my ear. "You know everything you need to at this time, Gwen. Understand? We're handling it."

Everett caresses his knuckles to my jaw, bending ultra-close to kiss me and whisper against my mouth. "The last few days have been stressful—"

"My whole life has been stressful," I argue, trying not to let them distract me. But damn it. It's working. I want to give in to their current need to ensure I can't think about anything.

I give one last fight, trying to spin around to face Bronx, but the bastard doesn't let me. He follows my movements, staying close to my back. Everett chuckles and steps back, watching me spin. So I lock my fingers to his towel and yank it away. He laughs and tries to move, but my dhampir speed kicks in and I manage to slap his ass.

"Hey, you got the wrong ass," Everett teases.

I huff and stick out my tongue. "Blame Bronx. Someone else besides me needs a spanking, and he keeps moving too fast."

"Here. I'll hold him," Everett says, trying to grab Bronx.

Bronx growls and dodges out of the way. "Hey, we're supposed to be a team, Ev. You said it yourself that she needs to relax, and she obviously plans to do otherwise."

I give up on chasing Bronx and bend over, shaking my ass. "Go on, Bronx. Test me. See what happens when you spank my dhampir side into full force."

"Dandelion, don't make me force you to relax. I will if I have to," he responds, swatting my ass cheek again before I can stand upright, my teasing him backfiring.

I spin faster than he expects and nearly knock him over with my belly. Widening his eyes in fear, Bronx drops to his knees and pulls me close by my waist, bringing his face to my stomach. His hands clutch my sides, and he presses the cutest kiss right to my outie, making me jump in surprise.

I comb my fingers through his hair and laugh. "You're so lucky you're cute right now or I'd tackle you into submission."

"Are you okay?" he asks without commenting on my quip.

"Have you forgotten I'm tough, and this bundle of a beast is apparently power-incarnate? Now take your own advice and relax. If you can do that, then I will join you." I smile and bump my belly against his chin.

"That sounds like an acceptable compromise," Everett says, rubbing his hands over my ass cheeks, cooling the sting of Bronx's playful spanks with his fingers.

"At least until Laredo returns," Bronx grumbles.

Everett whacks him on the back. "Even then, someone else can handle it."

Bronx releases a breath and scoops me up into his arms, carrying me to the bedroom.

Mikkalo smiles at me as he clicks the door to the hallway closed and locks it behind him, ensuring no one else will come barging in to interrupt us. Jameson shakes a baggy T-shirt in front of him, offering me his sexy smile. I flick my eyes around the room. Mikkalo and Jameson cleaned and disposed of the body faster than I expected. I'm relieved for it. If only they didn't have to deal with it in the first place.

"As much as I love seeing you in a sexy nightie, I really fucking want to see you in my shirt, Gigi. Especially when Laredo returns." Jameson's jaw twitches, and I feel the heat of his annoyance. Now that things have settled, I'm sure he's thinking about why everything turned into shit in the first place. Who knew a damn surprise kiss could end a vampire bloodline and summon rebels? Laredo will hear about it.

"Jamie," I say, reaching my arms up to let him slip his shirt over my head. "You don't have to be jealous."

"Oh, I'm not. I just want to remind him whose girl you are." Jameson flashes his fangs with his cocky-bastard smile.

"I think Mikkalo did a sufficient job with that." I meet Mikkalo's dark eyes.

He stands a few feet behind Jameson, his muscles bulging as I focus on him. "I could've done better."

I pout my lip and sigh. "I'm sorry you guys had—"

Bronx covers my mouth with his hand, cutting off my apology. The four of them surround me, smothering me between their bodies. "Whatever you think you need to say isn't necessary, Gwen. We've already talked about it with Laredo, and he's well aware that he was out of line. He vowed to never give you unsolicited affection again."

"Unsolicited affection?" I question with a frown.

Silence falls between my guys for a couple of seconds as they look to each other. They have a quiet conversation with their eyes, excluding me, and I try my best to wait patiently for someone to respond.

"All right, someone better spill. I'm starting to get bit-ey," I tease, trying to lighten the sudden intense shift in mood. I wiggle in Bronx's arms, stretching to nip his throat. "And you're about to be my first victim."

Mikkalo chuckles and slips his arm between mine and Bronx's throat. "I volunteer as your victim. Bite, suck, lick me all you want."

"Don't tempt me too much. You know what I'm like when I get wild now." I lock my fingers around his wrist and mold my lips to his arm, sucking hard enough to give him a hickey. "Now someone tell me what the hell is up with Laredo and his unsolicited affection?"

Jameson groans and puffs a breath through his mouth. "He thinks you have feelings for him and will eventually want to act on them."

My eyes widen. Holy shit.

Everett grabs my hand. "And before you start stressing out over anything, I want you to know that I've accepted you have history with him. What happened...just know I love you and our daughter. I also know you have so much love bursting from you that the idea of the slightest chance of Laredo being right doesn't faze me like I thought it would."

"We all feel that way, Gwen," Bronx says softly.

"As long as that fucking asshole doesn't try to push you or manipulate you or ever fucking try anything without your permission again," Mikkalo adds.

"Oh." I don't know what else to say or how to feel or think. This isn't the conversation I ever expected to have.

"Uh-oh." Jameson grabs my chin, turning my face to him. "She's stressing."

"I am not. I—" I snap my mouth closed and crinkle my

nose.

"Look at her eyes. Quick. Get her to the bed." Everett breaks the circle and bites his arm. "It's time she relaxes and enjoys some stress relief."

Bronx strides to the bed and sets me down, and the four of them run their gazes across me, resting on my elbows with my knees together and tipped to the side. It only takes a teensy smirk from each of them to figure out that they don't want to push the topic on me and would rather start in on their distraction mode, doing anything they can to drag my mind away from Laredo, the Barons, the rebels, and all the possible problems they can cause for us.

"Should I restrain her?" Mikkalo asks, lifting one of his sex restraints from its place hanging on the headboard. "She looks like she might argue about her health keeper's orders."

"Might argue?" Bronx says, plopping on the bed beside me. "She already is. Her expression says it all."

I glower and stick my tongue out at Bronx. "Well, I wouldn't if you'd stop treating me like—"

"Like you're about to give birth? Or maybe like you're about to overthink everything?" Everett asks, plopping down beside me. He holds a glass of blood to my lips and waits for me to drink the dark ruby elixir before offering me a glass of water next. "Perhaps we're acting like you are the most important person in the universe to us, and we need you to know that no matter what, we're your mates and your coven, and we think things will be exactly how they should be?"

I sigh and smile. "How the hell did we go from you guys wanting to keep me out of things to this? I might be all those things, Everett, but I'm still capable of helping, and I don't need to be coddled or distracted. And I definitely don't need you to restrain me to this bed for forced relaxation."

"Not relaxation," Mikkalo says.

"Stress relief," Bronx finishes.

I laugh. Fuck. Me. They're determined.

Jameson sits behind me and pulls me into his chest. "We know all that, especially now, Gigi. But just because you are capable and you want to keep being the badass you are, doesn't mean you have to be. Let us take care of you. You've been through enough bullshit this entire pregnancy that I'm afraid you never even got to enjoy it like you should've. I mean, that mini-beast is a fucking riot. You should feel the bed shake when she's partying all day long, preparing to ensure I don't get to sleep again."

I laugh again, shifting to look at him. "Jamie. I think you have that backwards. I'm the one with the milk jugs."

"If she even likes sucking on those bodacious beauties of yours. And even so, I bet I could figure out how to latch her on, make sure she gets what she needs, and give her daytime cuddles without waking you up. Everett said the numbing cream will work to keep your perky baby feeders from aching." The lightness of his voice sends happiness spilling through me. I can't—okay, I can—believe that he thought all of this through.

"Please don't tell me that's what my fantasies are going to turn into," I say, meeting Everett's gaze. "Numb boobs and assisted sleep feeding our baby."

All four of them chuckle and close in around me, squishing me in their arms as they hug me and each other. Joy and love pulse through me, and I take turns kissing each of them while they silently fight for belly space to feel our baby girl shifting and kicking in excitement like she can feel what we do and loves the hell out of it as much as I do.

I sigh in contentment, my muscles relaxing. "You guys are in trouble...later. Don't think I forgot about the rebels."

"Oh, we know," they all say in unison.

"But they won't be a problem." Laredo's voice steals my attention from my guys, and I jerk my gaze to the cracked open door. He waits in the hallway and doesn't look at us. It's not exactly knocking, and he was totally eavesdropping, but it was better than him acting like a creep and coming in uninvited. "Everything is in place, and we should be good until I can track down the location of the nest."

His words ignite a memory inside me, and I sit upright and frown. "What do you mean track down the location?"

"Finding where they hide isn't so simple," Mikkalo

says, answering for Laredo.

I scoot between Bronx and Everett to the edge of the bed. "That's not true."

"It should only take a day or so. They couldn't have gotten far." Laredo ignores me, speaking to Bronx. "I'll keep you informed when I figure it out."

I plant my feet on the floor. "Laredo, what are you talking about when you figure it out? You can—"

Again, he doesn't look at me. "I'll leave you be for—"

"Laredo!"

I rush across the room and into the hallway, locking my fingers to the back of his shirt. Spinning him, I force his chest into the wall, making him growl. My guys materialize around me and drag me away from Laredo like they're afraid I might punch his heart out or something. I squirm and wiggle, trying to break my arms free, but Mikkalo squeezes me tighter.

"Take Gwen back to the room," Bronx orders, his posture turning stiff.

"No! I swear to the damn universe if you don't all stop acting as if I've turned wild and am on a mission to kill Laredo, I will spank you all from here to the living room." I growl under my breath. "And Laredo, you better stop ignoring me because I *remember*."

"Remember what, Gigi?" Jameson asks.

I narrow my eyes on Laredo without answering anyone's curious stares. "Don't lie to them. I remember the maps. I remember that the Barons have every location of every rebel nest, and I damn well know they wouldn't have just quit tracking them. You're not going on some dangerous tracking mission. You know where they are."

"Gwen, it's—"

"Don't even try to make excuses. It's one thing for my mates to keep me on a need to know basis, but it's a whole other thing for you to do that shit to them," I snap, my muscles tensing in annoyance.

"Gwen, please. Let me explain," Laredo says, shifting under our heated stares. "It's not that I'm hiding things. It's just...I don't want you to consider me useless."

I clench my fingers into fists. "Are you kidding me? How am I expected to ever trust you again? If you think this is the best way to try to make things right or if you thought this would help me to forgive you, then you're wrong. You need to be honest, Laredo. Prove that you deserve an alliance with the Royales."

"Like you'll let me." Laredo growls under his breath.

"I'm trying!" I screech. "I've been trying. But you keep acting as if you're entitled to be here. You keep acting like the Royales are in the wrong and stole me from you, but fuck, Laredo! You abandoned me. You made me think you were dead. You—"

Pain swells through my belly stealing my breath. I bend

over and clutch my knees, crying out. Everett scoops me off my feet and rushes me into the room.

Bronx blocks Laredo from following them into the room. "You need to go, Laredo. Just go."

11

PREP WORK

BRONX HOVERS OVER ME, GAZING into my eyes. "Just keep your focus on me."

I do as he says, ignoring everything else going on in the room. A rush of emotion explodes between us, sending my heart rapping hard against my ribcage. Bronx holds his weight up on his elbow, propped beside me on the bed. His dark eyes shine silver as he prods into my mind.

"You are free to speak and move," Bronx says, stroking his finger along my jaw. "Just don't look away from my eyes."

"Okay." The word comes out automatically as he tests the malleability of my mind.

He graces me with a smile. "I want to practice keeping your focus and help you the only way I know how, especially with what your body will go through."

"Don't remind me," I say, my thoughts pouring from my mind without filter.

"Come on, dandelion. You can't ignore that this baby girl is coming soon." Bronx leans closer, sharing my breath. "If you tell us what scares you, maybe we can work through it with you."

"I think I'd prefer if you kiss me instead," I murmur, my body so relaxed that I feel as if I'm sinking into the mattress. "I need a better distraction at the moment. Everett's hand is inside me and not in the fun way."

Bronx groans and kisses me, keeping his eyes open and blurring my vision. "Ignore him," he commands. "You no longer feel what he's doing."

I inhale a gasp against his mouth, his mind manipulation acting like a block against Everett. I can't focus on what he's doing at all, and it weirds me out.

Wagging his eyebrows, Bronx asks, "Better?"

"Whoa." I search his gaze. "That's freaky."

"And necessary. If you'd watch the movies, you would be prepared. We don't even know how you want to go about things. Donors are creative. There are many ways to bring our baby girl into the world." Bronx purposefully brings it up, knowing I'm open to him in this moment. Usually, I'd cut him off before he can utter anything. Bastard.

"Did you know some expectant mother's birth babies in pools?" he questions, his jaw twitching as he feels my oncoming wave of emotions. "On their hands and knees too."

"I can't swim, and there is no way I'm pushing a baby out doggy-style." Thanks, mind. Glad I can count on you.

He chuckles. "There is no swimming."

I crinkle my nose. "No pools of whatever comes out of me."

"Seriously. I'm going to have to agree with Gigi, Bronxy." Jameson pops into view and kisses the top of my head.

Everett laughs and shakes his head. Bronx turns his gaze away from mine, breaking his hold on me. Scooting to the edge of the bed, he gets to his feet and crosses his arms across his broad chest, silently waiting for Everett to say something.

I clear my throat. "So, you want to give me a little rub after that, Everett? I think I deserve some sort of award." I grin at Everett and close my legs, trying to shove away the awkwardness of the exam.

Everett twists his lips and caresses his fingers over my

belly. Turning to Bronx, he refrains from responding to my joke and says, "Still no dilation, so I think you should be okay to go."

"Go?" I question, scrunching my nose. "What the hell? You didn't tell me you were leaving."

Bronx huffs in annoyance. "It was to be determined. I had to make sure I had time."

Jameson flops on the bed beside me and pulls me into his arms, trying to steal my attention.

His hand slides between us until he reaches the spot that'll make me tremble in pleasure. Brushing his lips to mine, he stifles my moan and rubs my clit with his index and middle finger. I ease my leg up to rest it on his hip, craving more.

"I'll give you whatever you want," he murmurs, breaking from my mouth to glide his tongue down my neck. "Just try not to give Bronx a hard time. He doesn't want to leave but we all agreed one of us needs to go."

I sink my fingers into his shoulders, locking him in place between my boobs. I trap his hand next, forcing my lust to settle down. "Why does Jamie make it sound bad? Where are you going exactly?" I ask Bronx, sensing Jameson purposefully trying to distract me.

Bronx sits on the edge of the bed again before lying down to snuggle me from behind this time. It doesn't go unnoticed that he doesn't meet my gaze. "I'm going with

Laredo to assess what we think might be the rebel nest where Silas is hiding. We won't be gone too long."

I try to turn, but he holds me still. "It's daytime, Bronx. I don't like it. You know rebels will—"

Bronx bumps his hips to my ass, play humping the concern right out of me. "It'll be dark when we arrive. Ashton will track us the entire time, so Mikkalo, Everett, and Jameson can focus on you."

"You mean Mikkalo and me," Jameson murmurs into my cleavage. "Everett is in health keeper mode. Just look at him."

I dart my gaze to Everett, tapping his finger across his com device. He winks at me and arranges a couple of things inside a huge box he keeps just out of my view. Whatever is inside must involve my impending labor and the mini-beast's birth, because he has been rummaging through it while talking on and off with Rio in medical terms that fly right over my head.

"I have to be completely prepared," Everett says, tapping his com device again.

"Yeah, you do," Bronx says, snuggling his face between my shoulder blades. "But don't worry. I'm nearly certain I can assist you with anything you need."

Everett chuckles. "Good. Gwen needs an excellent birthing coach. What you did during her exam was an excellent start."

A soft knock sounds on the door, and Mikkalo swings it open with Laredo standing behind him. Bronx snuggles me for a moment longer and kisses me softly before getting up to cross the room.

My heart pounds like crazy, my stomach twisting with nerves. Mikkalo helps Bronx load up with weapons and gives him a duffle bag with even more. Laredo's gaze burns into me, but I refuse to look at him. I can't. How Bronx can just go with him like he isn't a liar makes me anxious.

"Bronxy will be fine, Gigi," Jameson murmurs, pulling the blanket over us like he knows Laredo's stare gets under my skin. "Trust me. He can take care of himself."

"What if Laredo sets him up?" I question, my whirling thoughts making things worse. "Can't Laredo just go on his own?"

"Gwen." My name sounds like a plea escaping Laredo's mouth.

His presence latches onto my attention, refusing to let it go despite Jameson's persistent wandering hand mapping across my thigh like he wants nothing more than for me to continue to ignore Laredo and the rest of the world outside this makeshift blanket fort. The bed shifts as Laredo risks sitting beside me.

I stiffen and thrust the blanket away, glowering at Laredo for daring to get into my personal space. He hops back up and raises his arms in surrender. Silver flashes in his sad eyes, and it takes everything in me to remain expressionless. I refuse to let him see that his presence messes with me.

He swallows and steps back, giving me even more space. "I vow that I will ensure Bronx returns to you safely. You were completely right before. I was being unfair and an asshole, thinking that just because we have history it meant I still deserved you. Please forgive me. I want to start over."

"I can't act like the bad things between us never happened," I say honestly, tightening my fingers through Jameson's as he quietly offers me his support.

Laredo nods. "I suppose you're right. We can't really do that now, can we?" His gaze travels to my bulging belly. "But maybe you'll be open to moving past things. Let me earn a place in your life, even if it's strictly as someone who just wants to protect you. Maybe you'll have me as an ally and a friend."

I don't respond right away. Is that even possible for Laredo? He mistook a hug as an opportunity to progress with his affection.

"I don't know if you're capable of that. You always loved to test boundaries." I lock my eyes to his. "Wouldn't you prefer to see if you can find happiness outside of me? I'm not your responsibility."

Laredo rubs the back of his neck. "Gwen, you know me better than that. There isn't even a world outside of you for me."

This guy. Damn him and making my heart skip and race in overdrive loudly enough that Everett, Bronx, and Mikkalo all turn to look at me.

I try my best to remain expressionless, knowing they're waiting to see my reaction, but I'm fucking certain that my damn body gives me away.

And I'm pissed.

How could he test my resolve like this? How could he put me in this position to question myself and my feelings?

I remain silent for a long moment, gathering my thoughts, until I decide I don't have to respond to his comment at all. "I'm trusting you to take care of Bronx. He means the world to me and our daughter."

Laredo straightens his back, realizing that he failed to get to me. "You have my word. I will protect him with my life."

Laredo vanishes from the room, leaving me gasping. Everett rushes to my side and cups my cheeks in his hands, examining me with his senses.

Bronx and Mikkalo join him, and Jameson snuggles his face between my shoulder blades. They all silently wrap me in their arms, cuddling me close until I manage to suppress my trembles.

I blink my eyes and squeeze Bronx's hand. "If you come back with even a scratch, I will spank the hell out of you."

Bronx chuckles. "I spank back."

I groan and throw my arms around him, letting him pick me up. Clinging to him like a sloth, I kiss his throat a dozen times and work my way to his mouth. "Please be safe. I've already faced losing you too many damn times. I don't think I can survive another."

He pouts his bottom lip, his handsome face turning oh-so-broody. "Dandelion, it's just a night. I'll be back in no time."

I sniffle. "I love you."

"I love you more," he teases, kissing me again.

"Impossible," I say, stealing one last kiss.

Bronx hands me to Mikkalo before I refuse to let him go.

With a brush of his lips to my forehead, Bronx leaves the room, meeting Laredo in the hall. The two of them disappear, and I feel as if Bronx takes a piece of my being with him.

"Come on, let us feed you," Mikkalo says, stroking his hand down my spine.

I can only nod and keep my gaze on the door. I expect Bronx to return at any second, declaring he changed his mind, but he doesn't.

"Can I feed you guys too? Just a taste?" I ask, trying to hide my worry.

Jameson pulls me from Mikkalo and yanks his shirt off,

flexing his muscles. "Whatever you want."

If only he could drag Bronx back. Because right now, all I want is for the five of us to be together until our daughter comes, turning us into six.

12

SURPRISE

"DON'T MAKE A SOUND AND stay here, my beautiful dhampir. I will only be gone a few minutes." Laredo vanishes, leaving me frozen in place and unable to move or speak if I wanted to.

Soft moonlight shines overhead, casting the orchard in an eerie glow. Shadows dance and move, prodding at my fear instincts. Laredo will pay for this, leaving me exposed and vulnerable without a way to protect myself from shadow dwellers roaming this damn grove.

"You're late, brothers," Laredo's voice trickles through the trees to me.

"If you had suggested somewhere...not so close to Red Canyon Crest Grove, then we might've been on time," the familiar voice of one of Laredo's coven brothers sends panic rushing through me. "The outcasts have grown in numbers and don't make it easy."

Did he just say Red Canyon Crest Grove? Or what my brothers call The Orchards? Laredo brought me here? To the one place he swore he'd never risk taking me. The rebels in this community would lock me away and insist I procreate with one of their soldiers to ensure the power of the Gallagher dhampir line remains strong if they found me. It's why my dad fought so hard to keep my brothers and me away. But now—

"She's here." Laredo's deep voice cuts off my train of thought.

Another man huffs. "What? Are you certain?"

"Yes, Galveston. Look. I have proof." Sticks crunch on the ground, and I try to break free from the mind manipulation Laredo forced onto me. "Here's a visual of the Gallagher brothers with Trix. You know Gwen would be with them too. They would never leave her alone."

"When? Last I heard, their numbers were so depleted that they aren't even considered a threat anymore. Donor Life Corp took care of them," Thaxton says, his familiar voice scaring me, reminding me of other moments Laredo hid me away.

"Exactly. Which makes Gwen the exact person they need," Laredo says. "If you don't locate their whereabouts, they will find Gwen the perfect soldier to bond with."

Galveston growls. "I'll devour them all. Gwen is mine. Our bloodline will not be sullied with that of a donor."

"Then we must hurry," Thaxton says. "Give us the co-ordinates, Laredo."

"On one condition," Laredo replies.

"What?" Galveston's annoyance rips through the air.

"When you get what you want from Gwen, she is to be mine."

What the actual fuck. I try to move and fight, do anything I can to break through Laredo's mind manipulation. I don't know exactly what he's planning, but he's a dead vampire if he thinks he can arrange anything without my permission.

"Shit. Shit. Shit." Mikkalo's voice drags me from my dream. "I'm sorry, Gwen. I'm so fucking sorry."

I flutter my eyes open and try to push up on my hands, but something locks them in place. Fear prickles through me, my body screams to fight the mind manipulation, but Mikkalo offers his bleeding arm to me.

It was a dream.

I'm not being mind manipulated by Laredo.

I'm safe and with Mikkalo, his presence alone chilling me the hell out. Exhaling a long breath through my nose, I admire the rivulets of his blood flowing across his velvety dark tan complexion. It snaps the panic from me completely, igniting a deep-seated hunger all the way to my soul.

"I'm so sorry," Mikkalo repeats, pressing his arm to my lips, allowing me to drink. "I didn't know what else to do. I've been trying to wake you up for minutes, but you were...fucking wild. Look at this."

Leaning over, Mikkalo gives me a view of his ravaged neck and shoulder. If I didn't know any better, I'd guess he was mauled by some massive animal three times his size. I don't know what a ferocious beast attack looks like, but I'm nearly certain that this is worse.

"Fuck." My voice murmurs against his skin as my mouth refuses to release him so easily.

Mikkalo smirks and shifts, bending his leg up to kneel on the other. He frames his muscular, bleeding thigh with his fingers like he wants to ensure the mark is highlighted and on full display. I gasp and release his arm, trying to bring my hand to my mouth to cover my surprised expression. The chains clink, the leather restraints tightening, and I give up and settle on shuddering a breath.

"*I* did that?" I don't know why I even ask, because I know it's true. "In my sleep?"

His smirk widens into a full blown grin. The cute bastard is proud of himself like surviving a day with me is some kind of competition to prove only the toughest vampire makes it out alive. Shifting, he tugs down his briefs and reveals teeth marks on his tight ass. "After you did this. You should've heard yourself. You were snarling and everything. I've never wrestled anyone like that in my life. It was hot."

"Fuck," I breathe. "That's not hot. That's...brutal. I'm a monster."

"You're far from it. It was fucking exhilarating. I need you to spar with me when you're awake and aware because I was worried I was going to accidentally hurt you pinning you down. Plus, it wouldn't make me feel so bad for doing...this." He twirls his finger at the restraints, and I realize my ankles are bound to a bar, keeping my legs spread open. Following my gaze, he strokes his hand along the shiny metal and it extends wider, surprising me.

Heat travels up my chest to blush across my face. "Don't feel guilty, Mikkalo." My voice comes out funny, breathy. "You did what you had to do. I'm the one who should be sorry. I mean...I missed all this fun."

Thinking about my sleep-aroused blood hunger doesn't exactly sound fun to me, but now that my racing heart settles and I can think clearly, my current position seems like the perfect reward for Mikkalo having to deal with my crazy ass.

"I can make it up to you. Show you what you missed."

He shifts back to his knees between my legs, his desire now hard as fuck, stretching his briefs to enormous proportions. "I think it might be safe to release you." He roams his eyes from one knee and all the way up and then down to the other as I lay stretched and exposed on the bed.

I test the strength of the restraints. "You might want to reconsider. I don't think it's safe." I rub my lips together with my words, my body humming with lust, the lingering taste of Mikkalo's blood still buzzing across my tongue. "I might bite you again. On your other thigh. Maybe your other ass cheek." I hum and squirm, trying to fight the restraint to rub my legs together but the bar doesn't allow me. "Your pecs, too."

He raises his eyebrows at the playfulness in my voice. "I can't let you do that now."

"At least, not until after you retaliate, right?" I love the excitement rippling across Mikkalo's body. I know he's been dying to treat me like the wild one he teases I am, and I want to give him whatever the hell he wants in this moment.

I might not look sexy with my pregnant belly and blood smeared face, but I sure as hell feel like the hottest woman in the universe with the way Mikkalo reacts, his gaze heavy with his desire.

"You naughty, beautiful, wild dhampir," Mikkalo murmurs, shuffling closer to me on his knees. "Are you asking me to punish you?"

I grin. "If you think I need it."

His eyes spark silver. "I can't wait to give you what you deserve. Just tell me one thing."

"Hmm?" I question, squirming under his intensity, my body begging for his closeness and for more of his taste.

"Are you sure you can handle this?" Grabbing each of my knees, Mikkalo adjusts my legs even wider. The bar between my ankles clinks and locks into place again.

I wiggle my hips, the sensation of cool air caressing the damp warmth building between my thighs making me moan. "I'll tell you if I can't. I'll say banana."

Mikkalo cocks his head and laughs in surprise. "What have I missed? Is that your safe word with Bronx?"

I grin and shake my head. "We've only watched a couple movies, and every time I heard one of the donors use one, I thought about what mine would be."

"I like it. Can't ever let Bronx get away with his food choices for you, either." He chuckles again and leans over me, resting his palms on each side of my head. Brushing his lips to mine, he kisses me softly, teasingly. "Banana it is then. Use it if you need me to stop at any time."

I suck my bottom lip between my teeth. "I doubt I'll want you to." I bite his bottom lip and stretch it between my teeth. "Like you said. I'm a naughty dhampir."

"And I plan to bite you all over because of it." Mikkalo

extends his fangs, pricking my pouty bottom lip with them. He crashes his mouth to mine and glides his tongue across my blood coated lip.

Moaning, he sucks harder until my lip tingles, swelling from the pressure. I try to flick my tongue across his to deepen our kiss again, but he pulls back and smiles. A dozen thoughts light his expression. He gathers the fabric of my shirt between his fingers and tears it in half, taking a moment to rip the sleeves and pull it off my body completely.

He leans down and flicks his tongue across my nipple before blowing a cool breath, watching them pebble at the sensation. My skin buzzes with electricity and anticipation for what's to come, and I arch my back. Nipping the top of my breast, Mikkalo hums as blood pools. I stretch my neck to look, sending two streams around the curves of my boob.

Mikkalo kneels next to me, staring down at what I've done. Sliding his hand under me, he curls me up until the blood from his bite mark travels over my belly and to my hip, trickling all the way down to—

Tingles burst between my legs, my mind struggling to keep up with Mikkalo's sudden speed to get between my legs. He flattens his tongue, widening it, and licks across the seam of my body. I moan and wiggle, trying to reach down to grab his head. The restraints prevent me and my movements only expose my body more until Mikkalo glides his tongue over my clit and sucks it into his mouth.

"Mik," I gasp, the pressure of his tongue and lips exploring my body setting me off. "Oh, fuck."

He hums his satisfaction as I plead his name. "I'm going to bite you right where I want."

"Where?" I ask, panting, arching and trying to cage him in with my legs.

He taps his finger to my hip. "It could be here." Leaning over, Mikkalo extends his fangs, turning me on with the expectation of his bite, but he stops short and kisses the buzzing spot instead.

I shiver under the sensation. "This is torture."

He peeks up at me, his eyes flickering with his metallic desire. "I might do it here." This time, he caresses his fingers over my nipple in a smooth circle. If he does, his fang punctures will mirror the ones in my other breast. "Would you like that?"

"Yes," I say, my chest heaving with my deep breaths. "I need it. Right now. I crave it."

Once again, Mikkalo stops before sinking his fangs into my flesh and kisses my nipple hard enough that I might feel it in all its sensitive goodness tomorrow.

"Too bad," Mikkalo teases. "Naughty dhampirs don't get what they want."

Whoa. Yes, sir. I think the words, but I don't say them, my voice shaky with just the thought of pleasure Mikkalo will arouse inside me.

I yank my hands against the restraints, trying to see if I can break one of the cuffs from my wrists. "You're going to set me off, teasing me like this."

He glides his tongue over my side and gets between my legs again, stretching my hips open until they ache with effort. Cool air caresses the heat of my body, and Mikkalo undresses from his briefs, giving me a view of his body. Stroking the length of his thick girth, he pleasures himself while looking at me, driving me wild.

"I thought you were going to bite me," I say, my voice rising with my dare. "Are you too nervous now? Do you think that will kick on my dhampir strength to break myself free?"

He positions himself closer, sliding his hands under my ass to lift me a couple inches. Flexing his body, he taps his hard cock on my clit, using it to spank my aching, sensitive skin, craving for more of the ecstasy Mikkalo elicits.

I moan. "Whoa."

Mikkalo does it again, setting off a shockwave through my entire body. "You'll have to ask me if you want more like that."

I close my eyes and nod my head. "Yes."

"Ask," he persists.

"Will you give me more? I really, really need for you to bite me." My plea comes out a whimper, my voice breathy with the desire Mikkalo makes me crave.

"I'll bite you when I'm ready. Right now...I just want to see you squirm." Mikkalo positions his body, aligning his hard-on to sink between my legs.

He doesn't thrust or rock his hips and instead just gives me a view of his hot body. Stroking himself again, he teases me for a minute before using his other hand to rub back and forth over my clit. I moan so embarrassingly loud and arch my back, the sensation getting under my skin in the best way.

"I want more of you," I gasp, yanking harder against the restraints. The chains clatter with noise, but I don't stop. "Please, Mikkalo."

"Not yet." Picking up the pressure of his hand, he rubs my clit harder and faster until I scream out and fight harder against the chains. I'll break free of the restraints to pounce on him and have my way if he doesn't give me what I need soon.

Spasms tense my muscles with my orgasm, and Mikkalo bends forward, sinking his teeth into the soft, smooth skin of my groin. My body tightens even more, the pleasure bite lengthening my orgasm. He hums as he drinks from me, and I scream my ecstasy at the top of my lungs and yank my wrist restraints so hard that one snaps.

It swings at Mikkalo, and he swears and ducks as it ricochets like a chain whip, ready to lash through the lust permeating the air.

A door slams, and Jameson materializes on the bed, snatching the rogue chain and locking me back in place. "Fuck, Mik. Are you okay? You should've called me if you needed help..."

Jameson's voice trails off as he realizes what he interrupted between me and Mikkalo. Groaning, Jameson flies off the bed and puts space between us. Silver lights his eyes and he huffs a deep breath, trying to calm his nerves, thinking I was on a rampage to murder his brother in a blood lust frenzy.

I pant, slowly inhaling and exhaling with my still buzzing body. "Jamie—"

He turns to me and combs his fingers through his hair. "I'm fucking sorry. I didn't—"

"Mean to abandon me like you're afraid I'll go after you next?" I tease, flashing him a smile. "What do you think, Mikkalo? Should we punish him and let me bite him?"

Mikkalo lifts an eyebrow and glances at Jameson. "Do you hear our girl? She thinks she's in a position to hand out punishments."

Oh, fuck me.

"It seems that way, brother. What do you think we should do about it?" Jameson tugs off his shirt, effortlessly joining in without even missing a beat.

And damn it.

I'm so hot and turned on.

"I plan to punish her naughty mouth," Mikkalo says, grabbing the chains of my restraints and shortening them, forcing me to sit up, spread wide, for the both of them to get a view. "Those pouty lips keep getting her in trouble. Isn't that right, Gwen?"

I grin and nod my head. "Be careful, Mikkalo. I bite."

"Good. You know where I like it."

Jameson chuckles, utterly amused at how we continue to keep up our game.

"What about you, Jamie? How are you going to punish me?" I suck my lip between my teeth with my smile. "You can't exactly spank my ass."

He play-growls and crawls forward, kicking from his pants and boxers in the process. "Want to bet?"

Mikkalo surprises me by hoisting me up by my arms, grazing his cock between my boobs. A cool hand swats my ass, and Jameson takes me from Mikkalo and aligns my body to his. My body zings with desire, and I try to yank my hands free to grab Mikkalo to pull his hips to my face. Jameson sinks me on top of his raging boner.

I gasp only to have Mikkalo guide his cock into my open mouth, and I moan and lick the sweet, smoothness of his skin, the taste of his pre-cum like a dessert sauce across my tongue. I drool, unable to wipe my mouth, and Mikkalo slowly tests me to see if I try to speak. I don't, instead wrapping my lips around his shaft, letting him cup my head to guide my mouth the way he likes best.

Jameson bounces me on his lap, the pressure igniting fiery passion through my body, and he reaches around with one hand and plays with my exposed clit. I lose myself to the pleasure Jameson sends cascading through me and the taste of Mikkalo's desire teasing my tongue as he savors that I give him what he wants and needs.

The sounds of our satisfaction and bliss muffle through the air, and I find joy in letting them use me like this, taking away some of my control, and getting me to experience what it's like to just let someone handle my pleasure along with their own.

It's hotter and more deliciously exhilarating than I expect. My trust in Mikkalo and Jameson allows me to open up and enjoy anything they have to offer.

Mikkalo murmurs he's going to cum, and I voice my agreement, bobbing my head so that he doesn't think he has to stop. Increasing the pressure of his fingers, Jameson picks up speed, rubbing my clit while thrusting into me over and over again until my whole body tenses. Mikkalo cums first, his sweet, spicy flavor like cinnamon and sugar floods my mouth, and I swallow. He eases away, and I lick my lips, my brows scrunching with another orgasm.

With a few more bounces, Jameson finishes with a rumbling moan, and hugs me from behind, nipping my shoulder to taste my blood. Mikkalo releases my restraints, and I melt into Jameson and shift my hair, inviting him to bite me for a better taste. Mikkalo frees my ankles and sits between my legs, hanging them over mine and Jameson's to get ultra-close to sandwich me between them.

I cup Mikkalo's cheeks and kiss him, sucking the blood-offering he leaves coating his lips from a nip of his fangs to his tongue. I reach between us and stroke my hand across his cock, already feeling my desire rise.

He hums. "Do you want more?"

I bob my head. "I ache for you." Shifting, I turn my head just enough to peek at Jameson. "Will you feed me?"

"Fuck yeah." Happiness lightens his voice and he extends his fangs, the click sounding in my ear.

This is how I imagine life should be. Just giving in to our desires and natures and just being together without worrying about the rest of the world. Parting my lips, I prepare to bring Jameson's arm to my mouth while Mikkalo positions himself between my legs.

"I'm going to fucking kill you!" The familiar voice muffles through the room, sending a wave of ice through me, cooling my desire. "You're a dead man, Laredo."

I blink and jerk my attention to the door, listening as something crashes in the living room. "What the?"

"Shit," Mikkalo says, easing away from me. "I lost track of time."

"Ashton probably didn't want to interrupt us, either," Jameson adds.

"If you don't mind manipulate him to settle him down, I will." Brooklyn's feminine voice cuts over the commotion. "I don't care who he is. I'm not letting anyone attempt to hurt the father of my future niece."

"Just stay back! Go get Gwen and Declan," Bronx commands, his voice bellowing through the door. "Ashton, don't be nervous to show yourself. He could use a familiar face."

Snatching Jameson's discarded shirt from the bed, I rush to throw it on. My legs weaken the second my feet touch the floor, and Mikkalo catches me, holding me steady while he quickly puts on his pants. The three of us rush to the living room together, and I stop short, hovering in the hallway.

I don't believe my eyes.

"Porter?" I ask, my soft voice begging to stick in my throat.

My brother freezes and turns to me.

Before I can react, he sinks to the floor, bawling his eyes out.

I don't think I've ever seen him so broken.

13

BROKEN

"CAREFUL, DANDELION," BRONX WARNS, MATE-RIALIZING next to me to hook his fingers around my elbow. "Porter has been fighting us the whole way home. He's malnourished, traumatized, and can't seem to grasp what's going on. I don't want you to endanger yourself or our baby girl."

My heart slides into my stomach at his words, and tears burn in my eyes. I was afraid of something like this. Porter always relied on our family for strength. When we were separated, I feared he'd experience the worst. And now I feel horrible. How could I have been playing these twisted games with the Barons instead of demanding they bring Porter back? I have no excuse. Even if I thought being here with the Barons was worse, because they could turn him against me like Silas and Grayson, it doesn't make things better. Because if it was bad here, I'm sure that wherever he came from was far more torturous.

"Just let me talk to him," I say, yanking my elbow free from Bronx's tight yet gentle hold. I steel myself toward his protectiveness. "He needs me."

Bronx curls his fingers around the front of my shirt. "I get it, Gwen. I do. But this is not something I want you dealing with. Out of all of the things you choose to be stubborn about, think about the risk that comes with this one. Please. Let your brothers handle it. He could hurt yo—"

"No, I actually don't think he can. Look at him. I've never seen him so thin and weak. If anything, I could accidentally hurt him, so chill. I will be careful," I say, tugging from his hold. "He's my brother, Bronx. He needs all three of us. We're all he has left."

A rumbling noise escapes Bronx's mouth, but he doesn't try to stop me. He doesn't let me get more than a foot away from him, either. Our shadows blend together as one hulking entity, and I reach my arm behind me to flick him, silently warning him to stay back.

I shuffle the rest of the way to my brother, my legs still weak, and I pray I don't look like a mess. I shift my gaze to Laredo, sensing his attention on me. "Where did you find him? I thought he was taken out of the territory."

I had no idea Bronx and Laredo would show up with Porter. That must mean...fuck. Did the Blood Rebels do this? How can he look so filthy and thin if he was with them? They don't treat dhampir-mutation carriers like prisoners unless they've turned against the cause.

"I would think Silas would've—"

"I arranged a barter of sorts with some outcasts at the territory border," Laredo answers, cutting me off. "Your mates and I agreed it would be best not to tell you what we were planning as to not get your hopes up in case."

My brows pucker, and I swivel, tipping my head up to look at Bronx. "So you lied to me about hunting down the rebel nest?" Annoyance rises through me. I know I should be grateful they all went through this to help bring Porter home, but fuck. I feel so unprepared. If I had known...fucking fuck.

"Told you, assholes," Jameson says, hovering in the hallway. "She hates surprises."

"She also hates disappointment," Bronx mutters.

I inhale a few slow breaths. "I'm sorry. I just—I'm unprepared for this. It's like he's not even present." I force myself to look at Porter in the fetal position on the floor, continuing to sob and freak out, smacking his hands to the rug in an almost child-like tantrum.

"Make them stop!" Porter shouts, hollering and kicking.

I clutch my chest as if my heart might spill out. "What the hell is wrong with him? How do I deal? I'm unprepared," I repeat.

"You can't hold that against me. I didn't think you'd need to because—"

Jameson sneaks up behind Bronx and slaps his hand over his mouth. "Save that for later, Bronxy. This isn't the same as Gwen preparing for childbirth. At least she knows that's happening. This is far from a surprise bundle of joy. It's shocking to her."

I settle down, my annoyance dissipating as I focus on Porter. "Porter...?" My voice comes out as a whisper.

"Porter, shit! Oh, God. I'm coming," Declan says, rushing past me from wherever he was in the house to beat me to my brother, still hysterical and looking smaller than I remember. "Hey, it's okay, brother. You're safe now. We won't let anything happen to you. Try to take a breath."

"D-Dec?" Porter heaves and coughs. "Make them stop! Please!"

My insides clench at his desperation. "Who, Porter? Tell us what's going on?"

"They're hurting me!" he yells, swinging at the empty

air.

"Porter, look at me. No one is hurting you. You're safe. You're with us. Just breathe. Come on. In and out." Dropping beside him, Declan kneels close without touching him like he's afraid he'll set him off.

Porter heaves a few breaths, trying and failing to calm himself down. Everett materializes beside me and quietly hands me a glass of water. I take it, knowing it's for Porter, and I gather my nerves and force my feet to work to join Declan. Everyone remains utterly silent and watching us, all on edge and ready to rush in to intervene.

I clear my throat. "Porter?" I ask, my voice cracking at the mention of his name. "I have some water for you. Can you take a sip?"

"Will you let me help you upright?" Declan asks next. "Let me get a good look at you. I've missed you, little brother."

Porter coughs and heaves again, his thin arms shaking as he pushes his hands to the floor to get himself up. His eyes dart around the room, assessing everything. His fear instincts must settle, because he calms down enough to focus on my brother.

Declan carefully helps him to his feet and guides him to the sectional couch. I stay behind the two of them, quietly shadowing their movements, and Ashton finally pulls himself from against the wall next to Brooklyn and takes my hand, squeezing my fingers. I offer him a small smile, trying to keep my eyes from leaking. He doesn't have to say anything for me to know he's terrified Porter will hate him for the vampire he's become. I'm a bit nervous myself, but for my own reasons. I can't hide my big belly, even though Porter hasn't glanced at it with recognition yet.

"Here," I say lowly, sitting by Declan's side, knowing my guys would prefer someone else be between me and Porter. "You should drink something. When was the last time you've eaten?"

Porter opens and closes his mouth, his lips cracked and dry. "I don't know."

My eyes widen. "Jamie—"

"We're on it. Come help me, brothers," Jameson says, motioning to Mikkalo and Bronx. "They need some space. Let Porter settle down and eat. He seems like Gwen on an empty stomach."

Mikkalo nods and joins Jameson's side without complaint. He offers me a soft smile and turns motioning to Laredo and Brooklyn. Everett digs through his medical bag, preparing a couple things on a tray. I wouldn't expect him to leave, especially seeing my brother's condition, but unlike Bronx, he gives us space and doesn't even look anymore.

Jameson clears his throat. "Bronx?"

Bronx sighs. "I can't cook. I'm better use here."

Growling, Jameson materializes behind Bronx and

grabs him by the shoulders. He hauls him back, fighting against Bronx's stubbornness. "I don't care if you're a crap cook. I'll find something for you to do. Fuck, you can peel a damn banana."

A surprise laugh escapes my mouth at Jameson's comment. I slap my palm over my lips, stifling the noise. Everyone disappears, not letting me see or hear their reactions, and I shift on the couch and realize Porter gawks at my stomach like I have a deadly tumor or something.

"Gweny?" he whispers, clutching the glass of water. "Are th-they breeding you?"

I'm stunned speechless.

Ashton sits down on Porter's other side and clears his throat, gently touching Porter's knee. "Porter, no one is breeding Gwen. It's not like that."

"But the rebels..." Leaning forward, Porter hangs his head and stares into his glass. "Fuck. How long has it been? I'm so confused. It must've been so long with..." His words trail off as he looks at me. "Who's the dad? Do you think it'll be a, you know."

My heart breaks for Porter, watching him try to piece together everything he's missed. I so badly want to hug him and catch him up on everything, but I also want to know what he's been through to see if there's anything I can do to help.

"The baby belongs to me and the Royales. Bronx, Mikkalo, Jameson, and Everett will treat her, love her, and care for her as her dads. We're a coven and a family. And you're part of it now, if you want." I rub my hand across my stomach and flick my gaze to Everett ready and waiting for Porter to accept his help as a health keeper.

Porter's brows scrunch. "That still doesn't answer my question, Gwen. I thought you didn't want children. Have they manipulated you?"

I sigh a long breath, trying to remain even-toned. "I'm in love with them, Porter. They're my mates, and this mini-beast was a huge, unexpected, unplanned surprise. Laredo failed to mention that dhampirs could get knocked up by vampires."

The color drains from Porter's face and his head lolls as he faints. Everett materializes in front of Porter faster than I can call him for help and touches his fingers to his neck. Declan moves on the floor to kneel in front of us, giving Everett room to sit down.

"His vitals are dropping, Gwen," Everett says, quietly. "I need to give him blood."

"I'll do it," Ashton says, sinking his fangs into his wrist without hesitation.

Everett helps shift Porter in Ashton's arms to keep him upright. I clutch Everett's hand, my body turning wild with panic. This is my fault that Porter is in this position. Why he hasn't yelled at me and blamed me yet? I have no idea.

But I know it's coming. He's going to get his broken mind sorted out and when he does, he'll never forgive me.

"Declan, hold his hand. Talk to him. He needs someone familiar to him that still feels and looks the same from when you guys were still together." Everett stands and pulls me up with him. Instead of carrying me, he sets me on my feet. "Gwen, when he comes to, be prepared for anything. He doesn't know us like the rest of you do."

I rub my lips together and nod my head. "I know. It's just—is there any way to help him? Like how Laredo helped me?" I hate even mentioning it, but seeing Porter like this burrows into my soul and latches onto me. If there is something we can do to ease his turmoil, I want to try.

"That's a lot of damage to try to undo. I don't know if we should take the risk," Everett responds, keeping his gaze on Porter.

I inch closer, watching as color and warmth blossom in Porter's face and cheeks. His lashes flutter as a moan escapes his lips. Ashton keeps his arm in place, hugging our brother from behind. Declan grasps his hands and murmurs for Porter to wake up and to look at him. He repeats that everything is okay now that he's with us and how we'll get through this. The certainty in Declan's voice convinces even me.

Porter sucks on Ashton's arm for another few seconds, finally focusing his eyes and remaining conscious. A dozen thoughts flit through his sunken eyes. Bolting upright, he twists in Ashton's arms and narrows his gaze. Porter jerks his hand up and stretches Ashton's top lip, discovering his fangs on display.

"Whoa, shit." Porter turns to Declan. "You guys are vampires? Was this the Royales?"

Declan shakes his head and bares his teeth, flicking his tongue over them. "It's been a long few months without you, Porter. We have a lot of catching up to do."

"Fuck. Give me a summary. I can't stand this. The confusion sucks. You said I've been gone months? It feels so much longer. The fucking coven who bought my contract kept me in a dark room with two others during the day. And then at night—" He snaps his mouth shut and scrubs his face. "They used us for games. Sometimes as bait to lure outcasts to kill for sport. It was a nightmare. I wanted to die and they wouldn't let me. They—fuck. I don't want to think about it. I was so damn confused when someone dragged me out in the day and just abandoned me on a road."

I rush the few feet of space and can't stop myself from throwing my arms around Porter. My brother stiffens for a moment, sitting frozen. Everett touches my back like he'll drag me away, but Porter's embrace slackens, and he envelops me in his arms, hugging me with far more strength than he had before the blood consumption. Declan and Ashton join our hug, and I laugh and smile as Declan comments about getting kicked by my stomach. My heart swells with joy and relief, with more happiness than I knew possible despite Porter's condition. He still doesn't react as I had feared, and I want so badly to believe he never will. But dark thoughts flit through my mind, warning me that this could all go to shit at any second.

"All right, who's ready for some human food?" Jameson asks, his voice swirling through the air. "I made pasta with mushroom sauce. On top of the noodles for Porter and a vat of it on the side for the weirdo beast who would rather slurp it by itself and then eat the pasta plain."

I laugh. "Hey, blame the mini-beast."

Porter slowly nods his head and glances from our twin brothers and back to me. "The vampires cook for you?"

"Mostly just Jameson. It's his favorite thing—to fatten me up." I stick my tongue out at Jameson.

"Hey, I painstakingly put together a salad and removed all of the stalks from the lettuce because apparently you don't like them now?" Mikkalo materializes beside Jameson.

My grin widens. "You're the best." It's not that I don't like them, but anything that crunches when I chew is loud as fuck, and I hate it at the moment. "What about Bronx?"

Bronx huffs. "I poured the water."

Rolling my eyes, I shake my head. "How about some of your blood...and maybe you can give me a banana for dessert?" I keep my voice at a low pitch, ensuring my brothers don't hear the second half.

Bronx's eyes flash silver at my suggestion. My innuendo doesn't go unnoticed by Jameson, Mikkalo, and Everett, and the looks they give me send goosebumps over my skin. I don't know how Ashton remains straight-faced, his vampire hearing obviously picking it up, but he stands up and extends out his hands to Porter and Declan.

"We can catch you up and figure out what we should do while you eat, Porter," Ashton says, giving him a little shake. "If that's okay."

Porter bobs his head. "You have no fucking idea how good this sounds."

"I'd love for you to get to know my mates," I add, smiling at the four of them.

"That sounds...interesting. I guess I should've expected this, huh? You choosing a vampire—vampires. You did always have a thing for neck sucking. It used to drive Grayson crazy if he caught you with—" Glowering, Porter tenses and snaps his gaze to Laredo, quietly standing in the doorway to the dining room. "Laredo."

Laredo remains still, but he turns his gaze to me. "Perhaps I should keep an eye on surveillance until you can catch him up."

Porter fists his hands and pulls away from Ashton. No one moves. No one speaks, either. I know I should ask one of my guys to stop Porter, but another more dominant part of me thinks he should get to do what he wants after everything.

Laredo slumps his shoulders. "Porter, I—"

"You're dead!" Porter yells, swinging out to punch Laredo in the jaw.

Laredo lets him, not even turning his head at the weak gesture. "Actually, that was my brother Livorno. Whatever you think happened with me wasn't all true. We—"

Porter sucker punches Laredo in the mouth, socking the comment out of him. "This is your fault!" He reaches into his filthy jacket, Porter surprises all of us by pulling out a metal rod with a sharp tip.

Jabbing the rod forward, Porter stakes Laredo in the chest.

"You're dead," he repeats. "Fucking dead."

14

FAMILIAL BONDS

I PACE BACK AND FORTH in the dining room, watching Porter slowly pick at his plate of food. Mikkalo dragged Laredo out of the house, and the two of them still haven't returned. I know Mikkalo is fine. I can see him and Laredo having a conversation in front of one of the surveillance cams, but I really wish Mikkalo would come back inside.

"Come sit down with me," Everett says, drawing my attention from the com device I clutch in my hands. "I want to feed you a bit more."

"Watching Mikkalo help Laredo strategize how to get back onto Porter's do-not-kill list won't make it go any faster," Jameson whispers, pulling out the chair beside him for Everett to sit.

I nestle onto Everett's lap and turn my attention to Ashton and Declan. Brooklyn rests her hand on Ashton's shoulder, standing behind him, and I try not to think about the attention I'm just now noticing them giving each other.

"So, what do you think, Porter?" Ashton asks, drumming his fingers on the wooden table. "I'd really love to have you with me in Crimson Vista. You don't have to live with me if you don't want to. There are plenty of vacant apartments. I have to head back with Brooklyn in a couple days if you want to come and check things out."

"What about Declan?" Porter asks, leaning on his elbow. He no longer carries rage in his voice, but he's still tense, so it's hard for me to read him.

"I'll be going too, but my mister demands that I travel with Laredo...so I might just have to meet you there." Declan shrugs and twirls his last bite of pasta around his fork. "It's no biggie for me."

"And you, Gwen? Can you come?" Porter asks, staring at me without looking at anyone else.

I sigh and pat my belly. "My OB would prefer I not risk the travel, and honestly, Everett has everything already set up here. If we returned to Crimson Vista and I went into labor...I just don't know what to expect with the baby. She's half vampire."

"Oh." Porter slumps on the table.

"But we can video call any time. And then after, we'll see." I touch my stomach. "We're kind of just taking things a day at a time."

Porter nods without a word and Declan and Ashton begin to fill the silence again, telling Porter everything that has happened in the last few months. Biting his arm, Everett offers me his blood, and I bring his wrist to my mouth and suck, trying my best to ignore the hurricane tumbling inside me.

Jameson touches my knee, drawing my attention to him, and he bites his arm, ready to steal me from Everett next. Bronx joins in on the conversation between my brothers, going over anything Porter has questions about. It all sounds so strange, yet comforting, to hear plans being made for the first time in what seems like forever.

I slide into Jameson's arms and snuggle against his chest, keeping my legs slung across Everett's. Closing my eyes, I relax and savor what normalcy feels like for us. The baby kicks and moves, and Jameson taps his finger against my belly every time he sees a certain spot bulge out. I'm so consumed by him and Everett turning it into a game that I miss Mikkalo arriving until he touches my belly from over Jameson's shoulder.

I twist in my seat and spot Laredo just outside the dining room. He frowns at me when our eyes meet, and I lift and drop my shoulders. I don't know what he expects from me, because he's the one who fucked up to begin with.

A frown lines his face even more, and I swear Laredo looks ready to drop to his knees to grovel at my feet. It takes everything in me to find the nerve to twist on Jameson's lap and then it takes another moment of summoning my bravery to get my legs to work to stand me on my feet.

"I'll be right back," I mutter, bumping my stomach into Everett's shoulder as I try to ease between them.

"Want me to come?" Mikkalo asks, gliding his hand around my back, stopping me for a second.

"I'll be all right. It's twenty feet and you can see me." I stretch up and kiss his cheek, turning my attention to my brothers once more.

Ashton and Declan keep Porter engrossed in conversation, and I smile, hoping that it truly helps Porter the way I think it does. He's not as erect and stiff the longer they speak to him. Even when Bronx reaches and grabs a glass of gen. pop. blood from over Porter's shoulder, Porter doesn't flinch.

I waddle my way to Laredo, standing in the grand hallway outside the dining room. He leans his back on the wall and messes with the hem of his shirt. For someone who usually carries an air of confidence, Laredo looks defeated.

Why do I feel so badly for him? I wish I didn't.

Stopping in front of Laredo, I rest my hands on my belly and meet his gaze. His silver-flickering gaze drinks me in from head to toe like he can't help himself. I shift my weight between my feet at his sudden scrutiny. I despise and like the way he looks at me at the same time. My emotions confuse the hell out of me. I shouldn't even want him to keep staring at me, but I do. My rebel legs even decide there is too much space between us, so they shuffle me closer, nearly pressing my belly to his torso.

"I know I've asked so much of you already, my dhampir, but I have another favor to ask." Laredo brings his palm up to his chest and rubs the already healed spot from Porter's makeshift stake.

I let his use of his old term of affection slide and twist my lips. "It depends what it is. I'm not going to allow you to mess with Porter's head to force him into forgiving you."

"I've learned my lesson from that approach," he muses, inhaling a long breath through his nose. "I didn't even use mind manipulation to calm him down when we picked him up."

It's now that I realize I've been so overwhelmed and consumed by Porter's arrival that I haven't thought about exactly how he ended up here. To arrange for a donor to cross back into a territory had to have taken a lot of planning, collecting debts, and coercion.

Instead of arguing or asking him what he wants from me, I puff a breath through my lips and say, "Thank you for that. For arranging everything and bringing Porter home. I know you didn't have to do this for me. I don't even know why you wanted to after everything."

Laredo caresses his fingers to my arm, testing my reaction to find out if I'll allow him to touch me. I do. "My beautiful dhampir—Gwen—of course I had to do it, but it wasn't only for you. Porter didn't deserve the fate my failures forced him into. I know this might be hard to believe, but I enjoyed being around your brothers. They might've had their annoying quirks, but we got along for the most part."

"As long as you weren't trying to get in my pants," I tease, smirking with my comment.

"Which was nearly impossible not to. You've always had this presence about you. I couldn't help myself." His fangs peek from beneath his top lip. "Not to mention how often you loved to suck my neck."

Heat blooms from my chest to my cheeks, and I shake my head, suppressing the imagery that whirls through my thoughts at his comment. "Laredo..."

"I'm sorry, Gwen," he murmurs, trailing his hand up my arm until he plays with the strands of my blond hair on my shoulder.

I dart my attention back to the dining room, catching

Bronx watching me, though Mikkalo, Everett, and Jameson keep their backs to me. I know they listen to my conversation with Laredo, but I don't care. I share everything with them.

"I was only trying to remind you that it was more than about us. It was about your brothers too," Laredo says softly.

I nod. "You're right. I'll see what I can do. I honestly don't want to have to worry about Porter around you, anyway."

Laredo graces me with a smile. "If I didn't know any better, I'd think you might actually still care a bit about—"

"Oh, fuck. Fuck!" Declan's voice snaps through the air, the sudden panic lining his words startling me.

I rip my attention from Laredo and stride into the dining room, half expecting to find Declan injured. All of the utensils remain scattered across the plates, so I don't think he stabbed himself or something. To be sure, I close the space to him and spot his com device lit up on his knee.

"I have to go, Gwen," Declan says, waving his com device in my direction too quickly to see what freaks him out. "There's been an accident. Fuck!" Shoving his chair back, Declan nearly topples out of his seat. "I need to go now."

I bob my head, my eyes wide. Declan's urgency is enough to send my heart racing. "Is it Macon?" I clench my fingers into fists. The thought of something happening to

Declan's mister freaks me the hell out. If it did, that would mean his contract would pass on to the next vampire in line, and I don't even know who that is.

Declan wets his lips and shakes his head. "It's Jessa. She—fuck. Where's Laredo? I need to go."

Laredo materializes beside me at the mention of his name. Declan rushes around the table, looking ready to launch at Laredo, forcing him to carry him in his arms at vampire speed.

"We'll go with you," Ashton says, standing up. He surprises me by taking Brooklyn's hand. I thought he was talking about Porter. "I can arrange whatever you need."

My mind races as Ashton pulls out his com device and starts tapping the screen. Porter jerks his head back and forth between Declan and Ashton. Bronx slides his fingers through mine, his brows puckered. Jameson and Mikkalo disappear, only to reappear with duffle bags of things they might need for the long trip back to Crimson Vista. Everett adds a couple things to the bags and pats Ashton on the back.

"I—" Porter licks his lips, his voice faltering. "I want to go with you guys."

Declan and Ashton glance at Porter and then to me and my guys. Ashton presses his lips into a line like he's unsure of what to say. Laredo cracks his fingers and stares blatantly at Porter. I have no idea what Porter thinks about in this moment, but with his twitching jaw, I'm nearly certain it might involve trying to kill Laredo again.

"Thanks, Porter. Your support means a lot. I don't want you to think I'm abandoning you, either," Declan says, interrupting my thought before I can voice my opinion.

Laredo doesn't argue. "We need to get on the road now if we want to beat the sunrise."

"Can we walk them out?" I ask, sadness washing over me. I can't believe they already have to go. It's as if the universe wants to keep me from my family.

Bronx dips his chin without comment.

I hop up into his arms, knowing he prefers to hold me close in the safety of his arms. Mikkalo, Jameson, and Everett surround the two of us, and I watch from over Mikkalo's shoulders as Brooklyn lifts Declan into her arms as Ashton takes Porter. Laredo grabs the bags and slings them over his shoulders, leading the way.

The world blurs and cool air engulfs me. I snuggle my face into the crook of Bronx's neck, trying to suppress the sadness rising inside me. There is nothing more in the world I want to do than ask my brothers to stay instead of go with Declan, but that would be selfish of me. I have my guys and their incomparable support. Declan needs my brothers more than I do. I just don't want our time together to end. I'm afraid we might never get this chance to be together again.

"Let us know when you get into the city," Bronx says, turning to Ashton. "Please don't let the Barons' demise slip. I don't want the board to know until after our daughter arrives."

Ashton nods. "You can count on me."

A low growl reverberates through the air. Bronx tenses and tightens his arms around me. Mikkalo swivels, glancing around the property.

And then I hear it.

The rumble of a back-world car engine hums through the air. The tires crunch on gravel as it drives closer down the long road that cuts through an orchard of orange trees. Mikkalo and Jameson vanish without a word. They're sweeping the area to assess what we're dealing with. Brooklyn unsheathes a dagger and steps behind Declan and Porter while Ashton takes the front, sandwiching them in between their bodies.

"Misters Royale," a husky, raspy voice says, snapping my attention away from the intruding vehicle now illuminating the night with its headlight beams. "I have a message for—"

Mikkalo materializes behind a disheveled vampire, covered in dirt and dried blood. The tip of Mikkalo's sword pops through the front of the man's chest, and he hollers in surprise. Instead of cutting the fucker in half, Mikkalo restrains him in place.

"There are six outcasts gathering on the edge of the grove," Jameson says, popping into view in front of me. "Three rebel vehicles lie in wait. What do you want us to do?"

Bronx growls and looks to the intruder. "Who sent you?"

The filthy vampire flashes his fangs. "I have a message," he responds without answering Bronx's question.

Mikkalo twists his sword with a growl. "Answer us! Was it Silas?"

Screeching, the vampire nods his head. "You must deliver him his brothers or they'll attack."

Declan fists his hands. "We don't have fucking time for this!" Rushing out from between Brooklyn and Ashton, he yells, "Silas! Silas, you fucker! You're dead. I'm coming for you."

Tires squeal and a loud horn blares, stealing my senses.

A car barrels at high speed right for us.

15

REBEL INVASION

"SPLIT UP!" BRONX SHOUTS, UNSHEATHING his weapon. "Ev, take Gwen. Get her inside."

I screech in surprise as wind blows through my hair. Everett catches me and cradles me against him. Two vampires zoom from the trees, trying to cut us off. They hiss and growl and snap their fangs. Mikkalo roars with his swing, decapitating the two guys before they can even get within a foot of me.

Porter's screams rip through the air, stealing my breath

away. I dig my fingers into Everett's shoulders, trying to figure out where he is and who's attacking him. My gaze lands on his crouching form, hunkered near a tree. He covers his face with his hands, losing himself to his fear.

"Everett, we have to get him," I say, pointing in Porter's direction.

Without hesitating, Everett turns away from his beeline toward the house to get to Porter. Growls and snarls rip through the night as my guys fight the outcast intruders, seemingly coming in from all directions. The car horn blares again and remains on, stealing my chance of hearing anything else.

"Mikkalo, get the fucker in the car!" Jameson shouts over the discordant melody of rebel destruction.

I glance at Mikkalo disappearing into the grove and turn back to Porter. Everett kneels beside him without letting me down. Heaving, Porter grinds his teeth, his face red like he can't get any air in his lungs. A shadow casts over us, and Everett jerks upright, aiming a knife as Silas emerges from the trees.

"Baby brother, what the fuck happened to you?" Silas asks, baring his fangs. Turning his glare to me, Silas twitches his fingers. "Are you okay?"

"Sa-Silas?" Porter asks, his voice shaking.

"Get back!" I shout, tensing in Everett's arms. Silence fills the air, unnerving me. I don't have to look around to know that the others have gone after the outcasts. I'm not afraid though. Not of Silas. "You are not welcome here!"

"Aww, Gweny. How can you be such a bitch after everything we've done for you? I went through a lot of trouble hacking Declan's com device to get my brothers out, and honestly, I'm only here for Porter. When an ally informed me of his return into the Donor Life Corp Territory, I knew he'd be coming to you." Silas steps closer, making Porter wince. "Now get up, Porter. Grayson has been dying to see you. Let me take you to where you belong."

Porter remains still in his spot without acknowledging Silas's existence right away. Everett shuffles on his feet, trying to figure out how to keep Porter away from Silas without putting me in the line of danger. As for me, I'm currently weighing my chances of crashing into Silas to rip his heart out. Because I'm scared. What if Porter does want to go with him? He's been tormented and tortured by vampires and would make the perfect soldier to the rebel cause.

"Porter," I say, keeping my voice even. "Don't listen to him. He's changed. Silas doesn't care about any of us. All he wants is to use us to his benefit."

"Shut the fuck up, traitor!" Silas yells, flashing his fangs at me. "You're the reason why he can't even get up. You broke him!"

Porter tenses and whimpers, the noise breaking my heart. Fury ignites inside me, prodding at my dhampir nature. I want to protect Porter from the monster Silas has become. I never in a million years thought I'd imagine Silas's death, but in this moment, it's the sweetest thing to think about.

Launching from Everett's arms, I brace to tackle Silas. A deep, guttural growl escapes my lips, and I fist my hands for my oncoming fatal blow.

"Gwen, no!" Everett shouts, snatching me midair, stopping me from attacking.

It's the second Silas needs, and he hoists Porter from the ground and into his arms. "It's going to be okay. I'll get you out of—"

"No!" Porter jerks his hand at Silas, ramming a blade into his neck, sending blood spraying across the ground.

Silas's eyes widen for a split second and then narrow in rage. Silver explodes across his irises, and he extends his fangs longer than normal, preparing for a kill bite. My insides flip and twist, and I gasp a cry as pain shoots from my stomach and through the rest of me.

I can't do anything but scream in agony, watching Silas sink his teeth into Porter's neck. Crumbling to the ground, Porter falls to his side and clutches his throat. My heart explodes into a million pieces, and I try to get out of Everett's arms, but my body refuses to move.

"Porter!" I wail, a debilitating muscle spasm rattling me to the core.

I clutch my belly in pain, heaving a breath, feeling as if I might throw up.

"Fuck," Everett says, adjusting me in his arms. "Gwen, look at me. Look at me."

"Shit, what is that?" Jameson's voice muffles through the pounding in my ears.

"Take Gwen. Get her to the room, Jameson," Everett snaps, his voice deepening. "Mikkalo, keep pressure on Porter's bite mark. I need to give him blood."

I groan, another wave of pain tightening my belly. "Everett, something's wrong with me."

"Where's Bronx?" Everett asks instead of answering my question.

"He and Laredo are finishing the fuckers off," Brooklyn responds, her voice sounding strange and shaky.

"Well, fucking get him." Everett's tone startles me. "Jameson, what did I say? Get Gwen to the room. I'll be right there."

"Everett," I cry again. "Please. Something's wrong."

Everett materializes in my view. His brows furrow over his blue eyes, and he forces a smile on his tight mouth. "It's going to be okay. Your water broke, Gwen. She's coming."

"What?" Jameson and Mikkalo ask at the same time.

I clutch my arms around my belly and groan into Jameson's shoulder. "Shit. This can't be it. We're not ready."

I can't believe I'm about to have a baby.

"How's Porter? I need to know," I say, gripping Jameson's shirt in my fingers.

Cramps explode through my stomach, stealing my breath. I squeeze my eyes shut and jerk in Jameson's arms. I sink my teeth into his neck. Blood fills my mouth, coating my tongue with his sweetness, but it does nothing for the pain swelling through my middle.

I groan and gasp. "Fuck! How's Porter!"

Everett rushes into the bedroom. "Gwen, he's going to be okay. I promise. Let's worry about you." Pointing, he motions at the bed. "Jameson, help her get undressed and settled in the bed. I want you to time her next contraction for me while I get the equipment in here. I don't like where the Barons had the delivery room set up. There's a window."

"Gwen chose that location in case we needed to make a quick escape," Jameson comments, following Everett's instructions by carrying me to the bed.

"Good thing we have no need to escape now. Right, dandelion?" Bronx asks, appearing at the bed. "We got you. Brooklyn and Laredo are on watch. Your brothers are with Porter. Let's just focus on bringing our beautiful baby girl into the world now."

I glower at him. "Says the man who doesn't have to

push this beast out." Cramps seize my belly again, and I groan, squeezing Jameson's shoulders again.

"Count, Jameson," Everett calls, rolling in a machine. "Mik, grab some towels. Everyone wash up."

I lose myself to the pain clenching my body. What the fuck have I gotten myself into? I knew this shit would hurt, but damn it. I'm freaking the hell out. How are my guys remaining so calm?

"Try to breathe, Gwen. It'll stop soon. Remember, it won't last forever. You've dealt with pain before, but this time, it's for something amazing." Bronx squats next to where Jameson holds me on the bed, using his vampire senses to time what feels like the impending detonation of this mini-beast bomb.

"Forty-five seconds," Jameson shouts.

With his words, the contraction subsides, and I gasp and pant a breath.

What the hell? No way. That felt like an eternity. If this is how it's going to be...fuck my life. My poor body. Rest in pieces, vagina. I hope you'll forgive me for this trauma.

I stifle a sob of relief and rest my head on Jameson. "I can't do this. I can't give birth." I hold my belly and look down. "Do you hear me, baby girl? You just make yourself at home. It's cozy in there, right? You can stay in as long as you want."

Bronx chuckles, and I whip my head up and glare at

him. The smile startles off his face, his lips disappearing into a thin line like I'll bite them off if he dares laugh at me again. Reaching out, he touches my cheek and kisses my forehead.

"Trust us to help you through this," he says. "Now, let Jameson get you settled. Maybe you can take a quick shower with him. I read that it could help with the contraction pain until Everett can take care of you."

"I'm not going to last," I complain, pouting my bottom lip.

"Ev, hurry the fuck up," Jameson says, sliding me onto the bed next to him. He turns to Bronx. "You have three minutes before I sic Gigi on you. She's extra bitey."

Bronx kisses my forehead once more and joins the others to help set up. I thought it would be quicker than this, but they're not just getting ready for the delivery. Everett's setting everything up for after. Because really, only a small part of this is about me. It's about our daughter.

Everett carries medical equipment in his arms with Mikkalo and Bronx behind him. The three of them speed around the room too quickly to follow, and Jameson rubs his cool hand down my spine, getting me to raise my arms. He silently undresses me first, before doing so for himself. Carrying me to the bathroom, he brushes his lips to mine, keeping my focus on him and the softness of his mouth.

"You're amazing, Gigi. I want you to know that I'm

going to do my best to make this as perfect as possible, okay?" Jameson steps into the water and sets me on my feet. Steam wafts through the air around us, and he doesn't waste even a second before scrubbing both of us down. "I'm so fucking excited to meet our baby girl. I love her so much already. She's going to be as incredible as you."

His words sink deeply into my soul, and I can't stop a tear from slipping from my lashes. It blends with the water on my cheek, but Jameson must sense it's there, because he rubs the pad of this thumb under each of my eyes.

Mikkalo taps his fingers to the glass door of the shower. "We're ready, but Everett says you can take your time if you want to stay in here."

I'm about to open my mouth to ask him to join us when another contraction sends me bowing forward. A growl escapes my mouth with my groan, and cool air prickles across my wet skin as Mikkalo enters the shower in his clothes. He and Jameson each take one of my hands and use their free ones to rub soothing circles on my back. Jameson counts out loud this time, ultra-aware of what's going on. I pant and gasp, trying to force air in my lungs, but I can barely focus.

"That was a minute this time, Ev!" Jameson shouts over the sound of the running water.

"About five minutes since the last one," Mikkalo adds.

"Fuck," I mutter, remaining hunched over with the hot

water spraying on my back. "How much longer does this bullshit last?"

Bronx and Everett enter the small bathroom, already showered and changed into clean, comfortable looking clothing. Bronx grabs a fresh towel from the warming tray on the shelf, and it takes me a moment to catch my bearings to step out. Bronx helps me dry off, rushing as if he's racing to beat the next contraction. Holding out a robe, Everett bundles me up, cocooning me within the feather-soft fabric.

They let me waddle my way back into the bedroom, where the room has been converted for the delivery of the mini-beast. My heart skips a beat at the sight of a sleek, clear-walled bassinet next to a rolling cart of supplies I haven't even thought much about. Diapers, towels, tiny blankets, and the teensiest little onesie and hat set out perfectly.

Instead of going back to the bed, I stop in front of the make-shift nursery and run my finger over the soft fabric of the pink blanket with white flowers across it—the bloodroot blossoms like the ones on the Royale Coven Crest.

"Come on, Gwen," Everett says, touching his hand to my lower back. "Rio wants you on the monitors."

Shit. I nearly forgot about him. "Is he on his way? Do you think he'll make it?"

Silence greets me, and my heart slips into my stomach.

"The threat of rebels complicates things. Without his coven knowing, he'd have to travel to us alone, and I'm afraid the rebels aren't going to let him travel through their territory. They'll attack him if he tries."

I blink the tears from my eyes, knowing he's right. I just—I know what kind of pressure this puts on Everett, and I don't want him to have to stress about everything.

"Don't worry, Gwen. You're in excellent hands," Mikkalo says, strolling from the bathroom with a towel slung around his hips. "Everett knows what he's doing."

Everett smiles. "I thought I'd be a bit worried, but I'm excited. I never thought the first delivery I'd perform would be for our daughter."

"Now if only—" The words squeak from my mouth with another contraction, and I bow and brace my hands to the bed. I didn't think the pain could intensify anymore, but the cramps steal my breath and bring tears to my eyes.

Everett eases open the front of my robe and touches his hand to my stomach. "You're doing amazing, Gwen. Breathe in and out. As soon as this one passes, I'll give you something to help numb the pain."

I heave a deep breath as the contraction fades. Climbing onto the bed, I curl sideways and press my cheek to the sheets. Jameson perches near my head and gently starts combing my hair, twisting the blond pieces out of my face. Mikkalo silently joins us, twining his fingers through one hand, bringing it up to kiss my knuckles. Bronx eases onto the bed in front of me and presses his forehead to mine, locking me in his gaze. Our minds open to each other, and I inhale a small breath at the wave of love, warmth, and something indescribable washing over me.

"Focus on me, okay? You won't notice anything Everett does right now. He will take the best care of you and our daughter." Bronx's eyes flicker silver, blinking so fast that they look almost solid metallic.

"We're all here for you, Gwen," Mikkalo adds, releasing my hand only to stroke it across my back. He slides his fingers to my side to touch my belly. "You too, our precious baby girl."

"Fuck, I can't wait. What do you think, Everett?" Jameson asks, playing with my hair. "Is she as stubborn as her mama? What are we in for?"

"Ignore him if you want, dandelion." Bronx's breath mingles with mine.

Pain swells inside me again, clouding my senses. I miss Everett's response and snap out of Bronx's hold on my mind. I scream out, the intensity of the contraction growing worse by the second. I dig my nails into Bronx's hand and reach behind me to grab onto Mikkalo. Jameson murmurs something I can't process.

"Everett!" I yell, curling forward. "Make it stop!"

"Bronx, get her to focus on you again. Her pain relief isn't taking like it does with humans. Her dhampir nature must affect it. Only the topical cream will work, but that's not going to help with her contractions." Everett's voice cuts through my mind fog as my pain subsides.

"What?" I ask, my voice rising. "Are you kidding me?"

Bronx cups my face, guiding my eyes to look at him. "Gwen, don't look away from me. Open your mind and let me in completely. Do you understand?"

"Yes." The word comes out automatically.

"Now think of somewhere you love. Imagine it as best you can. I want you to take me there," Bronx says, his eyes turning silver.

I lose myself to their metallic depths.

16

ROYALE LOVE

"DAD? WHERE ARE YOU?" I can hear my voice, but it doesn't come from me. A strange sensation buzzes across my skin like tiny strings pulling me toward the familiar door of the bunker.

I stare in surprise as the hatch flies open, and I gawk at a short blond girl with round green eyes, a slightly turned-up nose, and gangly limbs she looks like she's still growing into.

"Dad?" she calls again, squinting her eyes to stare

around the bright sunshine illuminating the grass around the bunker.

"Over here, Gweny." The familiarity of my dad's voice sends my heart racing. This is the strangest memory ever. I've never been aware like this before, watching things unfold as a spectator, and it weirds me out a bit.

"You look just how I imagined you would as a kid." Bronx's deep voice hums from beside me. "I don't know what I was expecting, but I didn't ever think you'd choose to show me this."

I shift on my feet and meet Bronx's smiling face. "I don't know why I did. I should've thought of our room in Night Palms Castle with our favorite porno, huh?"

He chuckles and caresses his fingers to my jaw. A rush of energy zaps through me, and I gasp, feeling Bronx on a soul-deep level unlike anything I've ever felt. "Nah. The last thing I need right now is a boner for you."

I crinkle my nose. "Yeah, I'm not sure you're going to get your cock anywhere near me ever again."

"I guess it's a good thing I'm great with my hands." Tipping his head back, he laughs at his own joke and pulls me into his arms. He kisses my forehead and eases away, only to drape his arm over my shoulders. "They work well for both me and you."

Warmth floods my face, my soul reacting to his innuendo. If a giggle didn't cut through the air, I'd say some-

thing in response, but the younger version of myself beckons for my attention. Strolling forward, I pull Bronx along with me, following the familiar path to the nearby stream. I spot young me plopping onto a big rock next to my dad, dipping his bare feet into the stream.

I inhale a small breath. "I forgot how much Grayson looks like him," I whisper, my voice quivering as I'm overcome with emotions. "Fuck, I miss him. He'd be so happy to be a grandpa."

"Tell me what's up, Gweny. Is Kyler being a jerk-face again? Do I need to send him collecting two-hundred sticks this time to keep him busy from annoying you?" Dad bumps his shoulder to my younger self, a mischievous smile crossing his face.

Bronx chuckles and shakes me, guiding me to another rock to sit down. "He sounds like a good dad."

"The best," I say, resting my head on Bronx's shoulder. "He always knew exactly what to say and how to handle my brothers, especially when they'd gang up on me. They were little shits when we were young."

"I bet you were a handful too." Bronx graces me with a handsome smile. "Always wild."

I giggle and scrunch my nose without agreeing with him. "Let's just say that we're lucky there are five of us if she happens to be like me. But you know what? My brothers might've annoyed the hell out of me, but we kept each other entertained. They watched out for me. Even before..." I swallow, letting my comment hang in the air. Bronx doesn't have to ask to know I'm talking about my dad's death.

"Maybe that's reason enough not to banish my cock from you," he teases, grinning wider. "A sibling might be exactly what she's going to need."

I hang my head and crane my neck to smile at him. "Maybe even three or four."

His eyes widen. "Yeah?"

I laugh. "It's bound to happen with the way we live. I mean, think about it. Four sexy, mind-blowing cocks on constant rotation, vying for me. Soon it'll start being a competition. I know you guys."

Bronx's laughter fills the air, and he pulls me into his lap and kisses me softly. The trickling of the stream hums in my ears, and I savor the sounds brought forward from my childhood memory. Soft laughter and hyper voices cut through the comforting quiet of the woods around us, and I watch as my dad hops to his feet and splashes in the water.

"Come on and hide with me, Gweny. I think your brothers might need a little lesson, don't you think? Your mom used to always say that the best way to keep rebellious boys ready for anything was to always surprise them. We gotta make sure they can keep up with you. I don't want you to be stuck having to protect them for the rest of their lives." Dad holds his hands out, waiting for my younger self *to join him. "You'll be busy with your own life."*

I grin, watching younger me bounce on her feet in the water. "I call dibs on Grayson."

Dad laughs. "You remind me so much of my Demi, Gweny. Your mom always loved a challenge."

Demi? It's been so long since I thought of my mom's name that hearing how beautiful it sounds coming from my dad makes my breath catch.

"Bronx, what about Demi?" I ask, keeping my eyes on my dad as he leads my younger self deeper into the trees.

"Demi?" he asks, his face softening as he thinks the name over and over. "It's beautiful. The most perfect name I've heard apart from yours."

I smile. "Think your brothers will like it?"

"They'll love it. It's far better than calling her the mini-beast—"

A soft cry echoes through the air, and Bronx stills, cocking his head. I blink my eyes as the forest disappears from around us, and I find myself locked in his gaze. The silver fades, leaving me staring at the glassy pools of his dark depths. A tear trickles from the corner of Bronx's eye and streams down his cheek.

I reach up and smear the glistening path with my thumb.

"Fuck, Mik. Let me help you up," Jameson says, his voice tugging my attention from Bronx.

Another cry trickles through the air, and my heart picks up speed at the delicate, melodious sound stealing my breath away. I clutch the blankets and flick my gaze to Everett, quickly cleaning up the tiniest baby I've ever seen in my life.

He turns toward me, a dazzling smile crossing his face. "She's perfect, Gwen," Everett says, coming to my side. "Just look at her."

"She's tiny," Jameson says, his voice turning into a whisper.

Mikkalo sits on the floor, blinking his eyes in awe. "Look at all that blond hair. Just like her mama."

"Or you, Ev," Bronx teases, his smile beaming brightly.

"Yeah, brother. You and Gwen bone more than—"

I whack Jameson with a laugh. "Not in front of the baby."

Everett gently sets our daughter in my arms and fills the spot next to me. Mikkalo joins us, and Jameson teases him about fainting despite being able to handle ripping people apart. Bronx wipes his eyes on his sleeve and the four of them crowd around me.

"Isn't that right, Demi?" I ask, just holding her in my arms, frozen and unsure of what to do or think or say. "Do you like the name? It was your grandma's."

"Demi," all of my guys say in unison.

"I love it," Jameson says, reaching over to caress his fingers along Demi's cheek. "I love her."

I bonk him with my head. "And I love all of you."

"You're enjoying this way too much," I say, arching my back while Everett massages some numbing cream over my sensitive, swollen breasts.

He smirks, his eyes flickering with a blink of silver. "You bet I am. Whatever helps my girls. Demi is already latching like a champ."

"Well, look at who her mom is," Bronx murmurs, shifting on his side to smile at me.

"You say that like you guys don't survive by sucking every inch of me." I stick my tongue out and flick him.

Everett chuckles and slides between us, nudging me over onto my side to spoon me from behind. I hug his arms around me, loving how he cuddles me close. This is the first time he's relaxed in three days. Bronx reaches over Everett and sandwiches him between us to hold my hand too. I laugh and suck his finger into my mouth.

"Shit. I gotta get up or Everett's going to get poked." Bronx tugs away from me and bounces the bed.

I cover my mouth to suppress my laugh. Mikkalo hums under his breath from in front of me but doesn't wake up. My heart melts seeing Demi snuggled on his bare chest with her Royale Coven crest blanket wrapped around them.

Jameson sleeps on his other side, with Demi gripping his index finger in her sleep.

"Everett doesn't appreciate that as much as I do," I murmur, wiggling my ass against Everett, feeling his body awaken.

He groans in my ear. "Careful, Gwen. I might have to pick you up and carry you to the bathroom if you keep teasing me. I don't want you to wake Demi up with your moans. I'll never hear the end of it from Jameson and Mik."

I roll over and face him, grinning. "What would you do if I were purely human? It's been only days."

Everett licks his lips, closing his eyes as I slip my hand into his pajama pants, lacing my fingers around his hard-on. "I'm glad I never have to find out," he murmurs, hooking his fingers to my hip. Resting his head to the crook of my throat, he lightly scratches me with his fangs. "You're utterly irresistible."

"You think I'm irresistible? Because I'm addicted to you. I've missed you." I stroke him softly, teasingly, loving his reaction so much.

Bronx leans over and steals a kiss, his muscles rippling in his arms. If a knock didn't sound on the door, I'd roll on top of Everett and test to see if I'm healed and as sexy as ever like Everett claimed. Heat blooms over my body, and no one gets up. Bronx kneels beside Everett, looking ready to lift me to plant me on top of him if I don't move. This wasn't a perk I expected from drinking vampire blood and being a dhampir, but I'll take it. The only reminder I need about any of this is Demi and how adorable she looks in Mikkalo's arms.

I've never seen something so sweet in my life. All six pounds and seven ounces of her have captured my heart, and I could stay here all day, watching her sleep, feeding her and cuddling her when she fusses...and enjoying the fact that none of my guys have even considered having me change her diaper.

"Tell whoever it is to go away," Everett says, ignoring my slowing hand. He rolls me on top of him and gently bounces my boobs in his hands. "We're not ready for visitors."

An exaggerated sigh muffles through the door, and I grab Everett's wrists to stop him from locking me in place to test my resolve. Crinkling his nose, he sits up and adjusts his cock in his pants before snagging Mikkalo's shirt from the pillow above his sleeping head to tug over my naked body.

"Gwen's brothers might be too polite to speak up, but I'm not. I'm dying to see my niece, Bronx. Let us come in. Pretty please, brother," Brooklyn says, her voice edging on sounding whiny.

I glance at Bronx, but he shrugs. "Okay, but be quiet. Half of us are sleeping."

The door creaks open, and Brooklyn enters first with

the biggest smile I've ever seen on her. She usually gets under my skin, but her nearly palpable excitement softens my heart toward her. I know she disapproved of my relationship with Bronx and was always concerned about what he risked losing to be with me, and in this moment, I know that none of that matters to her anymore. Demi not only changed our lives, but she changed the dynamic of other's relationships with me. I can see Brooklyn claims Demi as family.

"Oh, brother. Gwen. She's so tiny. Gorgeous." Brooklyn hovers beside the bed, staring down at Demi sleeping on Mikkalo's chest. "Perfect."

Ashton, Declan, and Porter shuffle into the room with their arms full of big plates of food, setting my stomach off. Mikkalo and Jameson both stir at the sound, totally in tune to my body even in their sleep. Jameson rubs the sleep from his eyes and sits up. He offers my brothers a lazy smile and takes one of the plates, handing it to me.

"How are you feeling, Gweny?" Ashton asks, peering over Brooklyn's shoulder as she looks ready to wiggle her fingers to beg Mikkalo to let her hold Demi.

I scoop up a forkful of cheesy potatoes and savor the burst of flavor. "Mmm." I nod my head and quickly chew. "I'm great. If my boobs hadn't started leaking, I'd have thought the pregnancy was a vivid dream."

My brothers grimace and Brooklyn laughs, relenting to sitting on the edge of the bed to caress her dainty finger over

Demi's downy blond hair. Movement in the hallway draws my attention away from them, and I spot Laredo hovering like he can't decide whether or not he should interrupt.

I clear my throat. "You can come in, Laredo. I'd love for you to meet Demi."

Grabbing a vase of fresh flowers from a table in the hallway, Laredo smiles and brings the colorful bouquet he must've picked from the garden to the sitting area coffee table. I return his smile with my own and scoot to the end of the bed and out of Everett's arms. I motion for him to bring the flowers and stick my nose into them, catching the fresh scent.

"I love them. Thank you," I say, watching him return them to the coffee table.

I pat the spot in front of me as I face my guys still lying in bed. Jameson moves from his spot, giving Brooklyn his place beside Mikkalo. He grabs my abandoned plate and pulls me into his lap, not commenting that Laredo takes me up on my offer to sit.

"Mik, why don't you let Demi's auntie and uncles hold her?" Everett says, winking at me. "You know there might be a time in our future where we'd all like to enjoy some time with Gwen, and we want Demi to be comfortable with those who might babysit her."

Bronx, Jameson, and Mikkalo all look at Everett like he's said the most ridiculous thing in the universe, and I crack up and kick Bronx with my foot.

"Demi, you better start working on your daddies now, because they might chaperone you for the rest of eternity," I tease.

"It'll be tough when she needs a coven to satiate her. There will come a time in her life that she'll need more than what her parents have to offer," Laredo says, his voice serious.

I squeeze Jameson's hand, stopping him from saying something in exasperation, because I can already tell that he thinks Demi will never be too old to be taken care of by us.

"Can we not go there yet?" Mikkalo says, finally finding the nerve to hand Demi to Brooklyn to cradle in her arms. "She hasn't even had her first taste of blood. Who knows. Maybe she won't need it..." His eyes flick to mine, and I lift an eyebrow. He groans and adds, "Who am I kidding? She's going to be more ravenous than Gwen. She was suckling my skin in her sleep. Marked me."

I gasp a laugh of surprise, seeing the tiny bruise on his chest. "Oh, shit." I swing my attention to Laredo. "When do you think she'll need blood? How often?" I shift my gaze to my brothers. "Do you guys know?"

They shake their heads and shrug. "Grayson would know," Ashton adds.

I frown.

Laredo touches my knee and pulls something out of his

jacket. Holding a weathered, leather journal in his hand, he flips it open to show me intricate, swirling handwriting. "This will tell you anything you want to know. It's my journal. I kept one to document my sister's needs during her life. I have also included everything from my time as a Baron and from Gwyneth. I want you to have it. Add to it if you want, and that way, you can pass it along to Demi for me."

His words prod at something deep inside me, and I tilt my face toward him, peeking through strands of my blond hair veiling my face. "You make it sound like you won't be around, Laredo."

He hides his lips in a thin line. "I've realized you were right. I can't act as I always have with you. You've found your coven and will be an excellent mother to Demi. I just—I don't know, my dhampir."

"Oh." It's all I can think to say for a few moments.

Soft voices trickle from my guys and brothers as they allow me this private moment with Laredo. Jameson still holds me, but he doesn't speak. He doesn't show any emotions toward Laredo at all.

"What if I have questions?" I add, flipping through the pages. "What if—"

"Gwen." Laredo takes my hand and cups it between his. "If you want me to stay..."

Tears pool in my eyes, my emotions turning all out of

whack. Everyone falls silent. The heat of my guys' gazes prickles across my skin, and even my brothers and Brooklyn seem suddenly invested in the conversation they were pretending to ignore.

Demi fusses and begins to cry, her soft wail kicking me into action. I crawl across the bed and hold my arms out, needing to feel my daughter close. I blink through my unshed tears and cradle her in my arms, watching her suck on her fingers.

"Boobie time is coming," Jameson says, breaking the silence. "Daddy will help you latch to mommy, Demi. If you don't want to see your little sister's tits, I suggest you look away. This is a clothing-optional zone."

I laugh and swat Jameson's hand as he tries to pull the shirt off of me. I tug the neckline down instead and giggle as all four of my guys surround me, totally invested in making sure I don't grow frustrated like the first time.

"And boom. Milk time," Mikkalo says, holding up his palm to me. "Enjoy those delicious, bodacious tits for Mik-Mak."

I crack up and shake my head. "Mik-Mak, huh? I thought you more as a Daddy Mik."

"Before my transition, fathers in my community were referred to as *Makuakāne*. Mik-Mak reminds me of my dad, and I'd like Demi to know that part of our family too." Mikkalo smirks at me and kisses my cheek.

"What about you two?" I ask, turning to Bronx and Everett.

"Dad, Dado, daddio, pops," Bronx shrugs. "I don't care. I'll love whatever regardless."

"Dada for me," Everett says, snuggling his face into my hair, watching Demi suckle contently, her eyes fluttering closed. "It ups my chances of me being her first word. Isn't that right, Demi? You're going to say Dada first."

I smile, turning my gaze to everyone in the room. I had no idea this is how my family would be, but I wouldn't change it for the world. All I know is despite luck not always being on my side, I'm damn lucky now, cuddling my daughter, hugging my guys, and knowing my brothers, Brooklyn, and Laredo will be here for us.

One of the com devices chirps from their places lined up on the table. Ashton motions for Bronx to stay where he is and retrieves it for him. I adjust Demi in my arms, staring at Bronx as he reads whatever message displays on screen.

"What's up, Bronx? Does the board need something?" Ashton asks, crossing his arms over his chest. "We were going to head back to Crimson Vista tomorrow to get Declan home and give you all a chance to adjust. I can take care of anything you need."

Bronx scrubs his hands across his face and shakes his head. "It's not necessary. Just a notice for a board meeting I can attend remotely."

"Then what's up, brother?" Mikkalo asks, sitting up straighter. "You don't look happy."

Bronx sighs and shrugs. "I am utterly and completely happy. Happier than I have ever been in my life. Right now in this moment. The message just reminded me that this isn't how it will always be if—" He shuts his mouth and rubs his lips together. "I was just thinking...I don't want this position anymore. I don't want to be the head of a region."

"I was thinking the same damn thing," Jameson says, gripping Bronx's shoulder. "These last few weeks solidified it. And now that the Baron assholes are gone—fuck it."

Mikkalo nods his head. "Damn straight. I stand by your decision."

Everett takes my hand and squeezes my fingers. "I don't need the power or influence. We can handle this life without it. All we need is each other. All of us in this room. We're stronger than ever."

"We are, aren't we?" I say.

Bronx dips his head, his face relaxing with his gorgeous smile. "I'll submit our resignation then."

I hug Demi close. "Who knew this would feel so freeing?"

17

POWER PLAYS

I NEVER THOUGHT THE DAY would come for me to return to our home outside of Crimson Vista in the Night Palms Castle. My stay there was short in comparison to the penthouse suite of the Blood Match Center, where I had an entire floor with my guys. But I guess I should be used to things changing so suddenly. My life is constantly evolving, and Demi's birth finally ensured that I can and will adapt.

"We're getting close. How are you doing, Gwen? Can I feed you?" Everett adjusts me on his lap, turning me sideways and away from the expansive view of the city ahead.

I nod my head, absently stroking my fingers on his leg. "I'm a bit nervous, so just a little."

We've been in the car for hours, caravanning between Laredo, Mikkalo, and Declan in a vehicle in front of us and Ashton, Brooklyn, and Porter following behind us. Bronx remains rigid and aware behind the wheel, and Jameson cradles Demi beside us in a carrier he wears across his chest.

Children rarely, if ever, ride in vehicles, and it freaks me out just a bit watching the world zoom by. It's far better riding in Bronx's bullet-like, sleek, luxury car than one of the old back-world, gas guzzling, clunkers. At least now, we can hear everything in the world around us. No shadow dwelling outcast would dare try to attack us at the ridiculously fast speed we drive, making it feel as if we're flying on the smooth, asphalt road.

Everett sinks his fangs into his arm and brings it to my mouth. I mold my lips over the trickling blood, flicking my gaze to Bronx as he watches me in the rearview mirror. His jaw twitches, and he forces his mouth to smile at me, trying to reassure that everything will be okay. Just because we plan to give up the region doesn't mean much when we no longer face such threats like the Barons posed. The Royale name will still control their wealth and elite status, but instead of governing and controlling the general population, we will merely be a part of it.

Knowing that Demi isn't some freaky, fanged, vampire devouring beast also helps with all our nerves. She looks and mostly acts as a human baby should apart from her adorable obsession to suckle her dads if she gets close to their bare skin. I can't really blame her. They are fucking delicious.

"I've informed Viorica that I'll be joining the board meeting in person and managed to arrange it in our city. Apparently all of the City Heads will be joining us, and we offer the most neutral territories to satisfy each region's needs. It's not often everyone gathers, so we can assume it's something important." Bronx messes with the dashboard, turning on soft music to hum through the air. While he remains even-toned and expressionless, I know he's nervous as hell, only talking to keep out of his head.

"Yeah, our resignation," Jameson says, bouncing slightly in his seat. "It's going to be great. We won't have to concern ourselves with Donor Life Corp bullshit."

"Not like they've been much help to us, anyway," Everett murmurs, easing his arm away from my mouth. "They were ready to grovel to the Barons, and look who ended up being more fierce than the Vaduva Widows." He nuzzles his nose to my neck and kisses the skin below my ear, silently referring to me.

"Let's try to keep things cordial. I can't exactly blame them. If our positions were swapped, and someone demanded Viorica give away one of her coven members or face territory seizure, we'd hand over any one of them with a sparkly bow." Bronx taps his fingers to the steering wheel.

"Except we wouldn't sit around and act like nothing happened," I mutter, inhaling a long, slow breath to settle my nerves. "We'd strategize new defenses. Put effort into monitoring the enemies. Fuck, we'd figure out how to take care of the problem so it would never happen again."

"Which is why you're staying with Ev in the lobby," Bronx says. "I know you well enough to want to prove a point, and I'd prefer nothing involving us gets speculated. All I will say is that due to the dwindling number of Barons and their inability to control the rise in rebels that they succumbed to their much deserved fate."

"And Gwen?" Everett tightens his mouth. "It's not common for a new mother to bounce back so suddenly. It might raise some questions."

"Which is why she's going to be the one carrying Demi and also wearing my jacket. It'll be up to you to keep people away, Ev. I need Jameson and Mikkalo with me." Bronx taps the screen on the dashboard. A star lights up under his fingertip, and he enters something too quickly for me to see.

"I think it's best we remain in the car then," Everett says, his eyes flashing silver with his concern.

I shift and meet his gaze. "I don't want to be separated by more than some doors. We'll be okay. Laredo will watch our backs."

"I hope you're right," Jameson mutters.

I don't respond to his comment as the car slows and security personal check our vehicle, not even noticing Demi in Jameson's arms. Bronx hands a guy his com device to show Porter is registered as a Royale and also that Declan has a travel permit under our authority. Bronx offers the guard a tight smile and nods. Stomping the throttle, he drives forward, weaving around Laredo and Mikkalo to lead the way.

I don't know exactly what I expected in returning to Crimson Vista—maybe that everything would be completely unrecognizable—but it looks exactly the same as I remember. Even the line of vampires waiting for gen. pop. blood at the Donation Center seems familiar. Or maybe just their actions. Either way, excitement courses through me. All I can think is that I'm finally home.

"Everyone keep a lookout for donors out past curfew," Mikkalo says through the speaker of the stereo. His image pops up on the dashboard, but he doesn't look at the camera. "I don't know about you, but the drive was far too quiet. I'm sure the rebels were watching the place, and they might've decided to go for a different approach and call upon those hiding in plain sight in the city."

Damn. Now I'm nervous.

I don't get much time to think about it because Bronx slows to a stop outside the familiar tower. Dozens of vampires hover outside the building, looking as if they're anxiously awaiting to discover why all of the Region and City Heads have gathered in their city. Mikkalo and Ashton materialize outside my door. I catch sight of Brooklyn ushering Porter and Declan inside, where I spot Declan's mister, Macon, waiting for him with open arms. They slap each other's backs, and Macon grins at something he says, causing him to look in the direction of our car. Laredo stands just outside the glass doors, keeping an eye on the crowd.

"Time to gear up, Gigi," Jameson says, unhooking the buckles of the carrier from his shoulders. "Demi's ready for some mama cuddles."

I smile as Everett takes Demi to give Jameson a chance to adjust the carrier to my chest. Bronx shrugs out of his jacket behind the wheel and then spins the seat to face us. Leaning closer to Everett, Bronx kisses Demi on her head and helps Everett get her situated against my chest. Jameson kisses her next and tells her he won't be far. I kiss each of them next and shrug my arms through the big sleeves. Bronx and Jameson exit the car at the same time, and Mikkalo opens the door, letting Everett carry me and Demi out, keeping her tucked safely between us.

"Misters Royale," a man says just inside the chaotic entrance. "What's going on? What's this about?"

Bronx grumbles under his breath and keeps walking. "You'll find out along with everyone else."

The second we enter the elevator, I huff a breath of relief and settle my nerves. The last time I saw this many people gathered was when the board was planning a complete region overhaul to get rid of any and all traitorous City Heads who had fallen in line with the Barons. The thought still leaves a blip of cold dread in my heart, but I push it away as best I can.

"When we get to the lobby outside the boardroom, head straight for Ashton and Laredo," Mikkalo says, tapping on his com device. "They've cleared out a corner near the stairwell just in case."

I turn my attention to him. "Should I be worried, Mik-Mak?"

His lips quirk at my use of the nickname he chose for Demi. "I want to say no, but you know the drill, Gwen. Just be ready to go wild."

"She's always wild," Jameson murmurs, playing with my hair. "Just wait. Something's going to set her off and she'll turn into a monster mama bear and devour any asshole who gets within a foot of her or Demi."

I laugh. "You bet I will."

The elevator comes to a halt, and I tense and clutch Everett tighter, bracing to face...utter silence. The lobby outside the boardroom is nothing like the one coming into the building. Bronx straightens his back and heads out first, followed by Jameson. Everett carries me out next, and Mikkalo smacks his palm to a palm pad, keeping the elevator locked on this floor. It must mean we're last to arrive, and now I realize the lobby is far from empty. It's crowded and quiet because a few dozen eyes stare at our arrival.

Mikkalo, Bronx, and Jameson break away from us, and my chest tightens as the thick, heavy doors to the board room swoosh closed. I keep my eyes locked on Everett, afraid to meet anyone's gazes, despite them penetrating through me.

And then Demi releases a loud, startling wail.

Fuck. Fuck. Fuck.

"Gwen? Oh my God. It's you." The familiar female voice breaks the silence. "I thought..."

I swivel in Everett's arms and meet the wide blue eyes of the only other dhampir I've met. Jewel's smile falters, her brows scrunching together as she turns her gaze from me and to Demi bundled against my chest.

"I'm sorry, Mrs. Divine, but we must get seated. It's been a long trip for Gwen and her heir, and I'm sure they both need to eat." Everett remains on guard and moving, not letting Jewel block our path as he beelines straight to where the others wait. Neither Declan nor Porter is here, and I can only assume they're with Brooklyn since I catch sight of Macon in a chair a couple feet away.

"Her heir? I don't understand. I thought she was your coven's...mate." Her voice turns into a whisper, keeping it between ourselves.

"Hey, beautiful. Why don't you invite Gwen to sit down? You're attracting an audience." Diego Divine looks exactly how I remember him—as tall, if not taller, than Bronx with gray eyes that remain glued on Jewel. He hooks his arm around her slender waist and guides her away from us without waiting to see if we follow.

Everett clears his throat and motions for Laredo and Ashton to move from the seats Mikkalo picked out, and I wiggle in Everett's arms until he sets me down.

Demi continues to fuss, sounding exactly how I feel in this too quiet room. I haven't been around such a large group as this that I forgot how uncomfortably quiet they can be.

"Misters Divine," Everett says, remaining formal and on guard, despite knowing that Jewel and her guys could be some of our best allies if given the chance. "It's good to see you. How is Ombre Noire?" I doubt he cares about the city they run and is trying to deflect Jewel's obvious curiosity.

"I know you obviously don't want me to ask...but I'm dying," Jewel whispers, ignoring Everett's attempt at small talk. "The baby...?"

I don't get the chance to respond to say anything, because Bronx's deep voice rips through the air. The double doors swing open, and he stomps out of the boardroom with Jameson and Mikkalo behind him.

"You can't deny my resignation, Viorica!" Bronx shouts, fisting his hands. "That's not how this works."

"Mr. Royale, settle down. You haven't given me a chance to talk," Viorica says, her voice remaining even. "Now please. Don't make me ask my security personnel to—"

"Do not threaten me," Bronx says, flexing his muscles in anger.

Demi must sense the change in the air, because once again, she lets out a long, loud wail, stopping Viorica from arguing.

I don't have a chance to react or move as the beautiful red-haired vampire materializes in front of me. Her gaze travels to where Demi cries against my chest, and I do my best at trying to settle her down.

"Gwen, you've given birth already," Viorica says, her sharp tone softening. "Where are the Barons?"

"If you'd have given me a chance to explain my reasoning for stepping down, you would've known," Bronx says, annoyance sharpening his tone.

"They're dead," Viorica says like she can read my mind. "Now this makes perfect sense."

Swiveling on her feet, she turns to look at the rest of my guys. "Misters Royale, please follow me to my private chambers. I think it's time we sit down and talk."

"May I hold the child?" Viorica sits on the couch in the grand living room of her suite on the guest floor intended for board members. "Have you thought of a name yet, Ms. Royale?"

I bring my arms up and cradle them around Demi, sleeping in the carrier against me. "Demi, and no, I don't want to wake her. It's bad enough we had to stop by here to—"

"Please refrain from addressing Gwen. She's just given birth and has been through more than she ever should've been," Bronx says, stepping between me and Viorica to block her view of me.

"No thanks to you," Jameson mutters.

Someone knocks on the suite door at the same time Merrick, one of Viorica's daughters, hisses from her silent corner with who I think might be Heidi and...Layla. Sammy and her Blood Match aren't around.

Viorica sighs. "Come in, Misters King."

My guys suddenly surround me while Ashton and Laredo hover tensed and ready near the door. I clutch onto Bronx's shoulders to stand on my tiptoes to peek at the three security personnel who materialize in the room.

"Misters Royale, I'd like to introduce you to Berkeley, Aspen, and Torrance. They've come from the Blood Life

Corp Territory seeking refuge from a similar situation as you. You see, there are many covens against the territory boards around the world, and it seems that lately, they've grown tired of their lack of control and use Blood Rebels in an attempt to rise from the shadows." Viorica tightens her mouth even more, sharpening her features. "The reason why I've gathered you here was because I thought that perhaps you'd be interested in an alliance."

"You expect us to ally with a coven we've never met? Are you serious, Viorica? How long have you known them?" Bronx's voice rumbles with his words.

"Not long, but I've vetted them thoroughly, and they have proved themselves." Tapping her heels on the tiled floor, she steps closer. "I was hoping you could trust me as your board leader."

"I've already told you. We're resigning." Bronx steps closer, towering over Viorica.

She doesn't flinch or back down, maintaining her fierce persona. "Please, Bronx. Hear me out. We—"

A tap sounds on the door before it opens without waiting for a response. "I'm so sorry I'm late, Viorica. I had something come up..." A tall, slender woman with deep purple hair, soft golden-brown eyes, and full lips saunters into the suite. Her voice trails off as she stops short and faces our group. Silver flashes in her eyes, and she darts her gaze toward the Kings. "I'm sorry."

Viorica offers the woman a smile and motions for her to come closer. "You have rather impeccable timing, Fiona. You're exactly who I wanted to introduce to the Royales."

Fiona blinks a few times, slowly nods her head, and turns her eyes back to us. Her lips part in a smile and she stares at me and only me, acting as if my guys aren't surrounding me. "It's nice to meet you, Misters Royale. May I greet your...personal donor?"

Uh-oh.

Mikkalo growls at her word choice, which causes one of her coven brothers to growl—scratch that—not a coven brother. A mate.

My eyes rove over Fiona, and I realize all three of the men touch her, caging her within their muscular bodies. Coven brothers don't treat anyone like they do except a mate. It reminds me of...well, my guys.

Demi stirs against me, the growls sounding through the air scaring her. Releasing a wail of a cry, Demi fusses and screams her lungs out from her cozy place cuddling my breasts.

The growls immediately stop, and Jameson quickly unstraps Demi and gathers her into his arms, turning away from everyone to bounce her up and down.

Mikkalo steps forward this time, flexing his muscles with his movements. "I'm sorry, Viorica. We must go. Accept our resignation, and we will amicably part ways. Try to stop us, and you will not appreciate what happens then. Gwen and Demi are far too important to us."

"You would risk giving up your status and power at a time you need it most?" Viorica asks.

The Kings all remain silent, devouring the exchange.

"The risk is remaining here and as a Region Head. If there is a rising threat, we don't want any part of it. You were useless to us, Viorica. You stood by and denied our request for help. You allowed a rebel coven to take our mate. We nearly lost her. So no. You won't even approve of her Blood Vow contract because she selflessly gave it to her brother after you wanted to banish him." Bronx turns to me and holds out his hand. "Now, we are done here."

Lifting me into his arms, Bronx rushes across the room. Viorica materializes in our path, and Mikkalo unsheathes a knife from his jacket.

Merrick responds with a growl, coming up behind him, but Everett, Ashton, and Laredo reveal their weapons. I expect the Kings to join the Vaduva Coven, but they remain in place. I can't stop my eyes from turning to Fiona. All she does is frown at me.

"Everyone settle down," Viorica says, remaining composed.

"Move out of our way, Viorica." Bronx shifts me in his arms.

"No. I want you to understand the mistake you're making. Without the backing of the board, you might not have the future you desi—"

Laredo releases a guttural noise from his throat and slides between Bronx and Viorica. "The Royales will have everything they desire and need and then some. As the last Baron Coven member, I am registering in the territory and giving my inheritance to Gwen and Demi under the Royale name."

Viorica blinks in surprise, looking as if she just realizes Laredo was even in the room. "A Baron?"

"It's true. He was the one caring for Gwen and her brothers before we caught them in the city." Jameson steps forward, holding Demi against his shoulder, rubbing her back.

"I cannot fulfill such a request without a permanent alliance, Mr. Baron." Viorica crosses her arms.

Nerves bunch my stomach. I'm afraid Viorica won't give up, and the only way we will get what we want is to fight.

"And I'm not so sure I can agree to such an arrangement under these current circumstances," Viorica adds.

"Then I propose a Coven Union with Ashton Royale. Brooklyn Anderson, too." Laredo squares his shoulders.

"But—"

"Viorica, please. It's okay." Fiona's soft voice draws everyone's attention to her. "It's these kinds of strategic moves that threaten alliances. They obviously love Gwen, so why not just accept their decision? Your demands will turn a potential ally into an enemy. It also makes me question whether or not this could work between us as well."

Did she just stand up for us?

A small smile graces Fiona's beautiful face. She winks.

Ice washes through me at the realization. She knows. She has to.

Except I can't ask.

Viorica sighs. "You're right, Fiona. I suppose if I want things to change and to grow the strength of our territory, I must be open to change." Turning towards Laredo, she says, "I accept your request to a union with the remaining Anderson heir and Ashton Royale, if they agree."

"They will." Bronx strokes his fingers down my back.

"But I have a condition for you, Bronx," Viorica adds.

Everyone stiffens without responding.

"I want to arrange a Blood Vow for you and Gwen. Tonight. It will prove my good intent and allow you some time to think things through. You might feel differently after your beloved transforms." A soft smile lights Viorica's face. "It is what you want, correct?"

Bronx doesn't respond right away, just quietly letting her words sink in. Jameson, Everett, and Mikkalo gather close, waiting for his response.

And me? I'm nervous as hell. I can't even transform. If

Bronx agrees, our secret could come out. It would put Demi at risk.

I'm about to open my mouth to deny her, but Bronx says, "The Blood Vow must be to all of us."

Viorica's mouth twitches. "Done."

18

ETERNAL PROMISE

ASHTON SITS IN A CHAIR by the door, guarding it as Bronx instructed. My stomach twists and turns, doing nothing to help with the anxiety rising inside me.

I try my best to focus on feeding Demi, though I keep struggling getting her to latch like she's already grown used to her dads basically cheering her on. Damn them. They're lucky I enjoy the moral support, since I'm sure others would find it weird.

"Come on, Demi. Latch for mommy." Tears prickle

my eyes as I try to remain calm, but this shit is hard. I guess this is why newborn donors and their mothers get around the clock assistance their first year in Crimson Vista. I used to think it was to ensure the future blood supply, but maybe there is more to it.

"Hey, Gweny," Ashton says softly, drawing my attention to him as he watches the door. "Why don't I hold her for a couple of minutes while you finish getting ready and then you can try again?"

My lip quivers, and I nod my head even though he can't see me. I adjust my top and stroll a few feet before Ashton comes to meet me halfway. A smile lights his entire face as he takes Demi and nuzzles his nose to her. He peppers her cheeks with kisses and sways with her in his arms, getting her to settle down.

"Thanks, Ash," I murmur, turning toward the vanity table with all sorts of cosmetics I choose not to use. "I think my nerves are getting to her."

"You know it's going to be okay, Gwen. We're all here, and no matter what happens after tonight, we'll get through it. We're stronger than ever." Ashton comes up behind me, meeting my gaze in the mirror. "Just relax. Drink the blood your mates left you."

My stomach twists again. "I can't. I'm too nervous."

Ashton adjusts Demi on his shoulder and rests his free hand on me. "All right. Time for a serious brother talk."

"Uh-oh. Is this going to be like the passing on the dhampir gene talk? Because it's a bit late for that." A laugh bubbles from my throat at Ashton's unamused expression with his lips pursed and his eyebrows puckering together. "Hell, give it a month or two. I'll probably get pregnant again. You'll be an uncle of like twenty beasts before you know it."

He groans. "Gweny."

I laugh harder, practically cackling. "That's our plan, you know. Take over the world with an army of wild ones like me."

"Ah, hell. Stop it. You're screwing up my speech about how you shouldn't think about not transforming or what it means for you next." Ashton cuts off my oncoming comment with his hand. "Nu-uh. You're going to let me finish because the second you get the jokes out of your system, you're going to be wound up and nervous again. So let me ask you this. Did you only ever consider a Blood Vow as a means to shed your donor status?"

I grimace and shake my head. "It means more than that," I mumble against his hand.

"What does it mean to you?" He eases his hand away from my lips and shifts me to look at him. "Think about it. Why did you ever consider the Blood Vow?"

My heart picks up pace with my whirling thoughts. "Because it means a promise of forever with my guys. It'll officially bring me into the Royale Coven as their mate and equal. And of course, I'm madly, all-consuming, irrevocably in love with them. It means even more that they're the fathers of Demi. This will also ensure her eternity."

Ashton offers me a smile and squeezes my shoulder. "So think of what you've told me and forget everything else. Enjoy this. You deserve the happiness you've fought so hard for."

Tears rim my eyes and I hug Ashton, tucking myself into his side while burying my face next to Demi. He's right. And thank the universe for that. Because no matter what happens in the end, the Royales will belong to me and me to them.

"Thank you," I say, wiping my teary cheek on his shirt.

He chuckles and kisses the top of my head. "Anytime, little Sis. And you know what? This is for the best. I don't know if you've realized it, but I kind of have a thing for Brooklyn, and being a Royale complicated the shit out of it."

His admission sends all sorts of feelings through me, but no matter my opinion or history with Brooklyn, I'm happy for my brother.

"You're right. This is perfect. Better than I could've ever hoped for." I take Demi from his arms and bring her to my face, giving her a kiss on each of her cheeks. "Isn't that right, baby girl?"

I catch the sound of the elevator to the floor dinging, and I grin and stride across the room, finally feeling excitement over what's to come. Flinging the door open, I step into the hall and freeze. Ashton pulls me back and gets in front of me protectively, seeing it's not who either of us expected.

"You guys stay out here," Jewel says, motioning to the Divines.

I slide past Ashton and wave my hand, telling him it's okay. "Just give us a minute, Ash. Jewel is my friend. She's a dhampir like—"

"Damn, you were right, Fi," a masculine voice says, coming from the doorway of the stairwell. "Gwen is like you...and so is..."

Growls rip through the air before a shit ton of weapons are drawn. I squeak in surprise and clutch Demi, panic washing over me because my guys aren't here.

"Get back in the suite, Gweny. I'll call your mates," Ashton says, pulling me back.

"Guys, stop," Fiona says, extending her arms out, acting as a wall between the Divines and the Kings. She flicks her gaze to me and then to Jewel. "We're not a threat. I just came up here because I wanted to talk to Gwen."

"Me?" I ask, shifting on my feet. "Why me? I'm a donor."

She purses her lips and flares her nostrils. I don't even

have to hear her thoughts to know we both know I'm lying. She heard and her coven heard what I said. "You're not. You're a dhampir. Like me. I saw your eyes flash in Viorica's suite. That happens to me too when I'm upset."

Jewel inhales a small breath. "You're faking being a vampire too?"

A growl reverberates through the room. "Damn it, babe. How do you expect us to keep this up if you keep announcing it?"

Jewel points her finger, and I gaze at her black-haired dark-eyed mate, Kingston, as he glowers. "Quit it, dude. They're like me. This is everything we've wondered about."

"Jewel's right, bro," Austin, the blond health keeper, says.

Fiona clears her throat. "I'm not pretending to be a vampire. Viorica knows I'm a dhampir."

One second I'm gawking at Fiona, trying to process what she just said, and in the next, Everett holds me in his arms. Bronx, Mikkalo, Jameson, and Laredo all crowd into the hallway. I suspected this the first time I met Jewel, but now seeing another dhampir with her coven proves that we definitely have a type with our buff, broody, over-protective guys. And it makes me smile.

"Fuck," Bronx and Kingston say at the same time.

"Wait, Viorica knows?" Jewel asks, her blue eyes widening with worry.

"Yeah," Fiona says, nodding. "You said your name is Jewel, right?"

"Why?" all three of Jewel's guys ask in unison.

Fiona remains expressionless. "I've heard of you from..." Strolling closer to Jewel, risking her setting off the Divines, Fiona whispers something into Jewel's ear. "We should talk sometime. Viorica—"

Kingston scoops Jewel into his arms. "We do not want Viorica knowing anything. Got it? If you tell, I will consider it war."

The Divines disappear so quickly that my head spins as my brain tries to process that they're no longer standing a dozen feet away. Fiona wrings her hands together and steps back into a handsome man with a neatly trimmed beard and hazel eyes—Berkeley, I think.

"This is a test," Bronx says, clenching his fingers into fists. "Viorica must suspect the truth."

"We didn't tell her our suspicions," a tall, dark-skinned man says, stepping from their cluster surrounding Fiona. "We wouldn't, but we also wanted to know for ourselves."

Jameson groans and scrubs his face. "We have five minutes to figure out what to do."

"I say we just proceed. Viorica will know we are on to her otherwise. If Jewel and the Divines can play this off, so can we," Mikkalo says, running his fingers over my arm.

"At least until we can make our plan to leave. We can't

stay. Not with Demi." Everett takes the baby and hugs her like he needs assurance to make sure we're both okay.

"Demi is yours?" Fiona asks, inching closer again.

None of us have to say anything for her to know the truth. It's written over all of our faces.

"She's no different than me," I say, worried she might assume something wild.

Fiona smiles. "I know."

"You do?" I ask.

"My bio dad was a vampire too," she says, relaxing a little.

Bronx's com device beeps, dragging his attention to it. His muscles flex and he looks at his brothers and then to me.

"Viorica's waiting. What do you want to do?" he asks me.

The conversation I had with Ashton swirls through my mind. "I want to promise all of you forever. The world should know you're mine."

"You look stunning." Laredo extends his arm to me, escorting me down a short staircase. The candlelit room glows with soft light, and white flowers permeate the air with their subtle powdery scent. "I'm so happy you've given me this honor. Demi will be safe with me."

I rub my lips together and nod. "You know how hard this is for me, right?"

"Your brothers will be with me. We won't be far," he assures, lifting Demi from my arms. He holds her in front of him and smiles. "Trust me and enjoy your vows. The Royales are the luckiest men in the universe to be able to claim you. I'd be lying if I said I wasn't jealous."

"Laredo..." I try not to pout at his words.

He bends over and kisses my cheek. "My apologies, my dhampir. Just know how much you're loved."

Laredo starts to step away from me, and I reach out and grab him by the back of the jacket. Electricity buzzes over my skin, my heart beating wildly. But it's not about Laredo. This isn't my body responding to his sweet words. This is my fear instincts turning on at full force, and the thirty feet of space between me and where Bronx, Jameson, Mikkalo, and Everett stand suddenly seems like a mile.

Demi cries out in Laredo's arms, the sound of her voice tightening my chest. It's like she can sense it too. Snatching her away from Laredo, I spin on my heels and search the room behind me. Apart from my guys, only my brothers, Brooklyn, Macon, and the Vaduvas are present. I don't know if it's because this is a test or not, but something is wrong.

"Ms. Royale, come join your misters. They will help ease your nerves," Viorica says, her voice laced with annoyance. "I'd like to make it home by dawn, and I'm sure you'd all like to enjoy and celebrate this surely unforgettable occasion.

I clutch Demi tighter. "We need to go."

"What's wrong?" Mikkalo reaches me first, his dark eyes searching my face.

"I can't shake my fear, and it's not nerves," I whisper, trying to keep my voice low. The all-consuming feeling steals away my ability to think clearly. Closing my eyes, I bow my head. With my emotions running rampant, my dhampir nature might give me away. Fiona mentioned she saw my eyes flash. Fuck. What if one of the Vaduvas sees it happen again? "I feel like I'm being hunted and stalked."

Mikkalo touches my chin, getting me to open my eyes. He searches my face, his features sharpening. "I'll check it out."

Tugging his com device from his pocket, Mikkalo quickly taps on the screen, pulling up the security feeds. I can't see much from my position, but no matter how many breaths I take, my heart won't calm down. The trembles seizing my muscles grow in intensity, and I feel as if I might die at any second. Mikkalo pulls me closer, hugging me to his side protectively with Demi nestled between us.

"I think you might be right, Gwen." His eyes roam over each little video. I'm so thankful he takes my fears seriously. My gut doesn't let me down often.

"What is it, Mik?" Bronx says, clearing his throat.

I squeeze Mikkalo tighter, trying to get myself in control to look up. Narrowing my eyes a bit, I peek from beneath my lashes. Bronx stands rigid near a narrow, high table with a pillow on it with Jameson and Everett. Various expressions morph their features, but none of them rush to join Mikkalo, letting him handle my blossoming panic.

Mikkalo taps his screen some more. "I don't know. I think I see a shadow flicker in the corners of a couple of the cams. I'm trying to figure out if it's something concerning. Check the feeds. Tell me if something is off to you?"

Bronx tugs out his com device and glowers at it like he plans to crush it in his hand if he sees something he doesn't like. His features turn from sharp anger to head-tilting confusion. He widens his eyes and zooms toward me, unsheathing a dagger from his suit jacket. "Everyone out! There is a rebel on the premises. We need to sweep—"

The ground shakes beneath me, and I screech and stumble into Mikkalo. The door to the small meeting room flies off its hinges, and I recognize the woman who tried to kidnap me with my brother. She clutches some sort of metal canister in her hand, narrowing her eyes at me. Her ponytail swings with her movements, and a looming shadow creeps behind her.

"Five seconds to come with us, Gwen. If you don't—" A hulking man materializes behind the woman and engulfs her in his arms. The woman suddenly disappears as Jameson jabs a dagger in her empty space. The silver canister clinks to the tile floor, and a strange hissing noise escapes from it. Smoke pours into the room, stealing away a clear view of everyone.

Jameson snarls, the silhouette of his form remaining near the door. He coughs in the smoky air. "Protect Gwen!"

Loud pops sound through the air, and Jameson stumbles back into the room and out of the smoke. Several bullet holes ravage his chest, and once again, the smoke envelops him, stealing him from my sight. Bronx and Mikkalo tense and ready themselves for combat, unsheathing more daggers from hidden places on their bodies. Mikkalo hands one to me, and I adjust Demi in my arms, trying to keep the smoke away as it creeps closer, hazing the room. The Vaduvas follow my guys' lead, preparing to fight by their sides instead of running for cover.

"What the fuck? Gwen, here. I'm unzipping your gown. I want you to cradle Demi inside the fabric the best you can," Everett says, lifting me in his arms. "We're going to make a run for it. You two can't stay in here."

"The back is clear," Bronx says, helping me adjust the bodice of my gown over Demi. "They don't know our building structure or back routes. They're not from our city."

"Who?" I ask, trying not to inhale as deeply as my lungs want to. I cough, my throat starting to burn.

"Silas transformed a few dozen rebels," Mikkalo says, growling. "They're coming in with force."

Bronx turns to me and Everett and says, "Get Gwen out of here now. We'll catch up. Jameson needs backup."

I open and close my mouth. "But Bronx—"

Spinning on his feet, Bronx swipes a blade through the air, managing to stab a rebel vampire in the chest as he tries to get close to us. I screech in surprise, tightening my free hand around the hilt of my dagger, bracing to gut another asshole.

Bronx spins and shoves another vampire. "Go! The Vaduvas will get you out, Ev. Hurry! Don't stop until you're home."

The world blurs as Everett carries me and Demi through the haze and to a back entrance. Merrick holds open the heavy door. Heidi flashes her fangs, yanking a few throwing knives from built in sheathes on her tight-fitted dress. She throws them from her spot, the blades whizzing past us and into another vampire trying to stop us from leaving. My thoughts race a million miles a minute, and I try my best to suppress my fear instincts.

"Don't worry, Gwen. We'll get these assholes taken care of, so you can go through your Blood Vow," Heidi says, whipping her red hair over her shoulder.

"I will ensure they suffer for ruining the best day of your eternity." Merrick speeds forward to stay ahead.

I hug Demi close to me and whisper that no other day would ever be better than meeting her. It's all I can think about to keep my heart from exploding from my chest in worry. Where the upcoming exit should bring relief, knowing we're almost out, it actually makes my chest tighten.

"Careful. Someone's out there," I say, forcing my voice to project through the hall.

"How do you know? I don't hear anything." Heidi blocks Merrick from slamming the door wide.

"Just trust her," Everett snaps. "It has saved my life several times."

Merrick and Heidi slow and hesitate at the door, readying themselves to fight. Heidi stands off to the side as Merrick pushes the door hard, sending it flinging open. Cool, musty air wafts in from the underground garage. A shadow flies from behind a car and knocks into Heidi, sending her crashing into the wall. Merrick hisses and charges another rebel vampire, blurring in a fight.

"Everett, put me down and protect Demi. You know I can fight." I wiggle in Everett's arms until he sets me on my feet. He keeps close, practically flush against me. His heartbeat outraces mine. I don't think I've ever seen him this on edge with a threat, but I know he worries about Demi and my safety.

"I know you want to protect the both of us, but it's up to us to protect her, even if it means putting me in danger," I say, flicking my eyes to the shadows, searching for more threats.

Everett slowly nods his agreeance but doesn't comment, watching the Vaduvas fight their attackers. "The car's straight ahead. Keep your—"

A tall, lanky vampire bares his fangs in my face, startling me. I shove him back as hard as I can, knocking him off his feet. Launching onto him, I give in to my dhampir nature and pin him down with my strength. My fear turns to anger, watching as his lips curl into a smile.

"Don't move. Don't fucking speak," I command, locking him in a gaze. I grip onto the front of his shirt, getting right in his face. "You will obey my command."

He growls in response and breaks from my hold, linking his fingers around my wrist, pulling me into him. "Is that so, traitor?"

I glare and grip him tighter. "Let me the fuck go!"

Nothing happens. Our minds don't connect, sending my heart faltering at the realization that I'm within biting reach, outmatched, and looking death in its silver-flashing eyes. All he'd have to do is flip me off him. I'm not even that heavy. I've made it too easy.

"Ev," I whisper, my fear shooting through me.

The vampire doesn't slacken or stop smiling. Instead,

he extends his fangs more and tilts his head.

Shit. Fuck. Damn it all to hell.

Smacking the bastard across the face, I do the only thing I can think of. I bow forward and sink my teeth into his throat, surprising the hell out of him. The vampire snarls and tries to bite me back, but I shove my palm to his cheek.

"His heart, Gwen," Everett says, yanking the vampire's arm from me. He jerks it over the guy's head and stomps the man's wrists with his shoe to help lock him in place. "Take his heart."

The man hollers as his arm breaks under Everett's force.

"Now!" Everett commands.

Gathering my strength, I ram my fist into the vampire's chest, shattering his sternum and pulverizing his heart. The vampire stills beneath me, and I don't waste a second more getting to my feet.

"Gwen. Ev. Go!" Mikkalo yells, flying toward us from the entrance to the building. Another few vampires materialize behind him. "I'll keep them off."

Obeying Mikkalo, I grab Everett's hand and run with him in the direction of our car. Growls and hisses echo through the concrete garage. I remain tense, my fear trying to consume me. It sounds as if the fighting happens everywhere around us as the noise bounces off the walls.

Everett hands me Demi, and we climb into the car,

starting the engine. He activates the locks and blares the horn, the intense noise dropping a few vampires to the ground.

The last thing I see is a handful of rebels—both human and vampire—flooding into the garage, trying to bring the fight to us. Everett stomps the throttle, speeding toward the cluster of armed rebels. A man shoots his gun at the windshield, and the bullet ricochets off, leaving a tiny star in the glass. Everett honks the horn again, overwhelming their senses, stopping them from fleeing as we plow through the fighting crowd, knocking the rebels out of the way.

"Don't worry, Gwen. We're going to be okay. Our coven has this handled," Everett says, glancing at me in his peripheral vision. "Try not to worry. They'll be right behind us."

I hate leaving the rest of my mates behind. It feels as if I'm leaving a part of my heart with them.

What if being unable to finish our Blood Vow is a sign?

I'm terrified we won't get our forever after all.

19

FUTURE ROYALE HEIRS

"HERE, LET ME FEED YOU." Everett shrugs out of his suit jacket and starts unbuttoning his dress shirt. "I can hear your stomach from here."

I stare around Jameson's art studio, taking everything in like it's the first time all over again. I had no idea how much I missed living at the Night Palms Castle, but seeing the few sketches Jameson had to leave behind of me reminds me of how much fun we've had. Everett chose for us to wait here for our coven because it gives a view of the property and can only be accessed by a single road or climbing up the rough terrain.

"Come on over here, Gwen. Give me Demi. She'll be perfect and safe next to us." Everett gently takes Demi from my arms and lays her down on a blanket on one of the plush rugs on the floor. "Now, let me take care of you. It's all I can think about. We've been through a lot tonight and I want to do anything I can to make things better."

I swallow and nod, allowing him to pull me to the floor in front of him. Everett shrugs out of his shirt completely, revealing his perfect body to me. I kneel, giving myself more height, so he doesn't have to bow forward. Offering me a soft smile, Everett tries to calm my nerves by pretending the world isn't falling apart around us. I want so badly to push things away, but my nerves are shot, I'm freaking out about the rest of my guys, and I can't help but wonder if Viorica is going to blame me for my brother's wrongdoings. I mean, what the actual fuck was Silas thinking? Did he transform an entire rebel nest?

Cool fingers trail down my neck, and Everett slides his hand into my hair, guiding my face to his. I meet his beautiful eyes, and suddenly feel like drowning in their deep blue depths sparkling with silver like a stormy morning.

"Gwen, will you open your mind to me? Please. Will you tell me what you're thinking?" Everett's lips graze mine with his words.

My body relaxes as I give in to his need to connect on a soul-deep level. "I'm scared, Everett. Everything about tonight makes me feel as if the universe is just so against me and my desire to just live and love and spend our forever together, watching our children grow into powerful beings capable of thriving in the world I want so desperately to build for them."

Everett's brows pucker together, and he brushes the pad of his thumb across the unwanted tear splashing my cheek. "I'm afraid too, Gwen. But I don't feel as if the universe is against us. I think it just wants to push us and strengthen us, teaching us exactly what we need to know to change and create a world they can live in without the fears and dangers we face."

"So what scares you?" My voice whispers against his soft lip, puffing slightly to caress against mine with his breathing.

His eyes flick back and forth over mine as if he tries to find the answer to my question reflecting to him in my gaze. "Many things scare me, to be honest. I'm afraid of the uncertainty we face and how things could change if your dhampir nature got out. I'm afraid I might not be as capable as I thought I was in ensuring our daughter's health and wellbeing. I'm afraid of failing you and my brothers. Or that all of this could possibly ruin any chance you might want more children with us. Because having Demi, feeling how much I love her, I want more. I want a huge family with you. It's something I never thought about, and I was terrified of when we found out you were pregnant...but now? Losing it all freaks me out."

"You want more children?" I can't stop the smile crossing my lips at his admission.

He chuckles, a gorgeous smile crossing his face. "I know it's only been days...but yeah. I'm already thinking about it. It has been bliss."

I lean into him, kissing him softly, sensually, just savoring the sensation of his lips against mine without getting carried away. I wrap my arms around his neck and ease away to meet his eyes again, blurring them as I rest my forehead against his. "You know what?"

"Hmm?" he asks, brushing strands of hair behind my ear.

"You don't have to be afraid of any of those the things you worry about because I'm going to be by your side forever. Your brothers will make sure you never fail by helping you out when you need it, just like I know you'll do the same. You're not solely responsible for Demi as her health keeper, either. We're in this together." I kiss him again. "Always."

Everett nods and graces me with a smile that pushes away the worry lining his handsome face. "And to think I was supposed to be the one making you feel better."

I giggle and nuzzle my nose to his. "You did. I feel so much better."

"Mmm. Good." He sucks my bottom lip between his teeth, stretching it just enough to make me gasp and dig my fingers into his bare shoulders. "Let me feed you. I can't stand another second of hearing your hunger and seeing your need flickering silver in your eyes."

I slowly nod my head. "Will you check in on your brothers? I can't fully relax until I know they're safe."

"Anything for you." Hiking up my dress, Everett lifts me by my hips and sets me on his lap. "Now bite me. My brothers need to see that you're in good hands."

I laugh. "Are you trying to make them jealous, Everett?"

"Never. I just want to give them an incentive to hurry their asses up," he teases.

"That's actually a brilliant plan." I snap my teeth playfully. "Get ready. I want them to see me bite."

With a moan, Everett strokes his fingers across the back of my neck and tilts his head, exposing his throat to me. I listen to the soft tap of his finger across his com device and wait until I hear the subtle click of the line connect.

Everett groans as I sink my teeth into his throat, filling my mouth with blood. My body buzzes like crazy and I clutch Everett harder, shocked and thrilled at the pleasure igniting inside me.

"Fuck, Ev. Is she draining you?" Jameson's smooth voice erupts through the air. "Gigi, please. Save some room for me. We'll be there within the hour."

I pull away from Everett's neck with a frown and swivel to try to glance at his image. It's then that I see the projection on the wall with Jameson, Mikkalo, and Bronx watching the two of us with sexy looks capable of melting my dress right off, even through the line.

"That long?" I tease. "But I'm so hungry."

Bronx play-growls. "Fuck, I never thought I'd love hearing you tease me, dandelion. This attack is a fucking shitshow. We've sent Laredo and Ashton to guard you and keep an eye out on possible threats, so don't worry. I just— we'll be there soon. We have a few things to do."

"You good, brother?" Everett asks, knowing I need to hear his confirmation. "Anyone hurt? The Vaduvas?"

"We're all good. The rebels were sorely mistaken to think that just because Silas transformed them that they'd be all-powerful. Only a handful got out of the building. I doubt they'll even make it out of the city." Mikkalo remains expressionless as he speaks for Bronx.

"You sure it was Silas? Did you see him?" I ask, trying to keep my heart in check.

"Positive. Viorica took prisoners." Bronx tightens his jaw.

I can only nod, not wanting to think about what that

means. It's best not to think about it.

A familiar feminine voice sounds through the line, and I spot Fiona and the Kings come up behind Bronx. He sighs and gets closer to the phone, blocking my view of the dhampir. I have so many questions as to why she and her coven are with my guys, but one look into Bronx's eyes warns me I better wait.

"We have to go, dandelion. Give Demi big kisses from us, okay? See you soon." He turns his gaze to Everett. "Distract her or something. You know how she gets when she's worried."

I crinkle my nose. "Seriously, Bronx?"

He disconnects the line without responding.

Everett's cool fingers touch my upper back, and I shiver at the sensation of him dragging down the zipper on my dress. "He's super serious, Gwen. You're also not the only one needing distracting. I'm...in need of your affection after those assholes ruined our Blood Vow. I was looking forward to it. You're everything to me, and I wanted the whole world to know you are mine."

I hadn't thought much about what my guys thought about the Blood Vow and what it meant to them. We never expected to get the opportunity, and even though none of us were certain of Viorica's intentions and allowing such a thing to occur, it was still important.

I glide my fingers over the low neckline of my gown,

easing it off to bunch around my waist. "They will," I say, grasping his hand resting on my hip and guiding him to explore my body. "I'll scream it to the world if I have to."

"I'd love to hear it," he murmurs, exploring the skin across my stomach at a torturously slow pace, teasing the line of fabric slung over my hip with his finger.

"I'm yours," I murmur, gasping as he slides his hand lower and into my panties.

He moans his agreement. "You're mine."

Pleasure zings between my legs as he tests my body, needing to discover exactly how hot and excited he makes me with his closeness and the mere anticipation of his touch. I shift my weight on my knees, opening my hips wider, so completely turned on. I can barely stay still under his soft exploration. He only teases my clit, his touch light and torturous as he listens to the change in my breathing.

Bending forward, I flatten my palms to the ground, needing to set off his deep-seated nature and desire that'll turn him from playful and sweet to passionate and as wild as I feel inside. He hums in appreciation, lifting the hem of my dress to get a better view of my body. Sliding his finger underneath the back of my thong, Everett tugs it and snaps it against my buzzing flesh. I gasp and glance behind me, biting my bottom lip between my teeth at the sight of him unzipping and taking off his pants behind me.

Everett grabs my ass cheeks and spreads my legs, his

sensual touch turning demanding with his desire. He teases me with his cock, flexing it against my pelvis, just gliding it over my clit as he hooks his fingers to my dress. A loud rip cuts through the air, and the fabric spills to the floor, piling beneath me. Everett gathers my hair in his hand and tosses it over my shoulder to drag his hands down my back, leaving a trail of blazing energy in his wake.

"Fuck, I missed you," Everett says, hooking his hands to my hips. He lifts my legs onto his shoulders while I rest on my elbows. With his fangs, he tears the fabric of my panties to get them out of the way. "I need to taste you how I like."

Ecstasy explodes between my legs as he flicks his tongue over my clit, the thrilling position opening my body wide for him. The good ache sends goosebumps over my skin, and I'm sure I'll feel the memory of my pleasure in my muscles for days. Everett picks up the pace and pressure of his mouth, his tongue flicking me in just the right spot that I feel on the verge of an orgasm. I moan so embarrassingly loud that I slap my hand across my mouth to stifle the sound.

Everett hums at my reaction, the vibration sending me over the edge. My arms weaken, and I drop to the ground completely, bracing through the wave of pleasure cascading through me. The sound of Everett's fangs click, tightening my whole body even more in anticipation, and he sinks his fangs into my ass cheek, giving me the most incredible pleasure bite, shooting electricity to my very being that I can feel it in every cell in my body.

"Damn, amazing," he murmurs, easing me back to my knees. "You wet me."

I squeeze my eyes closed with a breathless laugh. "Everett."

He chuckles, rubbing his hands to my ass cheeks, aligning his body to mine. "What? I fucking love it. You're just as sweet as your blood. I want more."

I shake my hips playfully. "Only when you cum."

Everett play-growls and smacks my ass before pushing his cock deep inside me. I gasp at the mind-blowing sensation as he wastes no time to give me what I want. It's nearly impossible to stop my voice from screaming my pleasure, and Everett bends over me and presses his hand over my mouth while clutching my shoulder in his other, thrusting hard and fast and deep, turning my mind into a mush of lust-filled haze and desire that I never want to end.

And then Everett bites me again on my shoulder, and my body reacts with another wave of shuddering pleasure. His lips mold to my skin and he drinks my blood, satiating his hunger unlike he's been able to for months.

The pressure of his bite subsides, and he presses his cool fingers to his mark to staunch the bleeding. My whole body quivers with everlasting pleasure that I don't move until Everett slides out of me and flips me over to kiss him, tangling his legs with mine and showering me with his love and affection.

I sigh in contentment and rest my head on his chest, listening to his heart beating. "I've missed this. Being able to feed you how you want and need...it feels so good."

He traces his fingers over my lower back, teasing my skin. "I want this forever. Surviving on our love and bodies. Taking care of each other. This is how life will be. I don't care what it takes. I vow to you that our eternity will be everything you ever desire."

He sounds so certain that I do believe him. I know he's right. We will all do whatever it takes to make it happen. Not only for us, but for our family. For Demi. For all of our future Royale heirs.

Everett and I remain in each other's embrace until we hear the familiar sound of Jameson whispering our names through the door like he can sense Demi's asleep. The door eases open, and he peeks his head into his studio. His gaze lands on us, naked and cuddling on the floor, not even bothering to cover up. A lusty smile lights his face as he shuts the door behind him. He watches me with his steps, quietly making his way across the room. I purposefully rub my legs together before easing them open, waiting for his reaction.

He groans and grabs his now throbbing boner, pressing

against the fabric of his pants. "Damn it, Gigi. I want to tackle that seductive cute ass of yours but the others are waiting in the house."

I purposefully pout my bottom lip. "That's too bad. I've been dying to feed you properly like I've done with Everett."

Everett chuckles and rolls me on top of him, showing off the pleasure bite on my ass. "She tastes even more delicious now."

Jameson fake-glares and gently lifts Demi into his arms and kisses her sleeping face. "Hold on tightly to that thought. I plan to ravish you later when Everett takes day duty. There's no way we'll get away with fucking without waking her up. I don't even know how you two did it now."

I laugh. "You'll have to figure it out for yourself."

"You know I never tell," Everett says.

"Even for Demi's sake? You would deny me ensuring our daughter gets a peaceful, uninterrupted hour or two of sleep while allowing me to pleasure our girl?" Jameson snuggles his face into Demi's teensy chest. "You hear them, mini-beast? Rude."

I grin and open my mouth to respond, but a knock taps on the door.

"Gwen? I don't mean to interrupt, but I can't wait much longer," Ashton says, his voice muffling through the door.

I grab Everett's shirt and button it up. "What do you mean?"

Jameson groans. "Damn it. Sorry, Ash. I got distracted. We'll be right there."

I frown in confusion. "What's going on?"

Jameson adjusts Demi in his arms, his face remaining expressionless. "Just wait until we're all together. Bronx has called for an important coven meeting."

20

CHANGE THE WORLD

EVERETT HOLDS ME CLOSE, CARRYING me over the threshold into the grand foyer of the Night Palms Castle. It almost feels like another life since I laid my eyes on the huge crest on the grand wall. It reminds me of my first night here, annoyed and afraid, hell-bent on escaping. I can't believe how much has changed.

Like Everett and I share a mind, he says, "It's strange returning here after so many months. Zaire would..." His voice trails off at the mention of his former coven leader, and the reason I ended up with the Royales in the first place after Blood Matching with Zaire.

"He'd have never fucking survived any of this to even think anything anyway," Jameson says, strolling past us without giving the foyer any attention like he couldn't care less.

I squeeze Everett's shoulder and lean close to his ear. "It's okay to wonder. I can't help myself from doing the same with a million what-if questions involving my brothers."

Everett smirks in appreciation at my comment, and I kiss him sweetly until he sets me down in the grand living room with covers over the furniture, the artwork off the walls, and a layer of dust coating everything. It feels almost haunted. And maybe it is.

Mikkalo and Bronx speed in my direction, breaking away from my brothers, Laredo, Brooklyn, and Macon. I'm shocked to see everyone here. My heart skips into overdrive, pounding hard against my ribcage. I'm sure everyone can hear the erratic rhythm, threatening to weaken my legs.

"You okay, Gwen? Mikkalo asks first. He traces the silhouette of my body without touching me, like he's examining every inch of me with his eyes. "Everett? Either of you get hurt?"

"Jameson, I need to hold Demi," Bronx adds, the two of them looking as if it takes everything in them not to go blowing up the world.

"We're fine." I slide into Mikkalo's arms, knowing how much he craves to hold me. I savor the comfort his embrace brings.

"We were more worried about you. It took you longer than expected." Everett remains close, sandwiching me between him and Mikkalo.

Bronx loves up on Demi, kissing her awake despite Jameson begging him to relax. A smile splits across his handsome face, his love for her so palpable I can feel it in my bones. Where the world seems to constantly test him and try to bring him down, Demi will always lift him up in a way nothing else can. My heart spills with joy and warmth, and I feel as if I'll melt into a puddle at any second. I've fallen even more in love with my guys in the last few days than I knew possible. I can survive on watching them care for and love our daughter for the rest of eternity.

"Why don't we all sit down? I would like to let everyone know at once," Bronx says, turning away from us to look at the others. His face doesn't turn serious as he keeps smiling at Demi. "It involves all of us."

Nerves bunch in my stomach, and I follow my guys to the covered couch. Mikkalo tugs off the plastic and scoops me up, nestling me on his lap. His arms slide around me, hugging me close, and he kisses the spot below my ear. I rest against his chest, squeezing his arms to me like I might float away if he dares try to loosen them. Bronx plops down beside me, holding Demi to his chest, cradling her tiny head in his big palm. Her pouty lips suckle at the closeness of his skin, looking as if she's trying to shower him with her own kisses. Jameson perches on the arm of the couch and links his fingers through one of my hands, and Everett sits on the floor in front of us, crisscrossing his legs.

Laredo eyes me as he crosses the room and glances at the space on the couch before choosing to sit beside Everett. "I'm happy you're safe, Gwen."

I offer him a small smile, remembering his comment from earlier. He still confuses the hell out of me, but I will always be grateful for what he's done by accepting Ashton into his coven so I could officially be a Royale. And right now, it means the world to me. "Thanks for helping us. I know you didn't have to."

"It's the least I can do, Gwen. I feel responsible for a lot of this." He leans back on his palms and tips his head back. "I want to do right by your family—and I'm not only speaking of you and your brothers." Nodding at Bronx, he adds, "You can count on me as an ally with no strings attached."

Everett nudges Laredo with his knuckles. "We appreciate it."

"Yeah, man. I'm glad you're not acting like an entitled douche anymore. This is about Gwen and Demi," Jameson says, kissing my head. "They come first." A smile quirks the corner of his lips up, and I try not to react, clearly hearing the innuendo.

"Jamie, it's not just about me and Demi, though. It's about all of us and what we need for the future." I bump Bronx with my shoulder. "Isn't that what you said? We're here because it involves all of us."

Bronx nods but doesn't speak right away, just cuddling with Demi as he gathers his thoughts. I rest my hand on his knee in silent support, knowing that whatever is on his mind makes him nervous to say. I don't know if he's questioning himself or what, but it takes Mikkalo patting his back to get him to adjust Demi in his arms so he can focus.

Clearing his throat, Bronx finally looks up. "I've decided that if my coven and mate agree, we will be leaving not only the region but also the Donor Life Corp territory. Returning to Crimson Vista with Gwen has proven my fears right about how things would go. Being a Region Head while trying to protect her and our daughter will be nearly impossible with the constant threats from both rebels and other vampire covens seeking power."

I blink a few times and glance at Macon, my nerves getting the best of me. "Bronx..."

Bronx takes my hand and offers me a reassuring smile. "It's okay, dandelion. Everyone in this room knows our situation and about you and Demi. Macon has proven his loyalty with his Blood Vow proposal to your brother upon his thirtieth birthday to become his coven brother."

My eyes widen. "What?"

Declan grins and rubs his palms together. "Did you really think you were going to spend eternity without me? Macon's more than the guy I supply blood to. He's my best friend."

Ashton laughs. "You haven't been around much, Gwen, but he's right. They have a real fucking bro-mance going on."

I cover my chest with my hand. I shouldn't be surprised. Declan, like the rest of my brothers, carries the dhampir gene. And seeing all of us together like this, forming bonds with different covens, leads me to believe that the mutation attracts more than a coven to a dhampir. Maybe it's the universes way of preparing a future we can all live together in without worry.

Swiveling in my seat, I glance to Porter next. He hasn't been here long, and I doubt he'd want to leave my other brothers. "What about Porter? Is he coming with us?"

"I've secured a spot in the coven of one of my most trusted permanent allies for Porter. It was part of going through with the alliance, ensuring our loyalty remains strong. Until then, he will remain with Declan in my household without any donation requirements. Mr. Baron ensured it."

Tears rim my eyes, and I meet Laredo's gaze. "Laredo, I—thank you." I lean forward, stretching out my arms to hug him.

He relaxes as I sink against him, appreciating everything he's done for me. "I have wronged you and your family so often that I have a lot of making up to do. So please, don't thank me."

I swipe my hand over my eyes. "Too bad."

He chuckles and eases away, not allowing our hug to linger. I slide away from him and scoot between Mikkalo's legs, resting my back to the couch.

"So as I was saying," Bronx continues, like he's afraid if he doesn't spit out his thoughts now that he might never do it. "I trust Macon as our ally to ensure your brother's safety until—until it is safe enough to return."

I shift and glance at Bronx. "Are you sure that is the best plan? How long?"

He presses his lips together and holds my gaze. "Yes, I think so. We can't stay here anymore, dandelion. We just can't. It's not safe for us or Demi. At least for the time being. I'm sure there will come a point where we need to return, especially when she's an adult."

It's so hard to even think in that length of time. To my guys, years don't mean the same as they do to me. "But where will we go?" I ask, my nerves getting the best of me. "You said out of the territory. What if it's just as bad?"

"Where we go, we'll be on our own in one of the un-controlled areas given back to nature. You know outcasts flock to the cities and rebel areas. We're going to disappear. Completely. I've arranged for us to be removed from the system." He hands Demi to Mikkalo and holds his hands out, silently pleading with me to get up and sit with him. "As it turns out, the Kings aren't Viorica's perfect little security personnel. Their coven's technology lead hacked into the system and removed us. The board no longer has control over us."

"We're free, Gigi," Jameson says, finally speaking up. "Laredo has given us everything we need to survive outside the system. All of the old Baron maps and logs—everything they used to navigate and live unregistered—is ours."

"And we found the perfect uninhabited back-world town." Mikkalo grins as Demi looks at him. "We can settle down and raise Demi in peace and without the fear that comes with our position of power."

A dozen thoughts rush through my mind, and I scrub my cheeks with my hands, trying to process their words. Unregistered? Uninhabited back-world town? How can they be so certain such a place exists? Not to mention what it would take to get there.

"But the rebels. You know they're watching us," I say, my nerves not allowing me to even enjoy the idea of getting away from everything for even a second. "What if they follow us there? Or the board? Do you think it's even possible to disappear?"

"We've planned for that." Mikkalo rubs my leg. "And it is possible. We've gotten word that prior board members have returned to the shadows."

"Brooklyn and I will help," Ashton says, twining his fingers through Brooklyn's. "No one will see it coming."

I turn and look at everyone as they all train their eyes on me. "Are you all sure? I don't want my problems to mess up any of your lives."

"Gweny, we're family. We look out for each other," Declan says.

"He's right, little sis. Helping your coven and our niece is all that matters to us," Ashton adds. "I know you struggle to think this, but you guys will change the world."

Porter offers me a smile. "And I bet it'll be an amazing place."

I bounce on the balls of my feet, pretending to sway for Demi, though I only move for myself. I can't keep still. I can't concentrate on anything either. Not like I have to.

Everett and Mikkalo load up Macon's huge SUV, hidden in the vast garage with several other vehicles we could choose from. Bronx and Jameson stand close together, looking over a map while marking off all the different cities they could get in and out of without too much trouble.

"Gweny, we're going to head out." Ashton's voice draws my attention to him. He stands in the doorway leading into the den I never spent any time in. Declan, Porter, and Brooklyn hover behind him, all remaining expressionless as if one twitch of their face could set me off. And who knows? Maybe it would.

"Oh." It's all I can manage to get out of my mouth.

Striding across the room, I close the space to them and open my free arm. Ashton hugs me first, kissing my forehead and then Demi's, taking a moment to inhale a small breath like he needs it to help him remember us the best he can.

"It won't be forever," he says, sounding as if he's trying to convince himself more than me.

"I hope not," I murmur, motioning to my other two brothers to join us. "I'll miss you guys too much."

"Nah, you'll be too busy building a Royale army of dhampirs." Declan laughs at his joke, making Porter groan.

"Seriously, Dec?" Porter punches him in the arm.

I shake my head and cover Declan's mouth before he can respond. "No matter how busy...or not busy I am, doesn't mean I won't miss you."

"Damn it. We're going to miss you and Demi like crazy." Ashton takes Demi from me and snuggles her close. My heart breaks knowing that she might never get the chance to know what amazing uncles she has. All I can do is hope. Hope for a better future. Hope for a life where we're strong enough to handle any and all threats. Hope for a world where rebels won't deem dhampirs as traitors to humanity for loving the vampires they're drawn to.

My brothers each take turns holding Demi until Brooklyn takes her, so they can hug me once more. Macon materializes with Laredo, and my guys stop what they're doing to join our circle.

"Is everything set?" Bronx asks Macon, his jaw remaining tight.

Macon nods and pulls out his com device, handing it to Bronx. "These are where we've spotted rebels. They're preparing for dawn."

I frown. "Preparing for what?"

"They're going to attack." Laredo thins his lips. "We caught several soldiers and mind manipulated the information out of them. Apparently Silas transformed about twenty willing soldiers—all chosen for a suicide mission to get in here for an ambush."

Of-fucking-course.

"There are also a few others preparing another attack on Crimson Vista. They're going after the donor population to cause unrest. They want donors to think that they're in danger, so they fight instead of comply," Macon adds.

Shit.

"But don't worry about it, Gwen." Laredo straightens his shoulders, meeting my gaze. "I will take care of it. I promised to always protect you, so I'm doing it the best way I know how."

I grimace. "What? I thought you were coming with us? The journal isn't enough. Demi—"

"My dhampir," Laredo says softly, slightly herding me just outside the circle.

He touches my cheek, and for the first time in a long time, I don't reject his subtle affection. It doesn't confuse me or feel anything other than just like Laredo and all the time we spent together and how much I missed him. In what way? I can't say. I don't know the answer to that.

Laredo's eyes flash silver. "I will not abandon you forever, but I have a duty and a responsibility to do everything I can to protect you and Demi. I must stop the threat where it started, and I will not allow you or your mates—no one—to be put in that position."

He doesn't have to say the words for me to know he means going after Silas. I hate admitting it, but he's right. I wish it weren't true. I wish Silas and Grayson never fell into the Barons' hands in the first place. But nothing we have done or said could change their minds. And now that Silas is threatening the lives of innocent people, both registered donors and rebels, all in the name of the rebel fight, I know deep down he must be stopped. For everyone's sake.

Blinking the tears from my eyes, I throw my arms around Laredo's neck and hug him, burying my face into the crook of his neck. I breathe in the scent of his familiar skin, remembering the exact taste of his blood from the three years he not only manipulated me but also protected and prepared me the way he thought best.

"I swear you better not get yourself killed, Laredo," I murmur, easing back to meet his gaze. "I mourned you once already. I don't want to go through that again."

A smirk crosses his lips and he tugs away from me, turning toward my guys. "You are incredibly lucky to have been chosen by such a magnificent woman. Take care of her and your daughter—and also each other. A dhampir is as powerful as the coven who helps her rise."

Laredo caresses his lips to my cheek, the feather-light touch like a whisper of breath against my skin.

He disappears.

21

ALLIES AND ENEMIES

I CLUTCH DEMI TO MY chest, holding her close even though her carrier ensures she's not going anywhere. Mikkalo and Jameson sandwich us between them, keeping their eyes trained out the windows. Bronx drives the SUV in manual mode, not trusting the vehicles autopilot. Tapping away on his com device, Everett watches the outside cameras while also continuously checking on me.

"They're approaching the decoy." Ashton's voice hums through the speakers, his picture on the dash screen, but he doesn't look at the camera.

"Get ready to trigger the defense response," Mikkalo says, shifting in his seat to glance at Everett's com device. "They're going to attack the vehicle the moment the sun rises. Let's not make it too easy for the assholes. It'll buy some time before they figure out we're not inside."

"Gotcha. Activating it now."

A beep sounds through the car, and I straighten in my seat as if I need to prepare for something to happen. But we're far from the decoy vehicle Mikkalo set into motion, monitored by Ashton from the safety of his apartment in Crimson Vista. I don't know what I'll do when we have to abandon the vehicle and my only way of contacting my brother, but it's the only way.

Jameson quietly rests his hand on my leg, trying to give me his strength through his touch. If I wasn't dead-set on clutching Demi, ensuring her closeness, he would take my hand. I don't know how my guys manage to remain so calm. None of them ripple with tense muscles, which should make me feel better. But it doesn't. I feel even more on edge.

A thin line of light blooms on the flat horizon as the sun rises. I swallow and watch it grow, my whole body trembling in anticipation. The heavy tint gives me a clear view of the coming day without stinging my eyes. If only I felt better that the night disappears. It makes me feel far worse. Without the protection of night, my guys are vulnerable. If something happens to the SUV, they could burn.

So I do the only thing that'll ease my anxiety, even if just a bit.

Bending forward, I grab the sun-protection gear and start tossing the hooded sweatshirts to each of them. I expect at least Bronx to argue with me, but he puts the SUV into autopilot and shrugs his on first. Mikkalo, Jameson, and Everett follow his lead, and I pass out the full-coverage face masks next. They adjust them on their heads like hats without pulling them down to keep a clear visual of our surroundings.

"Better, Gigi?" Jameson asks, patting my leg.

I lick my lips and nod. "Just one more thing. I want you to each drink from me."

"We'll drink some gen. pop.," Everett says, swiveling his seat to face me. "We need you in perfect condition."

I narrow my eyes. "And I need to ensure you have the best blood in case. You know you heal faster after consuming my blood."

"But we're not injured," Mikkalo says, patting my other leg. "If we run out on the road or something happens, then we'll consider it."

I swat his hand. "Mikkalo—"

"Listen to your health keeper, dandelion. No need to be a pain in the balls already. We haven't even been on the road long." Bronx flicks his stare to the rearview mirror. "Now why don't you let Jameson feed you instead?"

"I'm fine." I fidget in my seat, my nerves choosing now to scream in fear.

Bronx huffs. "You are not—"

Ashton hollers in excitement, his cheer echoing loudly from the stereo system. "The decoy has been hit. Ten rebels. One in sun gear."

"We're bringing up the feed now. We'll call you if we need anything else," Everett says, hovering his finger over the dashboard screen.

"I'll be ready." Ashton finally looks at the camera. "Love you, Gweny. Don't forget to call me one more time before you guys abandon the vehicle. One goodbye wasn't enough."

Without waiting for my response, Ashton's image vanishes, leaving a video of a rebel approaching the camera of the decoy car meant to trick the bastards. Raising a gun, he shoots, sending a loud pop ringing through my ears. I startle at the noise and jump in my seat.

Jameson grabs my hand. "Turn off the sound, Ev. It's about to get really fucking lou—"

Bronx suddenly slams the brakes, sending the back of the SUV fishtailing. If Jameson wasn't holding my arm while Mikkalo clutches my leg, I might've snapped hard on my restraints. I gasp a breath and jerk my attention to the windshield. Up ahead, a familiar woman stands in the middle of the road. I can't seem to place her, but I don't think she's a rebel. Her dark, tight curls bounce with her movements, and her dark bronze skin shimmers with makeup, giving her a perfect glow. She's far too clean for the rebel life, dressed in tight jeans, a low-cut top, and stilettos.

"Fuck," Bronx says, smacking his hand on the steering wheel.

"How did they know?" Everett swivels in his seat, turning to look at Mikkalo and Jameson.

"I saw it myself that they left Crimson Vista last night." Mikkalo unsheathes a dagger, his bulging biceps flexing in anticipation. "Just give me the word, Bronx. The Vaduvas can't be far. Samantha would never agree to let her Blood Match face us alone."

That's why the woman looks familiar.

"Hang on, brother. I'm getting a call," Bronx says, stiffening in his seat. "It's Viorica."

Bronx connects the line, and Viorica's image flickers on the screen of the dashboard. She wears a pair of large sunglasses that reflects a view of a silver SUV and scattered trees as she holds up her com device. I'm surprised she stands outside, and only with a white hood and no head covering.

"Mr. Royale, I never expected you to be the type to give up when faced with difficult circumstances." Viorica's fangs peek out from beneath her ruby-colored upper lip. "Especially after you faced the challenge of your board seat by a more powerful opponent."

"Things have changed, Viorica. Now please ask your future heir to move out of the way." Bronx grips the steering wheel and revs the engine before lurching the SUV forward a few feet.

"Not until you give me the courtesy of a face-to-face conversation. Don't you agree that I deserve as much for not declaring you a traitor to the board? Deleting your coven from the system after gathering classified knowledge will not bode well with other members. It is even punishable by death, and you know it." Viorica's voice sharpens with her threat. "I'd like answers. A Blood Vow to Gwen was supposed to solidify a better alliance between us. Why would you abandon an offer when all you have been doing the last few months is fighting for the woman you love?"

"Viorica, we owe you no explanation. Any and all debts as well as a donation to keep our region intact and undivided until you find a new board member has been secured." Bronx drums his fingers on the steering wheel. "Now, have your future heir move. I will not ask again."

"Bronx, I'm asking for five minutes. Please," Viorica says, her voice softening. "Give me that and I'll let you go."

"She's setting us up," Mikkalo mutters, getting ready to fling the door open. "I'll move Evora out of the road myself."

Viorica disconnects the line with a huff, and my guys tense. Something slams on the roof of the vehicle, startling Demi awake, and she starts fussing. Heeled black boots jump onto the hood, denting the metal, and Bronx drags his head covering down and abandons us inside the car. Jumping from the hood, Viorica faces Bronx, aiming a dagger at him. She clutches an umbrella made of strange thick material, protecting herself from the sun instead of wearing sun-protective gear.

"I am not here to fight, Bronx," she snaps, her voice muffling into the car. "Now be reasonable and join me in the shade. Only Evora and Samantha have come with me to intercept your journey. I'm not your enemy."

"How can I be sure?" Bronx slaps the hood of the car. "Despite your position of power, you still run things like before The Divisions. I wanted a board seat to change things for the better so everyone could thrive, not to stroke your ego and take care of things you pretend don't exist because they're not happening in you region."

Viorica nods. "I admit, I struggle with my back-world ideologies, but that's why I'd like you to reconsider abandoning Donor Life Corp. I want our territory to thrive, and I need you and your coven."

Shaking his head, Bronx says, "I'm sorry, Viorica. With our daughter and Gwen's safety in jeopardy, I—*we*—can't agree to such things."

"What if I help you eradicate the—"

A horn honks, cutting Viorica's words off. Dust clouds through the air as a silver SUV peels out in the dirt. Evora stands in shock, watching what I'm certain is Viorica's vehicle barreling her way. A figure blurs from the cluster of trees, and tackles the donor to the ground. Smoke wafts from the unprotected vampire—from Sammy—as she drags her Blood Match out of the way. The two of them disappear from the road and back to the trees. The loud pops of gunshots echo through the air, and Everett growls, jumping into the driver's seat.

The silver SUV speeds in our direction, the front corner panel dented and the windshield smashed and broken. A man pops his head out of the passenger's side window and pulls the trigger on his gun, hitting Viorica.

Without waiting for Bronx, Everett slams the gear into reverse and stomps the throttle. The tires screech as he spins the seat sideways, keeping one hand on the steering wheel and his attention on the back window.

"Everett, turn!" Jameson shouts, wrapping his arms around me.

Jerking the wheel, Everett sends the SUV skidding. My head spins as we spin into the dirt, hazing the air.

"Get out!" Mikkalo shouts, flinging his door open.

Demi screams her lungs out, and I clutch her to my chest, scrambling to get out with Jameson as fast as I can.

An explosion of metal crashing into metal steals my hearing, and Jameson drags me by the wrists, trying to get me into his arms. I screech and squeeze my eyes shut, watching helplessly as the SUV and a back-world car tumble right at us. Spinning as fast as he can, Jameson throws me and Demi into the air.

I scream again, my fear instincts and desperation to protect Demi getting me to curl around her midair. Strong arms envelop me, and I yell again, but not in fear. In relief. I've never been so thankful for my guys' quick reflexes.

"I got you, Gwen," Everett says, relocating us into the shade of a nearby tree.

"The others?" I gasp, barely able to get my words out. "They're—"

Blood sprays across my face as a long knife impales Everett through the neck. His eyes widen and close. With my dhampir speed, I yank him forward, pulling him off the blade, so the fucker behind him can't try to behead him. Demi cries harder, her wailing lungs gutting me like Everett's crumpled body.

Fury blasts through me, and I charge forward and spin-kick like Jameson taught me, keeping my arms protectively blocking Demi. The vampire doesn't expect my move, and I stomp him in the stomach and then kick him in the side with all my strength, sending him flying out of the shade. My dhampir nature consumes me, not letting me back down from the asshole who thinks he can hurt my mate. I rush to him, stopping him from getting up, and grab the sun shield from his head, craving to watch him burn.

Silas hollers and flashes his fangs, the intensity of the sun burning and blistering his face setting him off. I expect him to run like the coward he is and to take cover in the trees, but he doesn't. He flies at me with outstretched arms. I spin on my boots to protect Demi, and Silas grabs my hair and drags me back.

"Gwen!" Mikkalo hollers, risking the sun to charge at me. "Gwen, fight!"

His words kick my ass in motion. Thrashing, I reach behind me and lock my fingers to Silas's wrists, jabbing my nails into his burning skin. He growls and tugs me off my feet completely, lifting me into the air. My scalp burns in pain, the weight of my body feeling as if it'll rip my hair out. Mikkalo roars and unsheathes his sword, getting ready to fight.

I buck and twist, using the desperation in Mikkalo's yells to break free. I land on my knees and fall sideways, screeching in fear of hurting Demi. Tears burn my eyes and I shove my hands into the hot compacted dirt, trying to push myself to my feet. Gunfire rings through the air in quick successions, and I tilt my head up, watching as a small army of rebels shoots from a speeding car, catching Mikkalo off guard.

"Gwen, run!" he shouts, his blood loss sending him to the ground.

The rebels blare their horn and stomp the gas, running over Mikkalo only to screech to a halt, trapping him beneath the car.

"No!" I yell, stumbling in his direction.

"Stop, Gwen! Run! Leave him! I'm coming!" Bronx's deep voice bellows through the air, punching me in the heart.

My jogging falters, and I spin to run in the opposite direction, but Silas materializes in front of me. He extends his fangs to their full length, the white of his teeth a stark contrast to the blackened, burning skin on his face and neck. Silver glows in his eyes, his vampire nature consuming him with self-preservation. I swing my fist, hitting him in the cheek, feeling this tender skin rub off with my force.

He screams at a pitch I never knew possible and grabs my shoulders, squishing Demi between us. I claw at his face, his eyes, everything I can sink my fingers into, but he doesn't back down. He bites my wrist first, and I automatically jerk my arm away, giving him an opening.

More gunshots and back-world car engines fill the world with noise, stealing away my hearing. The haze from dirt and a fire I can't see clouds the air. Coughing, I try to force Silas away by smacking my hand to his chest, but it doesn't work. The burning pain grows too intense.

Sharp fangs sink into my throat as Silas bites me so hard that I know he plans to rip my throat out. He plans to ensure I die in unbearable pain. He wants me to suffer.

"Get her in the car!" a woman shouts. "Now!"

The agony from the pressure of Silas's bite releases me, and I gasp, struggling to breathe. Hot blood pours down my neck. Shadows crowd my vision, and I wobble on my feet, my body still fighting to get away.

A figure closes in on me and two warm hands grab me by the sides. "Hold still, traitor. I don't want to hurt our baby girl."

Desperation and anguish collide into me at the loosening of Demi's carrier. I scream and try to grab her, but fingers sink into my shoulders, ripping me back.

"Don't!" I scream. "I'll kill you!"

"Use your venom!" a feminine voice yells. "Knock her out."

The last thing I hear is Demi's frightened wails.

Pain ignites through me.

22

BROKEN BLOOD BONDS

"DO YOU REMEMBER THE RULES, Gwen?" Grayson stands with his feet apart and his hands fisted in front of his face, ready to fight and shield him toward any attack I might have in store.

I nod and bounce on my feet, shaking out my tense muscles. "Flash my boobs and seduce them with my charm until I can punch my stake through their hearts."

"Gwen!" Grayson snaps, scowling at me. "You need to take this seriously. This isn't some practice run with a fangless outcast. The city is full of bloodsuckers who will try to capture you and cage you."

I roll my eyes. "Fuck, you need to lighten up and take a joke. You know I'd never flash some asshole."

"She's right. She's only allowed to show me those perky tits of hers if she's going to show anyone." Laredo materializes a few feet away and crosses his arms over his broad chest. "I have first dibs."

Grayson's face turns red, and he charges Laredo with his stake. Laughing, Laredo darts out of the way and vanishes at vampire speed only to stop behind me. I catch his scent and spin, swinging my fist at his face. He snatches my arm and drags me to him, lifting me off my feet. The world blurs as he relocates the two of us far enough away from Grayson that it'll take him at least a minute or two to catch up.

I whack Laredo's shoulder. "He's going to stake you for this."

My words only make Laredo smile wider. "Only because I'll let him. That's how you control your brothers, you know. You act as if they're braver and stronger than you are. They sometimes are so full of themselves that they think they have control over you and I, but it's all part of the game."

I narrow my eyes, crinkling my nose. "I should take your heart for even teasing that you're playing games with us."

Laredo leans closer, his handsome face filling my vision. "You already have it, Gwen. Now let me practice with you. You can test your theory."

Warmth blooms across my cheeks. "You'd love that, wouldn't you?"

Humming, he says, "I guarantee it'll work."

Ice water splashes my face, jerking me from the dark recesses of my mind. The weight of my memory crashes down on me, stealing my breath. I thrash and try to push myself up, but heavy shackles lock me to the wall. I blink a few times in confusion, staring down at my belly, expecting to see me pregnant and only woken by a horrible night terror.

Dirt and blood stain my clothes, and my heart shatters into a million pieces, seeing the broken straps of the baby carrier hanging down my body.

"Demi! Demi!" I scream, fighting against the metal restraints. They bite into my wrists, shooting pain up my arm as they rub against the venom bite Silas gave me.

"Gwen, knock it off. Those restraints have been used to trap vampires for more than a century. The Barons would never half-ass something that keeps prisoners contained." Silas's husky voice snatches my attention from the restraints and to him. His burned face looks far better than it had, but he still has grotesque, red patches and scratch marks where I tried to claw his face off.

"Where is she!" I yell, my fury and panic hitting me in

wave after wave of anguish. "Where did you take her?"

Silas lifts and drops his shoulders. "It's none of your concern. She'll be far safer and better raised than with you and your asshole coven. She's where she belongs."

I can't stop the sob from escaping my mouth, my eyes burning with tears. It feels as if he cuts my heart out and plans to stomp on it until nothing remains. "Silas, please. She's my daughter. She needs me. How could you do this to me?"

Silas's eyes flash silver and he bares his fangs. "You did this to yourself, Gwen. You should've never let the Royales get to you like they had. You ruined everything for our family. You're why Dad and Kyler are dead. And when Grayson and I tried to save us all, you fucking turned your back on us. So don't give me this shit. You must die for your actions, you fucking traitor. Demi is ours. She's a Gallagher of the rebel dhampir bloodline and will be raised as such."

I scream again and yank the restraints, willing to risk breaking my wrists—hell, even cutting off my hands—to break free to go after Silas and get Demi back. He is out of his damn mind if he thinks he can get away with this. My guys will come. Even if the rebels kill me, they will tear the world down for her. I will do everything to make sure they can. Starting with ripping Silas's head off.

My dhampir side grabs hold of me, tensing my muscles and giving me strength to yank one of the chains free of the wall. I swing my hand and whip the chain across Silas's face, surprising him. Roaring, he stumbles back to catch himself on a metal table, which looks prepped and ready to slice me apart inch-by-inch.

He grabs a blade from the table and rushes me, slamming my back into the concrete wall. Holding the dagger to my throat, he gets in my face and tries to lock me in his gaze. My muscles slacken, and fear steals my breath. Without the power Demi gave me while pregnant with her, I can't resist his attempt to open my mind. My panic gives me the will to fight, and I bash my head forward, hitting him hard in the nose. Pain stings my throat from the long cut from his knife, but I grind my teeth.

"You fucking bitch! Now I'm not going to let you see Demi one last time," Silas shouts, materializing in front of me. He snags the loose chain and jerks my arm back over my head, securing it in place. "I'll ensure the elders make you suffer for your crimes against humanity. I was going to ask for mercy on your behalf, but that's the last thing you deserve."

The thought of not seeing Demi steals my breath and sends my mind spinning. I feel as if I'll die at any second. My body trembles, grief and sorrow gripping me tightly. I can't believe this is happening. I can't believe my own brother turned into one of the true monsters we were raised to fight against. He might be with Blood Rebels, but he's far from a crusader to save the human race. He wants nothing more than to control it. He's letting the rebels think they're in control as he plays his games.

Games.

The word swirls through my mind over and over again as I remember the memory of Laredo teaching me how to control my brothers. I thought it was ridiculous at the time, but now, as I stand here, broken and weak, I realize that Laredo was right. Vampires love games, and I know Silas. I know exactly what he needs to drop his guard. He needs to feel powerful while seeing me weak.

"Silas, I'm sorry! Please, don't do this. Please don't deny me seeing Demi. I'm begging you." My voice shakes with my real desperation, and I sink into the torture of grief he wants me to lose myself in. "Please."

Silas's anger morphs into satisfaction, and he steps closer. Swiping his finger across my throat, he runs the tip across my trickling blood. He pops it into his mouth and hums under his breath, and it takes everything in me not to try kicking him in the balls for being a disgusting creep. He does it again like he knows it gets under my skin and his twisted ass wants to see me suffer like a weak piece of prey at his feet.

"Please," I beg again. "I'll do anything. Just let me see her."

Silas doesn't respond, standing utterly still with his

head cocked. A smile stretches even wider across his face, showing off the sharpness of his fangs. His eyes flash silver, and he gives me a slow once-over, taking in the sight of me like he enjoys seeing how much I tremble and wobble from pain and blood loss.

"You know, Dad always said you'd be the strongest of us all." Silas aims his knife at my throat again, nicking my flesh.

I wince and press myself to the wall, cowering away from him, trying to act as scared as I possibly can despite my rising urge to hurry the hell up and rip his head off. "Silas..."

Shaking his head, he adds, "He was a fucking idiot."

He licks my blood off the point of his blade and pricks himself on purpose. A drop of blood splashes on his bottom lip. He smiles, stretching his skin to send it dripping onto his chin. My gaze darts from his mouth, chasing the blood drop like it's the one thing I need to get out of here. My stomach screams, clenching and twisting, begging me to risk losing my arms to launch at him to satiate the blood hunger stealing my breath.

Shuffling a few feet back, Silas moves out of my reach. I realize he must notice the predator flashing in my eyes as he realizes his attempt to torture me only awakened my beastly nature. The potent scent of his blood trickles to me, and I flare my nostrils, narrowing my focus on him.

I try to remain calm and keep my cool, but the hunger roars in my belly, turning me wild. "S-Silas, you're right. He was an idiot to ever think that I was more powerful than any of you. Look where we are. Look at all of the things you accomplished."

He smirks, unable to steel himself to my words. "I'm going to change the world, Gwen. You should be honored that our heir will rise to help."

My insides clench at his words. "Will you please let me see her? Please."

His features sharpen and he scowls. "No. It's best this way."

The beast inside me roars, giving me the strength to break free of the restraints. I launch forward, my mind hell-bent on biting Silas's throat out. He spins out of the way and grabs one of the loose chains, swinging me off my feet. I collide into the wall and crash to the ground. Heaving, I try to catch my breath, but the air refuses to come.

Silas looms over me and kicks me in the stomach. My vision blurs and the world spins as I struggle to stay conscious. I can't move or fight as he lifts me up and returns me to the gross, bloody spot on the floor where I woke up. He adjusts my chains and pinches my chin, glowering into my gaze.

"I'll take good care of my heir, Gwen," he says, growling with his words. "Think about that when they come. The next time I see you, I'll drain you dry."

"My dhampir, drink. Hurry."

Sweet liquid coats my tongue, stirring me awake. I latch my fingers to Laredo's arm and suck hard and fast, quenching the burning need for blood inside me. My eyes blur with tears. Confusion muddles my mind, messing with my head. Is this a memory? A twisted last-ditch trick of my mind to save me from the misery of my fate?

"I'm so sorry. I should've known better than to ever leave you." Laredo strokes my dirty hair, watching me drink from him. "The second I realized Silas wasn't heading out with the rebels, I knew he was going to go after Viorica. The bastard got lucky that she led them right to you."

I blink my eyes a dozen times, trying to process his words. Easing away from his arm, I lick my lips. "We need to find Demi," I say, instead of asking him why Silas would do such a thing.

I already know the reason. He was probably seeking revenge for what she did by banishing him. He always did hold a grudge. He also probably thought the rebels could handle us. The fucker.

"Your mates are on it now," he whispers, using his sleeve to wipe the blood staining my lips. "They wanted to split up to look for the both of you, but they're quite injured from the attack. I thought it would be best if I came for you."

My lip trembles at his words. "We have to find them. If they're injured, they could—"

A door slams from outside of this dank basement, cutting off my words. Laredo growls under his breath, and he looks ready to fly at the door to devour whoever stands on the other side.

But a soft cry freezes him in place.

My heart clenches, hearing the already familiar fussing of my daughter, and I snatch Laredo by the sleeve. My chains rattle, and I cringe. I'm still restrained to the wall because Laredo wanted to give me blood, his innate need to take care of me distracting him.

"Gwen? Don't scream or anything. We can't let anyone know I'm here." Grayson's velvety soft voice hums through the door as he eases it open.

Laredo abandons me to hide, his movements too fast for me to follow. My heart aches, each beat more painful than the last. Tears spill down my cheeks seeing Demi in Grayson's arms as he cradles her against his shoulder. His brows furrow, and he looks thinner, his eyes sunken in, and his skin paler. Dozens of scars from bite marks pepper his neck and arms. It looks as if his sole purpose in life is now exposing his neck to Silas as his personal blood donor, and Grayson is close to receiving his final donation.

"Fuck, Grayson. What happened to you?" I can't stop the question from escaping my mouth. I remain in my spot, afraid that if I rattle my chains or make any sudden movements, he might flee and take Demi with him.

His hazel eyes meet mine, and a frown wrinkles his saggy skin. "I fucked up. That's what happened."

I have no idea what he means, but I don't care to ask. I can't take my eyes off Demi. She's close enough that I can smell her fresh scent. I want so badly to hold her and kiss her, to hug her and protect her while I start ripping out the hearts of everyone here. The desire grows so intense, that I bite the inside of my cheek to try to chill myself out.

Demi releases a small cry, prodding at my instincts, and I stretch my arms out, silently begging Grayson to bring her closer.

"Please, give her to me, Grayson." My voice cracks, and I try not to tug on the restraints.

He shuffles closer and gives me a once-over, eyeing all of my injuries. "Shit. That fucker. I want to kill him."

I frown. "It was Silas who did this."

Grayson grumbles under his breath, summoning his energy to stride the rest of the way. "I know. That's who I was talking about." Adjusting Demi in his arms, he reaches into his pocket and pulls out a key. "Power has gotten to his head, and he doesn't ever think things through."

The shackles pop open, releasing my wrists. I fight

through the ache and force my muscles to work, stretching out my arms. "So why do you stay? Why don't you stand up against him?"

Grayson's face slackens, a strange expression stealing away his scowl. "Because I can't leave. I'll die without Silas, especially because I can't transform into a vampire. He tried. Look at all his effort."

Oh, shit. Without having to confront Silas, I know he mind manipulated Grayson. Fuck, he probably did so to the whole community, taking after the Barons, the only vampires he ever really knew.

I grab Demi from Grayson, afraid something Silas manipulated into his head might make him snap and run away with her. He stands frozen and watches me as I bury my face to her chest, just breathing in her scent and listening to her heart beating. My whole body aches to get out of here with her, and I run a dozen strategies through my mind.

"Okay, Gweny. I'm really sorry, but I need to take her back." Grayson's words stab me through the heart, setting me off.

I release a scary-ass growl, startling him. "Like fucking hell am I letting you take her."

Grayson scrambles back, reaching for a gun on his belt. Snarling, Laredo zooms from his hiding place and stands between us, baring his fangs. Grayson can't even remove the gun from its holster in time to fight Laredo. Grabbing him by the throat, Laredo lifts Grayson up and slams him to the ground.

"Gwen, take the tunnel!" Laredo commands, jerking his attention to me. "Yell for your mates the second you get outside. They'll come for you."

Turning on the balls of my feet, I spot the access to the hidden tunnel near an empty shelving unit. I swipe a knife from the metal torture table and adjust Demi the best I can in one arm.

Grayson hollers from behind me, pushing me to summon my dhampir speed.

I flee.

23

REBEL FIGHT

I TAKE THE STAIRS LEADING up as fast as I can until I reach the door to where I pray is the outside. Yells sound from behind me from Grayson for a moment, clenching my chest. He falls silent, and I push my body to hustle my ass up the last few steep steps. Using the hilt of my knife, I thrust the door open, and it clatters against the ground.

I peek my head out slowly, peering around. Cool, fresh air engulfs me, the dim purpling of twilight like a kiss of energy to keep my body moving. I gawk at the sight of the vast yard for a moment, recognizing the Baron Coven's property. I had no idea I had been taken here. That section of the basement must've been behind a door I never cared to enter.

Silas's mention of the century-old restraints belonging to the Barons didn't even click in my head. Shit. I should've known I was here. I could've better strategized where to go from here. Now, I freeze, wasting time trying to figure out the safest direction to hide as I yell for my guys.

Inhaling a deep breath, I scream, "Jamie! Jamie, I'm near our hiding place!" We had several, but hopefully he can narrow it down to the one closest to the house.

My brother's stupidity in thinking he could start a rebel colony here gives me the advantage I need. Jameson knows this property as good as Laredo does, and he will know exactly where to find me.

I rush forward and toward the cascading low branches of a lush tree, ducking under to get out of view. There's no doubt in my mind that my yell could be heard by everyone on the property. If I've been sentenced to death, there is no way they're going to not try to kill me on sight.

I clutch Demi. "Jamie! Hurry—"

Sharp pain explodes in my lower back, and I scream in terror, pulling Demi up and away from me. My blood coats the bottom of her blanket, spilling from around the point of a knife, impaling through my skin.

"Get the baby before she drops her, Trix," Silas commands, his voice deep with sadistic sharpness. He slides his knife from my back and points it at two men. "You two go inside. Find out who let her out. She didn't break the restraints. They were removed."

The familiar woman, Trix, who attacked me with Silas before snatches Demi from my arms. I yell and thrash, launching forward to tackle her. Pain slices through me again, dropping me face-first to the dirt. My eyes burn with tears, blurring Trix's figure as she ducks under the low branches, stealing Demi from me.

"Fucking hell, Gwen. You're not getting out of here. Stop trying to fight." Silas bunches the back of my shirt in his fingers, hoisting me off the ground.

The world spins as he tosses me from the covering of the trees, and I cry out, rolling across the grass. Fiery pain courses through my body, igniting agony deep in my soul. It takes everything in me to push from the ground to get onto my hands and knees. I will fight to get to Demi until my last breath. I will not give up and accept this fucking fate.

"Spread out, soldiers! A traitor is among us. They attacked Grayson and freed Gwen." Trix's voice drags my attention from the ground in front of me. She cradles Demi, glowering at her crying face, looking as if she already holds a grudge against her.

I grind my teeth and crawl forward summoning my

dhampir nature to give me the strength I need as my humanity curls up and dies inside me. I need my beast side. I need the part of me who will do whatever it takes to save my daughter from these monsters. I need everything untamed in my soul to unleash. It might be the only way to save us.

"Grab her!" Silas yells, his shadow stalking me from behind. He doesn't rush to attack me, using his predatory nature to taunt me. He's trying to set off my fear instincts born from my humanity, but it's too late for that.

My vision shadows, my blood hunger ripping through my body, tensing my muscles. I push to my feet and scream in fury. Curling my fingers into fists, I spin and sucker punch Silas in his bastard face, jerking his head to the side. He stumbles from the force of my punch and flashes his fangs.

Two rebels grab me from behind and each take one of my arms, forcing me to the ground. I buck and kick, thrashing and fighting to break free. I'm going to murder these fuckers. I don't care if they're human. I will rip their throats out and feed them to the outcast population. I will take the heart of every last rebel. They're not fighting for humanity. They're fighting for the same damn thing vampires fight for—complete control. If they weren't, they wouldn't give their lives so readily. They wouldn't agree to turn into the supposed monsters they fight against.

But here they are. I can smell a collection of scents, stirring my dhampir nature even more. It turns my blood hunger to blood savagery, and I use my strength to flip one of the fuckers onto his back.

A loud alarm rings through the air, stealing my hearing for a moment.

Trix waves her finger, pointing to a few men. They vanish at vampire speed, abandoning the human rebels. The cluster crowds around me, caging me in, glowering down at me like I'm the worst, vilest person they've ever seen.

"Gwen Gallagher," Trix says, shifting Demi in her arms. "You have been sentenced to death by stake. You will die like the blood sources you serve."

Pulling a shiny silver stake from a weaponry belt around her waist, she hands it to Silas and nods. Silas snatches the stake from her fingers and spins it in my face like the sheer sight will make me cower in fear.

I growl, the deep noise reverberating through my bones. My chest heaves as I inhale angry breaths, my muscles spasming and begging me to fight. Gunshots ring through the air in the distance, and it's enough to kick my ass in gear. Because my guys are coming. I can sense it.

"Do it now!" Trix shouts. "End her. We have to move!"

More gunshots blast through the air, and two of the men drop to the ground. Trix yells in surprise and rushes back right into Laredo's rippling muscular arms. She screams, trying to run away with Demi, but Laredo grips his hand around her ponytail, jerking her back.

"Hold her still," Silas commands, crouching down to straddle me.

Two gunshots pop through the air, and the fuckers holding me drop dead, falling back. The second their grip loosens, I swing at Silas, socking him in the jaw. I jerk my other hand forward and grab the stake, using my burst of energy to sink it hard enough to impale him with the blunt end in his stomach.

Silas roars and chomps his fangs into my shoulder deep enough to penetrate my bone. I wail in pain and swing my fists, trying to get him off of me. Laredo shouts my name, chucking a throwing knife at a shooting rebel, keeping him away as he protects Demi.

Silas yanks back, ripping a chunk of my flesh away. Blood pours from the wound, soaking into my hair.

"Silas, no! Don't!" Grayson's yell echoes through the air.

Grayson fires his gun, and Silas jerks and snarls as the bullets ravage his back. My head pounds, my body weakening. The only reprieve I feel is when Silas's weight vanishes, leaving me staring at the stars overhead.

I roll to my side and press my cheek to the grass. Silas lifts Grayson off his feet and hollers into his face. My arms shake as I try and fail to push from the ground. Someone calls my name, but I can't find the strength to turn.

I watch in silence as Silas sinks his fangs into Grayson's neck over and over again, sending his blood splattering across his face. Ice flows through my veins, stealing away my warmth. I close my eyes, cutting off the world. I can't watch Grayson die by Silas's hands. I can't.

"Gwen, here. Drink." Everett's melodious voice wraps me in his familiarity.

His sweet blood trickles across my lips, gushing warmth across my tongue and into my throat. Growls and gunshots continue to fill the air as the fighting draws closer to us. Fluttering my eyes open, I meet Everett's beautiful blue eyes, his handsome face pink and blistered from some time in the sun. Dried blood stiffens his shirt, and his throat still shows the damage done by Silas's blade.

Fury and the warmth of Everett's blood settling in my stomach gives me the will and strength to push up.

"Demi," I say, gasping a breath.

"She's safe. Laredo has her," Everett says, lifting me into his arms.

"The others?" I can't seem to speak more than a few words, my voice straining to escape with my painful breaths.

Everett releases a guttural noise from deep within his chest. "We're overwhelmed. Fighting the best we can. I barely managed to get through with my brothers' help. Silas transformed more than we thought. Like half the rebels we've come across here."

What the actual fuck. This is worse than I thought.

A couple of rebel vampires? Not a big deal.

But when they're a trained army and not starving out of their minds? Fuck this shit.

"Everett, to your right!" Laredo shouts, his voice reaching me from somewhere near the house.

Spinning, Everett summons his inner Mikkalo and swings me out, using the force of my legs to knock a vampire off his feet. Throwing me over his shoulder, I cling on to his back, cringing and aching as my wounds still heal. Everett disarms the vampire and uses the machete to chop the fucker's head off.

"More, incoming," Laredo calls, throwing a knife at a vampire closing in on us. "Take Demi and get Gwen out of here. I'll handle it."

Swinging the machete again, Everett cuts a man's arm clean off, sending him screaming to his knees. Laredo steps from the shadow, clutching Demi in his arms, searching the world around us for more incoming threats. I see the figure materialize behind him before he can even glance to look.

"Laredo!" I scream, holding my arms out.

His eyes widen, and he tosses Demi to me a split second before Silas stabs a blade through him. Everett tries to lift me to my feet, but I hold Demi out to him.

"Get her out of here. Find the others," I command, turning too quickly to hear him try to argue.

Anger rushes through me, and I catapult toward Silas and Laredo, my mind and body desperate for blood and revenge. Silas shoves Laredo, yanking the blade out of his back to swing it at me. Ducking, I crash into Silas, ramming my shoulder into his gut. We smash into the side of the house together, and I pin him to the wall.

Without hesitating, I lock my fingers to his hair and bend his neck. I bite his flesh as hard as I can, ripping and spitting exactly how he did to me. He will experience every single instance of pain he's ever caused me until he begs for death. It's all I can think about.

My wild nature consumes me, and I pull back to bite him again.

Silas yells and yanks his arm free, locking his hand around my neck. He squeezes, choking me, and I have no choice but to release his other hand to fight him. Throwing me off, he rolls on top of me and flashes his long fangs, preparing for a venom bite. I tense and shield my throat. Pain burns through my arm, and I cry out, knowing that I might only have seconds. The venom floods like lava through my veins, shadowing my vision.

Silas yanks my arms from my throat and roars in my face. Twisting my hair in his hand, he bends my head, exposing my neck. I scream and clutch his shoulders as he bites me and latches his mouth to my skin. My body slackens, the pain cascading over me muddling my thoughts. I can't fight. My body doesn't even try.

Demi's soft cry trickles through the air, and Jameson shouts my name. Growls and shouts of pain cut through the pounding of my head. My guys try to fight to get to me, but they won't be fast enough.

My body gives up, and I lose myself to the sound of my daughter's voice. I imagine the beautiful, powerful life ahead of her, knowing she will be well taken care and taught by the best and most loving men I could've ever asked for to be her fathers.

The thought comforts me as my heartbeat slows.

I always knew I'd die by the fangs of a vampire.

I expected to have a short life.

If only my brother's betrayal didn't hurt so deeply.

Opening and closing my mouth, I manage to push air from my lungs. "You're a monster. They'll come for you."

Silas yanks back and meets my gaze. "I'm saving the future, Gwen. Demi will have the life she deserves."

Her soft cry pleads with me. She screams for me.

So do my guys. I can hear them coming as a couple bodies thud.

They beg me to fight.

"I'll be a hero. All you'll ever be is the dhampir who bowed to vampires. A fang fucking slut," he adds, extending his fangs again, going for the kill bite.

His words ignite a fury unlike anything I've ever felt in

my life, and I yell and break my arm free, using my last bit of strength to punch my fist into his chest. Silas stills above me, his eyes widening. Yanking back, he tries to break free of my hand, but it's too late.

I clutch his heart in my hand and crush it until it splatters all over me.

"You're right," I say, falling slack under the weight of Silas's dead body. "Demi will get the life she deserves, even if it takes my very last breath."

Darkness claims me.

24

ROYALE ETERNITY

COOL FINGERS GLIDE OVER MY chin, softly stroking my cheek. The sensation draws me from my dreamless sleep. Another hand rests on my leg, and I stir and reach for it, lacing my fingers through Everett's hand.

"Gwen, hey. Demi's hungry. Are you feeling well enough for her to latch?" Jameson asks, running his finger over my cheek again. "If not—"

I clear my throat, my voice still hard to find, raw from screaming. "I'm good. Only thirsty."

I flutter my eyes open and let Jameson sit me up against a stack of pillows. It's strange to be in my old room at the Barons, but my guys didn't want to risk leaving until I was completely healed. As for the rebels? Most died. The smart ones abandoned the fight after I took my brother's heart, but they won't get far. Mikkalo promised.

Sitting on the edge of the bed next to Jameson, Bronx holds Demi in his arms. Mikkalo stands on the other side with Everett, filling up a glass with his blood. Motioning to Laredo, Mikkalo gets him to move from his spot against the wall. Without hesitation and zero looks from my guys, Laredo bites his arm and blends his blood with Mikkalo's.

"Any pain?" Everett asks as Bronx hands me Demi.

"I feel much better than yesterday." I get Demi to latch and try to take the glass of blood from Jameson.

He holds it to my lips and tips it slightly, filling my mouth with the sweet mixture. I swallow and hum. Warmth floods through me, and tingles blossom from my middle and travel through the rest of me.

"The only injuries left are the venom bites. Want me to apply some numbing cream?" Everett already squirts some into the palm of his hand, not waiting for me to answer his question.

I finish gulping the blood and smile, shivering as he rubs it over the bites. "What about you guys? You were hurt too."

Bronx sighs and rubs my arm. "Don't worry about us, dandelion. You went through far worse than any of us could ever imagine."

"And we never, ever, want you to have to face something like this again," Jameson adds, pouting his bottom lip.

"Fucking same," I say, mirroring his expression.

"We are working on ensuring it." Laredo gently touches my knee, a soft smile turning his broody face handsome.

I glance to each of my guys and down at Demi as she drifts off to sleep in my arms. "How?" I ask, lowering my voice. "I'll do whatever it takes. If we have to burn down—"

Mikkalo chuckles and slides in front of Everett, leaning down to kiss the threats from my lips. He nips me with his fangs, teasing just enough to get me to slide my tongue into his mouth, devouring his affection. He groans in his throat, not even caring that he interrupted our conversation with the others. Right now, I don't care either. All that matters is expressing my love and appreciation, showing my guys exactly how much they mean to me and how I'm ready to take on the world.

"Damn, Gigi," Jameson murmurs. "I want in on that."

Everett glides his fingers along my leg. "Tell me about it."

I giggle against Mikkalo's mouth and ease away. Desire flashes across everyone's faces, and I can't help but flick my gaze to Laredo and back to my guys. It's strange, yet comforting, having him here, knowing that he kept his promise to never abandon me.

"I can take Demi if you want," Laredo says, keeping his face expressionless. "I know you all have been through so much. I won't go far. I love her as much as—I love her already."

Bronx beams a smile. "It's impossible not to. She's as tough and beautiful as her mom."

My heart swells at their words and how matter-of-fact they sound. I never in a million years expected Bronx to be so relaxed and unthreatened by Laredo, but here he is, treating him as if they've been friends forever.

"So, do you want me to?" Laredo asks, shifting on his feet as I stare at him in silence. "Or I can just go. I have some things to arrange for our travels."

A dozen thoughts cross through my mind, and I don't even know what to say. I trust Laredo. I trust him more than I ever had before, and my guys trust him too. But a part of me doesn't want Demi out of my sight. The other part of me doesn't want Laredo to leave either.

"Hey, man. I can set Demi in the bassinet. She's not going to realize anything," Jameson says, taking Demi from my arms.

I slowly nod my head. "He's right."

Something flickers in Laredo's eyes, and he scratches the back of his neck. "Okay, if you need anything. You know where to find me."

Laredo strides across the room and to the door.

I can't stop myself from looking at each of my guys. We need to talk about Laredo and the mixed feelings rising inside me, growing more intense by the second. As much as I want to ignore them, the thoughts badger me, begging to work this shit through.

Because eternity is uncertain, and living in a state of confusion isn't how I want to start the rest of ours. I almost lost my life. I almost lost my guys. And Laredo.

"Laredo," Bronx says, his deep voice snapping my attention from my whirling thoughts as Bronx stops Laredo from leaving. "The travel arrangements can wait. I think Gwen wants us all to talk."

My heart picks up pace at his words, and I sink deeper into the pillows. Mikkalo slides next to me, pulling me into his arms, and Everett links our fingers together. Jameson sets Demi in her bassinet before returning to my side.

Bronx rubs his big palm over my leg. "I know you better than anyone, dandelion, and I think it's important for you to know my feelings. Laredo should hear them too."

I swallow, my stomach bunching with nerves, but all I can do is nod.

"I was uncertain and feeling a bit threatened when Laredo returned to your life. But I now recognize that just because he was a part of your past doesn't mean things could ever change between us. You two have an undeniable bond, and he has proved he makes more than a good ally. He will make an invaluable member of our coven." Bronx stretches over and leans in to kiss me. "You're the love of my life and the mother of our daughter. I care about you and want you to be happy. What happens from here is up to you two. We're a family regardless."

"We all agree with Bronx," Jameson says, grinning at me to prove he means what he says.

"I'm good if you're good," Mikkalo adds.

Everett bows and kisses my lips. "You have so much love to give. It's one of the things I adore most about you, Gwen."

Laredo clears his throat, getting the five of us to look at him. "I'll be whoever you need me to be, Gwen. Your friendship is the most important thing in the world to me."

I smile, my heart swelling at his words. "We always had a lot of fun, huh? I'd love for you to be able to share that with my guys. I think we could all learn so much from each other as a coven. As a family."

"I'd like that," Laredo says.

"Me too."

I extend my arms out, and Laredo sinks against me, hugging me close. I inhale a breath of his scent, setting my stomach rumbling like crazy. With all the blood loss, it seems I can never get enough of it.

"Uh-oh. Back away slowly, Laredo," Jameson says teasingly. "No sudden movements or she'll sink her teeth into your neck."

I laugh and snatch the front of Jameson's shirt from over Laredo's shoulder, tugging him to me. Laredo chuckles as I squish him between us and link my fingers to the back of Jameson's neck. He tilts his head in offering, and I bite down, making him moan as his blood fills my mouth. My skin buzzes, the taste of Jameson's sweet blood awakening my dhampir nature.

"Fuck, I love when she makes that noise," Mikkalo says, hooking his arms around me from behind. "Like she can't get enough."

I tip my head back until our lips meet. "It's because I can't. You're all so fucking delicious."

"Not as amazing as you," Everett says, his fangs clicking with his thought.

Bronx's fangs extend next, and a shiver runs through me as goosebumps prickle over my skin. Silence falls between us, their blood hunger igniting as strong as mine, and I ease myself from their arms to lie flat on the bed.

I rub my legs together in excitement, my body begging for their fangs to tease my skin, to let me give them what they all desire.

"Can I feed you all?" I ask, my words breathless and pleading. "You've taken such good care of me that I want nothing more than to do the same...if that's okay."

Bronx's smile fades as lust and desire wash over him at my words. "It's better than okay to me. We should have a little celebration."

I laugh and nod, hooking my fingers to the hem of my shirt. "That's exactly what I was thinking."

I pull my shirt over my head, exposing my body to them without an ounce of hesitation. Five pairs of eyes burn over me in their heated intensity, and I squirm in excitement and desire. Everett takes the initiative and tugs off his shirt next before leaning down to kiss me. He explores my tongue with his, setting off a wave of desire to shoot right to my clit, making me moan.

"Speak up if you're not okay with something," Bronx says, stripping out of his shirt next. "You're in control, okay?"

I dart my gaze to Mikkalo. "I'll say banana."

Mikkalo tips his head back with a loud laugh that swells happiness in my heart. Jameson cracks up and whips him with his shirt before discarding it on the floor. Mikkalo leans into me next, gliding his tongue over mine as I pull his shirt off and break away from his lips to kiss his taut skin, rippling with desire for me. Turning to Laredo, I curl and uncurl my finger at him, sending silver lighting his eyes. I kneel beside him and undress him next before patting his cheek with my hand. He cups his over mine, stopping me from pulling away. Turning my gaze to his mouth, I remember the dozens of kisses we've shared and snuck late at night on our travels together. I try not to think about my brothers, the memory threatening to awaken sadness in my heart.

Grazing his lips to mine, Laredo pushes the sorrow away, igniting something else inside me. The feral feeling wraps around me, and I moan and pull away before I sink my teeth into him. Lips caress my shoulder, and I tip my head back, savoring the sensation of Bronx's full lips mapping my skin. He guides me to sit between his legs, and I pant with anticipation, so turned on by their rippling muscles and hard bodies all desiring me.

Everett kneels between both our legs and drinks me in, his hard-on pressing to his pants. I can't stop my body's reaction and lift my hips, giving him silent permission to undress me. Jameson moans and rubs his hand over my leg and between my thighs, discovering exactly how excited I am.

"I can't wait another moment," I murmur, squirming more, purposefully grinding against Bronx's cock as it flexes against my back. "Bite me."

Laredo twines our fingers and eases my arm to his mouth, kissing my wrist. He doesn't bite right away like he wants to savor the taste of my skin. Jameson draws my other arm up and brushes his lips from my elbow to my wrist.

Moaning, I arch my back and ease my legs open until Everett nestles between them. He kisses my inner thigh, and I gasp in excitement, the anticipation making my body tremble. Mikkalo grasps my ankle and stretches my leg higher, dropping to his elbow to lick and nip the skin where my ass cheek meets my leg, helping Everett hold me in place while he chooses not to bite me and instead traces his tongue along the seam of my body until he sucks my clit.

Jameson, Bronx, Mikkalo, and Laredo all bite me at once. If Bronx didn't slide his arm in front of my mouth, offering me his blood in return, I'd scream my pleasure to the universe. Instead, I sink my teeth into his flesh, turning my blood hunger into blood lust, and I roll my body harder, more desperately, until an orgasm seizes my muscles and I arch and break my arms away from Jameson and Laredo.

"I need more," I gasp, desperately trying to rip Jameson's pants off.

Everett surprises me by flipping me over and rubbing his palms to my ass cheeks, spreading and closing my body while teasing me with his finger. My mind races with a dozen thoughts, but Bronx scoots down beneath me and kisses me with so much passion that I'm left breathless and ready to give them anything they want.

"Let me take care of you however you want," I murmur, arching up to kiss Jameson next.

Mikkalo quietly moves from the bed and returns just as

quickly. Touching my chin, he guides me to look up at him and leans down to suck my bottom lip between his teeth. He unbuttons his pants and kicks them off, stroking his hard cock until I take over, my hand slipping and sliding with lube.

Bronx nips my shoulder and whispers how beautiful I am into my ear, his hard body flexing between my legs. Cool liquid drips over my ass, and I gasp, squirming in pleasure as Everett teases me with his finger. The sensation thrills me, turning me on, knowing exactly what he wants to do. Jameson hums in appreciation, rubbing his own cock as Everett takes his time easing me into where he wants to takes things. I blindly reach out for Laredo, letting him take my hand and rub it over the length of his cock. I turn from Bronx's mouth and watch him for a moment, my attention split in five different directions as I relax and enjoy giving my guys what they want.

Adjusting my body, Bronx reaches between us and aligns his cock to enter me. I gasp at the pressure, increasing the pleasure of Everett's attention. Jameson tilts my chin up, kneeling at Bronx's shoulders. I rub my lips together and open my mouth, letting him control the ecstasy my mouth creates as I mold my lips around his cock. He guides himself in and out, moaning with pleasure, making me feel so hot and sexy and perfect in this moment.

Everett makes me shiver as he squeezes more lube, turning me dripping wet and ready. Reaching between me and Bronx, Everett rubs my clit at the same time he eases in. I moan with Jameson in my mouth, and he tightens his fingers through my hair, groaning at the sensation. The room fills with sounds of our passion, and I lose myself to the lust and love sinking into my very soul. I had no idea how much I'd love bonding with my guys at this new intimate level as much as I do.

An orgasm builds inside me again at the desperate touch of Everett's hand. He takes things slow, moaning and whispering how good I feel. Mikkalo rubs circles on my back, his body flexing. He moans as we cum at the same time, the warmth of him splashing on my back.

"I'm going to cum, Gigi," Jameson murmurs, and I hum in acknowledgement, letting him fill my mouth with his taste, sweeter than his blood.

I swallow and moan, my voice filling the air until everyone finishes, leaving me panting and buzzing and so in love.

Savoring their affection, I cuddle close with each of them, giving them all my attention. Satisfaction hums through me, and as I stare at my guys, at my mates, I know this is exactly what we've been fighting for. This is the future I want.

I plan to get it, no matter what.

I rock Demi in my arms, watching as a white SUV travels down the long driveway and toward the house.

"Gwen?" Jewel says, drawing my attention to the com device. "You don't have to go. We will stand by Bronx in his resignation and ensure Viorica doesn't try anything. You all can move to Ombre Noire. It's safe here, and your brothers are welcome."

I pucker my lips, flicking my gaze back to the SUV. Bronx, Mikkalo, and Laredo stand waiting together as it comes to a stop. "Thanks, Jewel, but we've made up our minds. There are still rebels out there, and...we're just ready to give all this up."

She nods. "I understand. You know how to reach us if you need anything."

The line disconnects, and I slide the com device back into my pocket. Jameson comes up behind me and wraps his arms around my shoulders. He kisses the crook of my neck and grazes his fingers over Demi's downy blond hair.

"Why don't you come inside with me and Everett?" he asks, kissing the spot below my ear next.

"I just need to watch to make sure they're okay," I murmur.

"They'll be fine, Gigi. Viorica came alone. Look." Stretching his arm out, he points as the red-haired vampire steps out from behind the wheel. She taps a button, opening the rest of the doors and the hatch, allowing Mikkalo to sweep the SUV to ensure she kept her word.

I sigh a breath in relief, releasing the tension from my body. I've always been on the fence with Viorica and the Vaduvas, and I haven't always liked the decisions the powerful woman made, but she has always been honest with us.

Viorica peers around the property, taking in the unsettling sight of the unmarked graves of the bodies of human rebels. In the corner, under one of the magnolia trees, a small marker points to where Grayson was buried. Tears burn my eyes at the thought, and I can't help wishing there was something more I could've done for him. But like Kyler, he made his decisions, and there isn't always a way to get out of facing the consequences. I'll never forget how he saved my life. I'll cherish our childhood memories for the rest of eternity, remember him as my big brother and not the man life turned him into.

"Gwen, I was so relieved when Laredo informed me you and your sweet daughter were okay," Viorica says, walking beside Bronx as he guides her toward the house. "I only wish I had known the true extent of the rebel problem. I'd have helped handle it far more swiftly."

I bob my head. "None of us could've truly known. The Barons..." I let my voice trail off. I don't have to remind her about the threats they made to get to me. "I'm just happy that I have such an amazing coven protecting me."

"As you should." Viorica smiles, showing off her fangs. Her gaze travels down to Demi in my arms, and she reaches to pet her fingers over her blond hair. "The two of you deserve the strength and backing of the Royales. You will need it to live up to the hearsay of your full potential."

I freeze in place and step back into Jameson's arms, a blip of fear squeezing my chest. Bronx motions for Viorica to follow him inside, and we all meet Everett in the living room as he disconnects the line with Rio Mercy. Viorica nods at him and saunters to where Mikkalo pours her a glass of blood from the gen. pop. stash the Barons stored in the grand kitchen.

"Let's just get straight to the point, Misters Royale. I know that Gwen is a dhampir and that her daughter is a Royale Heir." Viorica takes a seat on the couch, keeping her back straight while crossing her legs. "I also want you to know that your secret is safe with me. The rebels I collected from the attack have all been mind manipulated and registered to the gen. pop. donors of the Vaduva Region."

"So that's how you know," I say, my words coming out softly.

Her cheek twitches. "That's how I confirmed my suspicions. I knew something was...different about you. Unregistered vampires don't threaten to destroy an entire territory for an ordinary donor without prior attachments or blood debts."

"Oh." I don't know what else to say.

"You see, Gwen. Misters Royale. I've been alive a very, very long time. I know of the rumors and accusations from The Uprising and have known the Blood Rebels would eventually fight back, so it was easy enough to figure out." Viorica smirks, keeping her gaze trained on me.

I don't call her out on it, but I know she's only half telling the truth. Fiona told me she knew about dhampirs after meeting her, but I'll keep that information to myself.

"So why are you telling us all this?" Bronx says, perching on the armrest. The six of us form a semi-circle around Viorica, tense and waiting for her either to threaten us or prove that she truly can be on our side.

"I just figured since you invited me out here that you might have been preparing to tell me things I already know. And in all honesty, I think we have more important matters to discuss. Like your region." Viorica sips her glass of blood, giving my guys a chance to process her comment.

Ah, hell.

This is it.

"I don't want you to give it up," Viorica says, keeping her voice even.

Bronx releases a low growl.

Raising her hand, she adds, "I want you to agree to a permanent alliance with the Vaduvas, so I can inherit it with your deaths."

Oh, shit.

Mikkalo unsheathes his dagger, ready to fight.

She points at him next. "Hear me out, Mr. Royale. I'm not finished."

Mikkalo slowly lowers his blade but doesn't put it away, remaining stern-faced and prepared to fight.

Viorica sets her glass of blood on the coffee table. "I've realized that asking you to keep your position under these current circumstances was rather unfair, knowing the risks you face. I am a mother myself, at least, I was as a donor long ago, and I did everything I could to ensure a good life for my children, as I do for my coven daughters now."

I find myself leaning forward, devouring her admission. The motives of Viorica have always been a mystery to me, and things are finally turning clear.

"But why?" all of my guys say at the same time, asking the same question on my mind.

"What does a permanent alliance do for you?" Bronx adds.

"It will give me greater pull on the board, and also allow me to prepare for when you decide to rejoin the territory." Viorica says simply.

"But you said you'd get it upon our deaths," Jameson says, his brows puckering in confusion.

"Because the best way to ensure you can take the time

you need to raise your family is to fake your deaths. It's easy enough with the damage caused by the rebels. We will both get the things we want. Power for me, and a way out for you." Viorica folds her hands in her lap. "It's already been arranged. All you have to do is agree. It will be up to you if you choose to ever come back to Donor Life Corp, but I hope you do. You can let me know by tomorrow."

Viorica lifts her glass and downs her drink. Without a word, she slowly strolls across the living room and to the front door. I glance from Bronx to Mikkalo, and then to Everett, Jameson, and Laredo. Lastly, I peer down at Demi, knowing deep in my heart that this is exactly what we need.

No more rebel threats.

No more power struggles among vampires.

We fought so hard to get this moment, and now that one of the few allies in our lives offers it to us, I want to take it. I need for us to take it.

"Viorica," I say, calling out to her. "Wait."

She turns on her heels and smirks at me. "Yes, Gwen?"

"If we agree, I want it to be with one more condition," I say, adjusting Demi in my arms. My guys stare at me in silence, knowing that whatever I decide will be what's best for all of us. "I want my brothers to be your advisors. They know the rebel life like me. They'll help you turn the territory into something amazing."

Her face softens and she nods. "You have my word."

Vanishing, Viorica leaves us alone in the living room, and I release a breath and snuggle my face against Demi. Bronx and Mikkalo engulf me between them before the others join our group hug, showering me with so much love that I know I'll be able to survive for the rest of eternity on it.

"Have I ever told you how perfect you are?" Bronx says, kissing me. "Because of you, we'll have an amazing future."

"Our options will be endless," Jameson adds.

"Honestly, I just want to spend a few years in bed," Everett teases. "I want to enjoy the beginning of forever with you."

Mikkalo chuckles. "Damn straight. I love the sound of that."

I turn to Laredo. "What about you?"

He shrugs his shoulders. "My intentions have always been clear. I will spend the rest of eternity protecting you. And now, our coven."

"I'm down for that. For everything," I say, smiling. "But mostly, I just want to enjoy eternity as a Royale."

Mikkalo cuddles me close. "Nothing sounds better."

This was the last thing I expected from my life. I never dreamed I'd have a coven of perfect, protective, and powerful men who lift me up as their equal and stand beside me as we face the world together. These same men aren't just my lovers, but they're also the fathers of the most precious, beautiful dhampir in the world. They're my best friends and confidants. They're my family. My everything.

It's in this moment I know that no matter what eternity throws at us, we will stand strong and powerful.

We will take on the world.

We are the future.

Epilogue

POWERFUL FUTURE

COOL LIPS CARESS MY SHOULDER, drawing me from sleep. I flutter my eyes open and peer at Demi sleeping on Everett's chest beside me. My heart swells with happiness, and I lightly touch her tiny back, loving how she puckers her lips, dream suckling Everett in her sleep.

"She's so perfect, isn't she? I'll never take this for granted," Bronx whispers, sliding his arm under me to roll me to him.

I smile and stretch to kiss him, brushing my lips to his

until he pulls me completely on his body. "You're going to wake everyone up," I whisper, scooting back to feel his throbbing cock between my legs.

He hums and grabs my hips, rocking me back and forth, turning me on. "No, I'm nearly certain you will, dandelion."

"I guess it's time for their wakeup call, anyway," I tease.

He hums. "It's the best kind."

Bronx arches up and tugs my nightie over my head, arching forward to kiss me. I gasp at the sensation of his fingers shifting my panties, not even bothering to undress us, choosing to pull his cock from his boxer-briefs instead.

I clutch his face and kiss him hard, stroking my tongue to his as he aligns our bodies and thrusts inside me. Pleasure zings from between my legs and to the rest of me, and I moan so embarrassingly loud that I sink my teeth into Bronx's bare shoulder to shut myself up. He groans and guides my body up and down on his, hitting me in just the right spot that I tip my head back with my oncoming orgasm.

A silhouette hovers over me, and Jameson kisses the noise from my mouth as tingles explode through me, shuddering through my whole body. I ease my neck to the side and silently offer him a bite, loving how effortless it is to just be together. Jameson kisses the spot at the nape of my neck and then quickly pricks me with his fangs, molding his lips to his bite.

I pant and moan, enjoying the ecstasy and satisfaction, smiling and laughing as Mikkalo, Everett, and Laredo all stir awake, burning me with their lusty intensity. Morning wood throbs from each of them, and I bounce and ride Bronx, devouring the show my guys offer me until Bronx moans and slows, kissing me until he stops completely.

Everett scoots out of bed and quietly sets Demi into her crib, gracing me with a sexy smile. "I love waking up to the sound of your pleasure."

"I'm going to have to start setting an alarm to beat Bronx," Jameson teases. "It's like he's trying to knock her the hell up again."

Bronx chuckles. "I wouldn't mind."

I bite my bottom lip and grin. "Me either. I love you guys."

"We did say we were going to create an army of wild ones like our girl," Mikkalo says, sitting up to pull me off Bronx and onto him. "Isn't that right, Gwen?"

I smile as I lean in to kiss him. "Mmmhmm."

Jameson comes up behind me and slides his hand down my pelvis. "Then I guess we better work harder. It's a good thing we have this whole town to ourselves. We're going to need more room."

I hum under my breath and let them all surround me, showering me with their attention. "That sounds like the perfect eternity. You guys and me, this giant bed, our private piece of paradise, building a powerful future together...it's everything I could ever want."

They all chuckle and take turns kissing me until we all lie back down together, just enjoying the early evening in each other's arms.

"You forgot enjoying everything that happens right now, dandelion," Bronx says, sitting up to look at me from his new spot on the other side of Mikkalo.

I sigh in contentment and trace my finger on Jameson's chest. "You're right. This is utter bliss."

The End

Thank you so much for reading The Royale Vampire Heirs series! If you love the Vampire Heirs World, you can expect more dhampir stories in the future!

Join Ginna's reader group on Facebook called Paranormal Center for Matches and Mates to stay up-to-date on all things books, participate in tons of giveaways, games, and more!

THE MATES OF MAGAELORUM WORLD

The Pack Mates of Lunar Crest:
The She-Wolf Games
The Wolf-Mate Trials
The Omega Hunt
The Witch Chase

Fated Mates of the Dragon Clans:
Caged by Her Dragons
Freed by Her Dragons
Saved by Her Dragons

SEVEN SINNERS WORLD

Her Personal Demons
Her Deadly Angels
Her Darkest Devils
Her Sinful Saints
Her Twisted Sinners

About Ginna Moran

GINNA MORAN IS THE AUTHOR of over seventy novels, including the popular Vampire Heirs World series, The Pack Mates of Lunar Crest series, and The Seven Sinners of Hell's Kingdom Why Choose novels.

She always carried a fascination for all things paranormal and wrote her first unpublished manuscript at age eighteen. Her love of the supernatural grew stronger through her adult life, and she now spends her days with different creatures of the night. Whether it's vampires, werewolves, angel, demons, or mermaids, Ginna loves creating and living in worlds from her dreams.

Aside from Ginna's professional life, she enjoys binge watching TV, crafting and design, playing pretend with her daughter, and cuddling with her dogs. Some of her favorite things include chocolate, mermaids, anything that glitters, learning new things, cheesy jokes, and organizing her bookshelf.

Ginna Moran loves to hear from her readers so visit her online at www.GinnaMoran.com. You can also find her on Facebook, Twitter, and Instagram. To stay up-to-date on new releases, sign up to her newsletter. To interact with Ginna, join her Facebook Group Paranormal Center for Matches and Mates. You'll not only get exclusive access to extra stories, but you'll be able to participate in games and fun giveaways!